HIT GIRL

USA TODAY BESTSELLING AUTHOR
TIA LOUISE

Hit Girl
Copyright © TLM Productions LLC, 2018
Printed in the United States of America.

Cover design by Designs by Dana.

For the ones who never give up…

Contents

Chapter 1: A Hit

Molly

I study the couples moving on the dance floor as I wait.

Most keep a respectable distance, "room for Jesus," as the nuns would say—hands clasped, hers on his shoulder, his on her waist, six inches between the torsos. Others are hugged close, too close for propriety, dirty dancing in the dining room of this posh Seattle hotel.

An older woman sneers, and her cluelessness makes me want to laugh. *She thinks that's bad.*

Oh, to have such an easy life.

I guess I can't complain. As a nobody orphan from the streets of New Orleans, I've done pretty well for myself.

I've lived in Paris, Nice, Canada… Now I'm sitting in this marble-lined venue wearing a thousand-dollar Gucci dress and sipping a twenty-dollar glass of wine.

How times change.

"Shall we dance?" My escort's low baritone ripples across the table to me.

My blue eyes meet his dark ones, and I smile demurely. "You don't have to seduce me, Dennis."

He grins and holds out a hand. I allow my gaze to travel from his perfectly manicured nails up the line of his tailored gray suit jacket to a deep purple shirt with matching grey tie. A purple handkerchief peeks from his breast pocket.

I've never seen Dennis Langley in a suit before tonight, and in spite of what's to come, I'll give him points for his meticulous sense of style. Too bad he's an asshole.

"I like kicking it old school." Straight white teeth appear behind his full lips.

His face is clean-shaven, and he's slim, which will make my job easier.

I don't take his hand. Instead, I stand on red-bottomed stilettos and smooth my palms down the front of my thigh-length black dress.

"You're too young to be sentimental." I smile for him, let him think I'm amused.

"And you're in no position to argue."

With a shrug, I place my hand in his larger one. "Suit yourself."

Dennis is tall-ish. I'm petite, but in heels, my lips are at the top of his shoulder. He holds me close against his body, and his heat radiates into me. It's off-putting.

I don't want to inhale his spicy scent or feel the whisper of his breath at my temple. The breath is the essence of a person, and his essence is rotten despite his outward appearance of elegant propriety.

The song is "Moonglow," a piano standard, and he leans closer, his lips grazing the shell of my ear. "What do you do for a living?"

Blinking slowly, I put my private disgust aside and think about who I want to be tonight. "I'm in computer programming."

It's an easy lie and easy to believe in this part of the country.

"Were you born in Seattle?"

"Issaquah. I graduated Issaquah High, purple and gold."

"The Indians."

"It's the Eagles now."

"Is that so?" He leans back, and the grin curling his

lips tells me he's pleased with my ability to play the game.

He doesn't want to know my truth.

"Oh yes." I look over his shoulder again, away from his eyes. "Big local controversy, part of the district wide ban on racial stereotypes in local mascots."

"How very PC of old Issaquah."

We sway side to side, his hand moving farther around my waist, drawing me closer to his body.

"Do you have any brothers or sisters?"

I resist exhaling deeply. It's time to get this show on the road, give him what he wants. I'm glad, honestly, as it will get me out of this place sooner and back to where I want to be, back to the life I prefer.

"Only a step-brother. He was the quarterback of the high school football team until he blew out his knee. Now he works at Cougar Mountain Zoo."

"A stepbrother…" The word rolls from his tongue as if he's preparing for something delicious. "Were you home alone together much?"

He's encouraging me, and I continue unspooling the lie.

"Yes," I answer slowly, seductively. "Even after his injury, he was still so fit. He liked to walk from his bedroom to our shared bathroom in nothing but a towel… so I could see the *V* in his obliques."

"What else would he do?"

I make my voice breathy, high like Marilyn Monroe. "He would wait until I went to bed at night, then he would come into my room."

"How old were you?"

"Fifteen."

I know Dennis prefers them younger, but it doesn't seem to matter this time.

"What happened?" His voice is eager.

"He would get in my bed and slide my panties down my legs to my ankles."

"Then what?"

I speak right in his ear, a breath above a whisper. "He'd kiss me, sliding his tongue over and over. Then he'd touch me, circling and circling." I gasp and do a slight shiver as if I'm reliving this fiction. "The circles would grow harder, holding me down as my legs shook, and I cried out as I came."

Dennis steps back, dark eyes blazing. "You loved it?"

I bite back a smile. I've got this guy right where I want him.

Making a worried face, I continue speaking in my baby voice. "It was so wrong… so *dirty*… But it felt so *good*. I could never tell him no."

His large hand tightens on mine, and he turns leading us off the dance floor at a steady pace. I'm practically running to keep up with him, the long, gold chain around my neck swaying over my bouncing breasts.

We don't stop until we're at the shiny brass elevators. The doors slide open, and he growls when it's not empty. I'm inwardly relieved. I don't want him touching me any more than absolutely necessary.

Inside, he repeatedly presses the button for the tenth floor until the doors close. We rise, high and fast, gently slowing when we reach ten.

He holds my hand like I'm a child as he strides down the hall, fumbling with his pocket until he pulls out the door card.

"What about the bill?" I whisper, breathless, keeping up the charade.

"They'll add it to my room." His voice is gruff, Daddy.

An electronic *beep*, and he pulls me inside an open suite with a picture window offering a stunning view of the Seattle skyline. An ice bucket holds an open bottle of champagne on the far table.

I only have a moment to notice before he turns me, slamming my chest to the wall. He's on me at once, breathing down my neck and fumbling between my legs for the hem of my dress.

"Tell me about your toys." My skirt is up, exposing my bare ass. "Did you collect Barbie dolls?"

Manicured nails scratch at my thong, finding the scrap of material and ripping it away.

Closing my eyes, I calm my mind, centering my thoughts and summoning my strength. I move my focus away from his words and actions and toward my purpose for being here, just like I was trained to do.

Slow it down…

See the end.

I've been tracking this monster since a thirteen-year-old runaway named Brittanie cried in my lap and told me how he raped her.

It's been a year since that day.

We first crossed paths in the basement of a tattoo parlor. In a room with velvet couches and ornate chairs. It was an orgy, with men and women in various states of undress scattered around the room. He'd been on the couch complaining because there were no teenagers for him to fuck.

I was so ready to finish him that night.

Tonight, I will.

Expectancy floods my chest, radiating through my arms and legs, filling me with strength. I visualize my movements before I even make them.

"I played dress-up." The baby-voice drains away as I lift the thick gold chain from around my neck. "I wore combat gear and attacked the enemy with my bare hands."

In a fluid motion, I spin in his arms, whipping the chain off my neck and down around his, wrapping it repeatedly like a tourniquet.

Another spin, and I'm behind him, on his back, twisting the heavy metal tighter and tighter. My movements are so fast he doesn't have time to recover.

Surprise is my ally. By the time he realizes what I've done, it's too late for him.

The gold chain cuts into his skin, restricting blood flow, trapping the air in his lungs and preventing more from entering through his mouth. He drops to his knees with me on his back, gagging and struggling frantically to free himself, to get me off him.

Only he can't get me off him.

You are little, but you are fierce, Myshka...

I press my knees harder into his spine, twisting and pulling the chain, tighter and tighter as he snorts and claws at his neck.

My lips curl with a smile as his skin turns a darker shade of red...

Then purple.

Satisfaction is a rose blooming in my stomach, and I lean into his ear. "Now I collect the souls of men who rape thirteen-year-old girls."

He snorts one last time.

The chain links create oval-shaped black and purple bruises along his neck. So far, my plan is going exactly as it should — quiet, tame, final.

Dennis is the fifth predator I've successfully tracked down, but only the second I've killed myself.

The first put up a fight.

He was a big fat man, and I rode his back like a bucking bull at a rodeo around his stateroom on a train as he smashed lamps and overturned furniture until he finally fell.

Dennis goes down like a roped calf, mute and docile.

I'll hold him tight a few minutes longer to be sure he's dead. Then I'll meticulously clean his fingernails and all traces of me from his body with the tiny kit I carry inside my bra.

While I sit, I scroll through what I know of his crimes, the lives he's destroyed, and I give the chain another pull. Only one more, however. I don't want to cut his head off. That's a mess even I don't have the time or the energy to clean.

No, I'll walk out of this room without leaving a trace.

Like I always do.

No evidence; no looking back.

Another ten seconds, ten ticks on the clock, and my job here is done.

One less predator in the world.

One less little girl to be hurt.

* * *

At three a.m., I arrive at our apartment in the Capitol Hill neighborhood of Seattle.

Following cleanup, I walked around the city for a while to clear my head.

I inhaled and exhaled slowly as the light rain fell on my face and hair. I walked until the essence of Dennis Langley was out of my system, and I could breathe easily again.

I walked until the only thing left was the satisfaction of justice served.

Like Batman or Black Widow, sometimes it takes a

private citizen to do what the authorities can't accomplish...

And usually those private citizens have a reason.

A damn good reason.

Just like me.

The metal door of our two-story walkup scrapes when it opens. I hold it, guiding it closed so it doesn't slam. The huge warehouse studio is dark and quiet, and I step lightly doing my best not to wake Joshua, who's asleep in bed, lying on his stomach under a picture window.

In my closet, I take off the gold chain, and for a moment, I touch the links, allowing them to rest on my fingertips as I study them, savoring their lightweight strength. The necklace is a gift I only wear on special occasions. It's my weapon of choice.

The Louboutin heels are clutched in my hand, and I slip them in the shoe rack hanging on the door, then I kneel and dig behind the boxes on the floor searching for my sleek black case.

It opens quietly, cushioned. Inside is a tiny pink pistol, a Ruger LCP .380. It's the size of my palm and fits easily in my boot, but I'm not a shooter. This little weapon is only for self-defense.

Lifting it out, I take the yellowed sheet of paper from under it. Opening the note carefully, I study the list I made so long ago.

The first four names are written in a teenager's immature script.

~~Guy Hudson~~ (LH)
~~Robert Esterhaus~~ (MD)
~~Lewis Rain~~ (heart attack)
~~Gavin Hudson~~ (LH)
Dennis Langley

14

Dennis's name is written in a more mature hand, with precise, even lettering. Taking the small pencil from the bottom of the case, I put a line through it and add (MD).

Molly Dixon, cause of death.

Keeping this list is part ritual, part nostalgia. I started it when I needed a sense of control. I needed something concrete, confirming my plan. I needed something physical to hold, to take the idea out of my head and put it in the real world.

It was my roadmap to the men who'd hurt me, and even if I don't need it now, I respect the little girl who did.

I fold the paper and place it under the black velvet, return my tiny gun to its place, and arrange the chain in a circle around it. Then I close the lid and put it in the back of my closet behind the boxes and blankets.

Closing the door, I pause to *inhale, exhale* before going to the kitchen, where I take a bottle of wine from the refrigerator. It's a Willamette Valley pinot noir rosé—dry and cool, refreshing, and expensive.

I'm relaxed, breathing easily as I take a lingering sip. Sliding the zipper down the back of my thin black sheath, I let it fall in a puddle at my feet, leaving me in only a black lace bra.

I disposed of my ripped thong in a dumpster far across town, far from the hotel and any connection to where I live and work.

Unfastening my bra, I drop it on the dress and go to Joshua's dresser. I take out a white tank, a "wife beater," and slip it over my head.

I hate that expression, but I take another calming sip of wine before setting the glass on the table and walking to the bed.

For several seconds, I look out the window at the lights of the city. Our view of the park has become so familiar to me... I wonder if I would call this place home. It's been a year since I moved in here.

My eyes drift down to Joshua's bare back. The moonlight drenches his skin in silver, deepening the lines where he's attractively muscular. He takes a deep breath and rolls onto his side, and my stomach tightens when our eyes meet.

In this light, his gray eyes appear dark. Dark eyes, pale skin, messy, dark hair. He's my own private vampire, and a smile curls his full lips. I never believed I'd be sexually attracted to any man after what happened to me.

I was wrong.

"Where have you been?" His voice is husky but gentle.

Joshua doesn't challenge me. He only teases me, as if we share a secret—only, it's a secret he's never been told. I won't make him an accomplice.

"Working." My voice is low and even. Natural.

The muscles in his arms ripple as he pushes up to a sitting position, leaning his back against the headboard. "Late night."

"My client could only meet after hours." Reaching for the blankets, I move them away so I can climb into the king-sized bed beside him.

He slides down with me, resting his head on the pillow so our faces are close. I prop up on my hand, studying his expression, his square jaw covered in dark scruff.

Joshua is a rich boy, the son of a software developer who sent his only child into the world to do good with his obscene trust fund.

"How did it go today with the Realtor?" My hand is on the pillow, fiddling with the satiny-soft case.

"It's a big house—big enough for six girls—but it needs work." His eyes travel to my lips, to my hair. "Still, it's what we're looking for. It'll get them off the street and give them a safe place to crash."

When I moved into Joshua's apartment a year ago, he suggested we open a halfway house for runaway teens, girls who are too young to work, who need to finish high school or get their diplomas, girls who are at risk of becoming prostitutes or drug addicts or victims of crime on the streets. Girls whose lives wouldn't last long otherwise.

I agreed because it suits my goals. He can help them find a better life. I'll help them vindicate their past.

"It's finally coming together."

"Finally is right," he sighs. "After a year of permits and paperwork and tests and interviews... Jesus."

"Has it been a year?"

"It will be in a month." He stretches out a finger and gently touches one of the silver scars striping my skin. "One year, and I still don't know the story of this."

Silver-white lines hide across the inside of my upper arms, the inside of my upper thighs, my lower stomach. I only cut myself in places that were easy to hide.

My own family never saw them... or my adopted family—my one older "sister" Lara. I hid them until I found a better way to express my pain and rage. Until I was trained to stop hurting myself and start hurting the men who deserve it.

Joshua is one of two people who has ever seen my scars.

Tracing my finger along the line of muscle in his arm, I think aloud. "Why did you choose me that night?"

His dark brow furrows in confusion. "What?"

"That first night on the street, when you walked up to me and started talking. Why did you do that?"

His sexy grin appears. "That's easy. You're the most beautiful girl I've ever seen."

I shake my head, looking up toward the window. "Be serious, Joshua."

"I am serious." He scoots closer in the bed, sliding warm palms along the bare skin of my waist, higher under my shirt. "Have you seen your tits?"

"Stop!" Falling onto my back, I catch his wrists, pushing them down before he reaches my breasts. "I said be serious!"

He stops trying to grope me, but now he's on top of me, his warm body pressing down on mine, his weight supported by his forearms.

I love this feeling, surrounded by his juniper and citrus scent. Joshua's is the only body I want heating mine, the only breath I want mingling with mine.

"Okay, seriously? First, I love this cleft right here in your chin…"

"It looks like a butt."

"Does not. It's sexy. Superheroes always have clefts in their chins." He leans down and slides the tip of his tongue along the shallow line.

"Ew!" I push against him and wipe my face with my hand.

"Oh sure. Ew."

"I don't know where that tongue has been."

"It's about to be in your mouth." He comes at me, and I start to laugh, arching my back and pulling away.

"So I'm a superhero now?"

"Maybe." He props his head on his hand, a gleam in his eyes. "Maybe you're ambiguous, like Rogue. She's a southern girl, too."

"Ambiguous." My gaze drops to his full lips, away from his searching eyes.

"You definitely have that look." I frown, but he laughs, leaning down to kiss my collarbone. "That's the one, right there."

"What look?"

"Like you're seriously up to no good."

His lips travel to the side of my neck, higher into my hair, and I can't deny the heat following in their wake.

"Joshua…" It's a heated whisper.

How does he do this? He knows when to hold me close and when to give me space. A year ago, when I was alone, he gave me a place to live. He gave me his bed and then tried to sleep on an air mattress. It was the first night we made love.

"You never ask me what I do."

Lifting his head, his eyes meet mine. "Would you tell me?"

I don't answer.

He pulls out my arm and leans down to kiss my scars. "You'll tell me when you're ready."

Dropping beside me in the bed, he rotates my body so my back is against his chest. His palm is flat on my stomach, but he's not pushing for more.

"That's all?" I ask softly.

His voice is low at the back of my neck. "You're tired. I'll let you sleep."

"Until two a.m.," I tease.

"It's after three."

"Sorry, until five a.m."

"No promises."

Strong arms circle my waist, and he's so warm.

Yes, he's home.

A home I don't deserve.

I don't know what would happen if Joshua found out what I do. I've hidden it from everyone, but I can't hide it from him forever.

CHAPTER 2: A LOSS

Joshua

The sun is up, and I'm buried to the hilt in Molly's warm body. Her back arches, and I thrust rhythmically, meeting the tilt of her ass against my pelvis.

"Joshua," she moans, and I slide my hand around her hips, tracing my fingers along her skin to the place between her legs where she's wet and swollen.

That little bud is ready, and I pinch it lightly, circling and massaging. She moans again, and her fingers thread in the side of my hair, curling and pulling as our movements grow more focused.

Somehow I'd fallen asleep with her pretty little body spooned against mine, her back to my chest. She was only wearing my thin tank, and when the morning rolled around, I wasn't even fully awake when I reached for her.

Now I have the best view, looking down her shoulder at her body rocking with mine, those perfect breasts bouncing with my thrusts, nipples teasing at the thin fabric of my shirt. I pull it to the side so one spills out, and I swear, I almost lose it.

Cupping her soft, heavy flesh in my hand, I roll a taut nipple between my fingers. I kiss her neck, slipping out my tongue to taste her, grazing her skin with my teeth. Her insides clench in response and sparks of light go off behind my eyelids. The sound of her soft moans, the feel of her muscles massaging my cock...

"Shit, Molly." My voice is ragged. I'm on the edge, doing my best to stay with her until she breaks. "Come for me."

"Joshua," she repeats, and the desire lacing her tone is the best thing I've ever heard.

I thrust harder, and she whimpers. Her hand fumbles to mine on her clit, and I let her guide me, finding the right rhythm, the right pace, until she grips my hand and comes.

Her body goes rigid, and her mouth opens as her core shatters in a cascade of spasms around my dick.

"Yes," I groan, hopping on the wave of orgasm with her.

Her body bucks against mine, and I fill her, each pulse blanking my mind with intensity. We hold on tight through the crest of ecstasy until we're descending, floating back to Earth. All the way from heaven.

Her body relaxes; her fingers are still in my hair. We're panting and sweaty, and her hand slides down to my cheek.

"You are so beautiful." I kiss her palm, holding her against me as I cover her exposed breast with my hand. "Only bad thing about this position is I can't watch your tits bouncing."

"I wish you wouldn't say that word." It's a playful fuss.

I'm ready to play. "What? Tits?"

Her lips tighten, and I do my best not to laugh. "Does it bother you that I find you incredibly sexually attractive?"

She fights a smile. "No."

"You know how much I respect you as a woman..." I wait for her to say yes. "And I'd never do anything to hurt you."

"I know."

"Then you should also know I think you have the greatest rack I've ever seen in my life, and I've seen a lot of tits."

A laugh explodes from her. "Is that so?"

As much as I try to hold her, it's no good. My fading erection pops right out of that warm place I love. "Shit," I complain, and she laughs more, my badass girl.

I love the sound of her laugh. I love that I'm the one she'll let touch her, make her laugh.

Turning her to face me, I kiss her lips. I'm about to push them apart so I can go long and deep when she pulls back.

"Morning breath!" Her hand is over her mouth, and she blinks those blue eyes up at me. Those damn blue eyes that slayed me the first night I saw her, round and deep and full of secrets.

I reach up to slide a long, silver curl behind her ear. "Sorry. I also like kissing your sexy mouth."

Her gaze flickers to my lips. "I like kissing you. More than I expected I would."

"I told you."

She shakes her head, rolling those eyes.

My swagger is basically all an act. Molly has been a mystery to me from the start.

She's like a little bird I've managed to lure into my home, and I'm doing my best to keep her from flying away. After almost a year, I'm only a little more confident she's here to stay. Every new bit of information, every piece of the puzzle is a small victory.

Pulling out of my arms, she sits up and leaves the bed, walking to the kitchen.

I watch her cute little ass disappear under the hem of my shirt. "Are you going to the house today?"

While we don't have a permanent place for them, the most desperate of the runaways are in a small house near the park. We hired a social worker to act as their resident advisor, and she'll move into the permanent house as well once I find one I like enough to buy.

I think my dad would be pretty happy with how I'm spending his money now. I'm not dicking around in bars smoking pot all day anymore.

"Actually, I'm picking up my cousin Dean at the airport. He's moving back to Seattle. Want to come?"

She starts the coffee, and looks over her shoulder at me. "I can't."

I'm out of bed, giving the overcast day a glance before heading to the shower. "How come?"

The coffee pot gurgles and blows steam, and she's distracted, looking at her phone.

"Mol?"

Her attention snaps to me. "Oh, I have some research... I've got to check on a client."

"The one from last night?"

It's the closest I've ever come to pressing her for details, and as usual, she doesn't give up any. "Um, no. I'm not working with that person anymore."

She turns her back, taking the carafe out of the machine and pouring the dark liquid into a mug.

"Keep your phone handy. I'll text you where we go if you'd like to meet up later."

"Sure." She walks to the windows, and I wait a moment longer, thinking about the last time I saw Dean's dad, my uncle Jake.

It was right after Molly had attempted to shoot his boss, or I should say right after Jake's boss had tried to strangle Molly. What a clusterfuck.

I'd tried to save her, and he knocked me out with one punch.

Molly's "sister" Lara used her tiny pink gun to shoot him in the head.

"Jesus," I hiss, remembering the blood as I step into the shower.

I watch the rivulets of water trace down the lines of muscle in my torso. After all that, Jake moved back to Tacoma, and I started lifting weights. I gained about twenty pounds of straight muscle, so the next time Molly needs help, I'll be ready.

My phone alarm goes off, and I swear. I'll have to hustle if I plan to catch the train to meet Dean at the airport on time.

* * *

I'm surrounded by a herd of marble buffalo in the center of the Seattle-Tacoma airport when I hear Dean's familiar voice.

"Josh?"

Turning quickly, I spot him. "Dean." I hustle forward to give him a hug.

In five years, he hasn't changed much. His hair is ombré pink, and he's wearing a matching suit. "Who is this?" Dean puts his palm on his chest and walks around me, checking me out. "When I left here you were Gerard Way!"

"I wasn't Gerard Way."

"You had orange hair and you refused to eat..." He's carrying on like a mother hen — not that my cousin's flamboyance has ever bothered me. We've been close all our lives. "Now you're fucking Chris Hemsworth!"

"I'm not Chris Hemsworth."

"Liam Hemsworth?"

"I'm not fucking Liam Hemsworth."

"You'd better not be — I called dibs." His sharp elbow digs into my side as we walk quickly toward baggage claim.

"Shithead." That makes me laugh. I walked right

25

into that one. "How was your flight?"

"Good. The flight was good, my mother is good, and no, I haven't found a place to live yet." He nods as if checking off a list.

"Who pissed in your cheerios?"

"Forget it. Let's go to Pie Bar and get drunk."

"It's not even noon."

He checks his pale pink Swatch. "We've got five minutes. Come on. It's been ages since we've hung out. What else are you doing today besides spending Daddy's money?"

I scrub a hand in the back of my dark hair. "We can go to BRGR bar and have lunch."

"I can't eat hamburgers. I'm on a cleanse."

"In the Bowl has a vegetarian menu."

"Oh, cousin." He shakes his head. "What you don't know about your gut."

"I know we'd better hustle or we're going to be waiting a while."

The train ride to Capitol Hill is almost an hour, and Dean spends most of it talking about his senior year at the Savannah College of Art and Design. It's cool if he hogs the conversation—I haven't decided how much I'm ready to tell him about my last year. He'll just ask a bunch of questions I can't answer and then go off on how I don't know more about the beautiful girl sleeping in my bed. The girl I can't get enough of.

"It's on the coast, but the weather doesn't change there as quickly as it does here. Still, the college scene is edgy and awesome. You'd love it. Are you still hanging out at the bars, avoiding responsibility?"

"Not so much. I have a job." The scenery changes from run down to upscale the closer we get to my neighborhood.

I don't even notice Dean hasn't spoken for almost

fifteen seconds until I look over and see him glaring at me.

"What?"

"You have a *job*?" I start to answer, but he continues. "You left the band and now you have a job?"

I only laugh. "I was dealing with a lot of shit back then. I wasn't very happy."

"Does that mean you're happy now?" He inhales dramatically, placing his palm on his chest. "You've met a girl. It is a girl, right?"

Eyes narrow. "What do you think?"

He shrugs. "For a little while I hoped you might join my team. You were close so many times."

"I've always been straight."

"So, my cis-male friend, who is she, this girl who's stolen your heart?"

"And just like that, I'm reduced to a gender stereotype." Two can play his game.

"Stop dodging and answer the question."

I lean back, sliding my palms down the front of my jeans and choosing my words. Dean is someone I can trust, but I'm not ready to go all in yet.

"She's not from here," I hedge.

"What does that mean? Is she Canadian? You really are gay, aren't you."

"She's from the south. Louisiana."

"Oh!" His eyes sparkle with delight. "A southern lady!"

That makes me frown. "She's not a southern lady."

"She's a southern slut?" His eyes widen, then his hands fly up as if I've drawn a weapon. "Take it easy testosterone. I was only kidding!"

Glancing down, I see my fist has tightened on my lap, and when I go to speak, I realize my jaw is clenched. "She's not a slut. She's from New Orleans."

His lips tighten, and humor flickers in his eyes. "That explains everything," he teases, giving my shoulder a rub. "Oh, come on, Josh. You wouldn't hit a guy with glasses now, would you?"

"I guess I'm a little protective. She's had a tough life."

Not that she's told me any of the details. Still, I've seen her cutting scars, and I know how fast her walls go up. My girl has some pretty deep wounds lurking below the surface, and I'm doing my best to ease her into trusting me, to letting me in and telling me what happened.

When he speaks again, Dean's voice is quiet, serious. "Have you told her about your mom?"

My throat is immediately tight. "It hasn't come up."

"It's a big part of your history."

And just like that, it's all right in my face.

It's a memory I don't revisit often, but when it's triggered, all those feelings hit me like a brick wall. It's ten years ago, and my mom just went for her usual morning jog around the Japanese gardens, past the arboretum, near the university.

Nothing special, it was a day like any other day.

Until she didn't come back.

When her body was recovered in the Sound weeks later, raped and murdered, it was headline news... And my family was never the same.

My dad buried himself in his work and in making billions. I buried myself in music and drugs and hanging out on the streets, hanging with Dean.

Eventually, I decided staying sober and making real friends was a better alternative to whatever the fuck I was doing. I'm not sure my dad ever recovered. We never talk about it.

I never talk about it with anyone.

Perhaps it's time to change that. I can't expect Molly to open up to me if I don't open up to her. For a little while Dean and I ride in silence, listening to the rails, looking out the windows at the passing sites. The needle is in view. Mt. Rainier looms over us all.

Dean interrupts my thoughts, putting a hand on my shoulder, and his voice is kind. "Well, I can't wait to meet her. You think she'll join us for lunch?"

Pulling out my phone, I study the face. I'm a little shaken by having my own invisible scars dragged into the light. Those dark days aren't so far away I don't still feel them. Still, I have managed to find my way through the darkness.

Almost.

Maybe that old, deep scar is what drew me to Molly — I recognized the survival in her eyes.

"I'll send her a text."

CHAPTER 3: AN INVITATION

Molly

Mist coats my cheeks as I stand, gazing up at the high-rise hotel. The time for check out has come and gone, and I imagine housekeeping entering the room.

It's possible they won't understand right away that Dennis Langley, the former occupant of Room 1021, is dead.

Then again, it looks like they did.

I'm across the street as two police cruisers speed up silently like great white sharks and park along the side street.

Stepping farther back, I pass through the foot traffic moving up and down the busy city sidewalk to a courtyard with a pop-up Starbucks and a few burned-out hippies lying on benches.

Are they called hippies now? They have faded dreadlocks and Goodwill clothes, but they're not much older than I am.

By contrast, I'm wearing tight black pants, flats, and a beige trench coat over a black turtleneck. An unnecessary pair of dark shades is over my eyes on this overcast day, but I don't remove them.

A man I recognize steps out of the building and pauses at the entrance to speak to two uniformed officers. His name is Hendricks, and he's the police chief. He was on the scene the night Lara shot Gavin.

Gavin ran an underground sex ring specializing in fetishes, including sex with minors. It was where I first encountered Dennis in that room below the tattoo parlor.

When that party was raided, I ran after the leader. I was determined to kill him, but Gavin was too big and too strong for me. He saw me coming, and he knew what I wanted to do.

He had me by the neck against the wall of his office, and for the first time in my life, I was certain I was about to die.

Joshua tried to save me, but Gavin knocked him out cold. Gavin hit him so hard that even in my state, as the heat burned my eyes and I felt the life slipping away, I worried Joshua would die too.

Then a gunshot sounded...

As if drawn by the energy of memory or the magnetism of my gaze, Chief Hendricks looks across the street directly at me. It's impossible he recognizes me, but he doesn't look away. He returns my stare, and I hear the words of my mentor, *Courage, above all things, is the first quality of the warrior.*

I'm not backing down. For the space of several seconds, I feel proud. I'm glad Hendricks is the one on the scene, because the minute he runs a background check, he'll learn Dennis Langley was a known pedophile.

That's right, Hendricks. I did what you couldn't do.

And just like that, like the tide returning to shore, caution pushes me to fade into the background, disappear without a trace.

Not that I'm afraid to go to jail. I feel confident I could survive jail... It's not that. It's this weakness I've developed in the past year.

It's Joshua.

My jaw clenches, and I fight the notion the way I do every time it tries to come up. I can*not* be in love with Joshua. I can't be in love with anyone.

Still... it's impossible to deny how my body, my heart, and my soul long for him. When he smiles, it curls in the tips of my toes, a bubble rises in my chest.

Lowering my face, I turn away from the scene of my crime. I put my hands in my pockets and walk with purpose away from here.

Candi meets me at the door of the temporary shelter Joshua owns. He bought it when Gavin's sex club was exposed, and the runaways who sold their bodies for food (or drugs) fled to the streets. We found as many of them as we could and brought them here. He's using his dad's money for good, and I'm using the information I get from these girls to add names to my list.

"Where have you been?" Candi snaps at me.

"How is that any of your business?" My gaze is level.

"Joshua was looking for you. He asked if you were here."

"Was he here?" I ask it too fast, and her eyes narrow like she knows something.

She knows nothing.

"He texted me and said he said he texted you."

Shit. I pull my phone out, and it's on silent. "I switched off the ringer."

"Why?"

"Because I didn't want it to ring."

Don't pry into my business.

Want to meet us at ITB for lunch?

The sight of his words makes my stomach flutter. *Fuck.*

Sorry. Ringer off. I'm at the house. Come here.

33

It only takes a moment for him to text they'll be here in a few. My ears are hot, and I'm pissed Candi is watching the whole thing, seeing my control slip.

"You don't know anything about him." The superior tone in her voice pisses me off.

"I've been sleeping with him for a year," I shoot back. "I know him pretty well." *Take that, bitch.*

Yeah, Candi's got a crush on my guy, and I know it's cliché and stupid to fight over him. *Trust me*, I know. But this shit is her problem, and I never back down from a challenge.

"Has he told you about his mom?" Her arms are crossed, one eyebrow arched.

I press my lips together. Score one for Candi—I don't know what she's talking about. "Maybe."

Her eyes narrow like she isn't sure, but she shuts her big mouth and wanders off toward the kitchen. I'm left with her words stinging my mind. I've shared very little of my past with Joshua, and I haven't really thought about what he isn't sharing with me.

So far our relationship has been built on chemistry—in and out of bed. It's easy. We make each other laugh, and we have great sex... Still, sometimes the unspoken words are the loudest ones of all.

Brittanie silently joins me in front of the picture window. It has a view of the park and the large, glass conservatory. "You haven't been here in a while."

"Sorry about that." I take her hand and hold it in my lap. "I got some weird sinus infection that went into my ears. It made me so dizzy. I had to stay in bed a few days."

It also nearly ruined my plans for Dennis, but I don't share that extra bit of information.

"Are you okay now?"

"Yeah. Went to urgent care and got some meds.

How have you been? I've been missing you."

Brittanie is fourteen now—the same age I was when I finally started getting back on track. A runaway from an abusive home, she ended up walking the streets, finding work wherever she could. It was Britt who told me about Dennis and Gavin's parties, who told me what Dennis did to her.

I wonder what she would say if I told her Dennis Langley won't be hurting anybody anymore. I wonder if she would thank me.

"I thought you were mad at us." Her dark eyes are round, and like me, she's a master of studying body language.

It's a survival skill.

"What? Why would I be mad at you?" I smile and shove a lock of silver hair behind my ear.

"I don't know. You hadn't been here in a week, and then you only fight with Candi."

"That doesn't mean I'm mad at you," I say, forcing a laugh. "I like coming here. I want to be sure you're being taken care of. That's the whole point, isn't it?"

She shrugs. "I thought maybe you'd decided it was more Joshua's thing than yours."

My brow furrows. "No way. Joshua's the money guy, but I'm looking out for you. Don't ever forget that."

I can't tell her how I look out for them. Just like I can't tell her sometimes I need a little break. Being here with these broken girls brings my own past a little too close. It makes me frustrated more isn't being done, the wheels of justice turn too slowly. It fuels the rage I've worked so hard to contain and makes me antsy, makes me start looking for a way to implement change on my own.

At present, those feelings are satisfied.

The door opens, and a different emotion fills my

chest as Joshua and another fellow dressed in a pastel suit enter the living room.

"Hey!" Joshua crosses the space to me and kisses my cheek.

"Hey." My eyes close as I inhale juniper and citrus. "Sorry I missed your text."

"Don't worry about it." He takes my hand and leads me to the guy waiting, studying me intently. "Molly, meet my cousin Dean. Dean, Molly."

The guy doesn't smile. He waits, causing the tension to build in my stomach. It's the same tension I feel every time I meet a strange man, wondering what he'll be like, whether he'll try to touch me. Only this time…

"You're gay," I say softly.

As if I broke the spell, he starts to laugh. "You say it like you've never seen one before… which is hard to believe since you're from New Orleans."

Shaking my head, I extend a hand. "I'm sorry. I didn't mean to say that out loud."

"Good thing I don't mind." He walks around the house inspecting the place. "Joshua told me you're his partner here, in this idea for a safe house."

"It was mostly Josh—"

"Makes sense." Dean nods.

Joshua doesn't say anything beside me, and I see he's watching his cousin, waiting for the verdict.

Dean continues through the downstairs floor then looks into the kitchen. "Interesting development." He picks up a textbook left behind on the dining room table. "Interesting."

"That's mine," Brittanie interjects. "I'm working on my GED."

"You're so young." I think of myself at her age.

Lara and I moved to Paris when I was thirteen to get away from the men abusing us in the theater, but the terror and the rage of what happened there moved with us. It haunted me. It chased me during the day, whenever we were in crowded places. It woke me at night screaming, until we finally left the city to live down by the beach in Nice.

It was beautiful.

It's where I found a cure.

Only *cure* isn't quite the right word. I found a way to get even.

"It doesn't matter how old you are," she continues. "I just have to pass the exam, and then I can apply for college."

"I didn't know you were coming for a visit!" Rebecca, the social worker we hired to live in the house, trots down the stairs. "The girls and I could have pulled together some lunch."

"No worries," Joshua answers. "I wanted to show my cousin Dean the place. He's just moving back to the city. Dean, Rebecca is the resident mom here."

She laughs. "I'm not sure I'm old enough to be a mom. More like a big sister… but I am a therapist, and I am here to look out for the girls, counsel them, give them advice."

"I'm very impressed." Dean turns to Josh. "Have you ever considered adding art therapy to your services?"

Rebecca is excited by his idea, and as Joshua starts to answer my phone goes off. I wave, "Be right back." Lara's picture is on the face, and I tap the green button as I step out the front door. "Lara? What's up?"

It's unusual for her to call me, and when she speaks I can tell something is off. "Hey, I was just thinking about you. We haven't talked in a while."

She's speaking too quickly, almost as if she's nervous. "Are you okay? Is Mark—"

"We're fine. Mark's fine. Jillian is starting to walk, and she's getting into everything."

A smile tightens my lips as I think about her baby with her police detective husband. Honestly, I've done my best to pull away slowly from them. Hanging around with Mark is a complication I really don't need in my life.

"Why are you calling then?"

"Do I have to have a reason?" Her laugh is defensive, but I don't feel like arguing.

"No. It just seems like you probably do."

The front door opens, and Joshua steps out, coming to me and putting a hand on my waist. His dark hair makes his gray eyes glow, and his smile reveals straight white teeth. "Everything okay?" His voice is nice and low.

I only shrug, putting my hand on his where he's touching me, sending electricity humming in my veins. *It's Lara*, I mouth.

"Is that Josh?" Lara says on the phone. "Oh, good. So why don't the two of you come for a visit? It's Mardi Gras weekend, and I haven't seen you since the wedding."

"Oh, I don't think we'll be able to—"

"Molly." Her voice is a gentle scold. "I want you to come home."

Joshua frowns, and I can't help thinking how much he's changed since the last time we were all together, how this lion emerges whenever he senses I'm feeling threatened.

"I am home." My voice is quiet. Joshua's brow relaxes, and his expression changes to something I'm not ready to face yet. Turning my back, I try to salvage what I just did. "I mean... I don't think of New Orleans as my home anymore."

"Okay…" She's processing this new development, this crack in the wall. "Still, we need a visit, and now is the perfect time. I miss you, and I want Jilly to know her aunt Molly."

"I'm not really her aunt."

"What difference does that make?"

Exhaling, I pinch the bridge of my nose. "I'll talk to Joshua about it and let you know."

"Perfect!" Her voice is louder now, as if I've already said yes. "You can stay with us!"

"We'll get a room in town… If we decide to come."

"Just tell me when you're getting here."

The call disconnects, and I'm still standing with my back to Josh. He steps up behind me and grasps my upper arms in both hands. The heat of his body behind me reminds me of this morning in bed, and my nipples tighten. Turning me gently, our eyes meet, and I feel the flush on my cheeks.

A sexy grin curls his lips. "What's going on? What do we need to talk about?"

"Lara wants us to come down for Mardi Gras."

"Let's do it!" The loud voice almost makes me jump out of my skin, and Dean practically skips onto the porch. "I miss the floats and the costumes… Mardi Gras is *gorgeous*."

From what I remember, it's a drunken mess.

Joshua steps between me and his cousin and surveys my face. "I think it sounds fun. Is there a reason we can't go?"

Chewing my bottom lip, I think about the prospect of leaving Seattle for a few days, especially in view of recent events. I remember the way Hendricks looked at me from across the street.

I shake my head. I could be imagining the whole thing. "I guess not."

Dean makes a little cheering noise, and Joshua glances over his shoulder. "I thought you needed to find a place to live?"

"A place to live will be waiting when we get back. Let's go party!"

Joshua laughs and returns to me. I force a grin, but Lara's nervous voice is in my head.

Was it because we haven't spoken in a while? But she's never been nervous talking to me. The guys continue ahead, discussing flight times and options. Joshua's dad has a private jet he says we can use... My mind is far away, trying to sort out why Lara called me out of the blue and what she might be hiding.

Returning to New Orleans always makes me uneasy. So many dark memories lurk in that sweltering city. The monsters are dead and gone, but there's no way I'll go back there with my guard down.

I'm not that little girl anymore.

CHAPTER 4: A MEMORY

Joshua

The sky is lit up purple, green, and gold when we arrive at the Hotel le Marais. Through our window balcony, we can hear the noise of Bourbon Street. The party is in full swing a half-block away and will be for the next seventy-two hours from what I understand.

Dean rolls his suitcase past us down the hall, waving his free hand over his head. "I'm headed to Oz. Text ya later, freaks!"

Molly doesn't answer. She's been quiet the entire trip, her guard firmly in place.

I understand it, I guess. This town holds a lot of bad memories for her.

The door closes behind me, and I linger a moment watching her cross to the window. She's wearing tight dark jeans and a maroon tunic sweater. Her long hair hangs in loose waves down her back, and she looks down to the street below.

Closing the distance between us, I place my hands on her waist and my lips briefly against her neck. "Do you want to see Lara tonight?"

She leans her back against my chest, and my hands slide to the front her waist. I can think of something I'd rather do instead of going out, but as quickly as she lets me hold her, she steps forward, out of my arms and turns to face me.

"I'm going for a walk."

My eyebrows rise. "Now? In that mob?"

Molly has always steered clear of large crowds and

unpredictable situations.

"There's something I need to see."

Intriguing choice of words. *Need*...

"Let's go." I slip the door card into the pocket of my jeans.

Her lips part, exposing the white tips of her bottom teeth. "I want to go alone."

Fuck that. "I want to go with you."

"Joshua —"

"I know you're perfectly capable of taking care of yourself, but I don't know this city as well as I know Seattle."

"I do." She starts to pass me, but I catch her hand.

"Which is why I want to go with you."

Her eyes linger on our connection, and her lips tighten. I'm ready to argue. This isn't the time or the place for her to be running around alone at night. But she doesn't make me.

With a little sigh, she nods, and I follow her out to the street below. It's a cool, damp night with rain hanging in the air.

Molly doesn't carry a bag of any kind, but I know she's armed. She slipped her little pink gun in her boot before we left the apartment in Seattle. I'm not sure if she knows I know.

We head two blocks northeast until we're just at the edge of Jackson Square. The noise of Mardi Gras is like a football game happening right on the other side of the tall, stone buildings. Echoes of laughter and music greet us around every corner. The black edge of a mob of revelers is at the top of the intersection ahead. Like a bubble it swells toward us then recedes from view again.

Molly doesn't hold my hand. She takes a sharp left, and I drop from beside her to behind her. The streetlight casts yellow halos in the heavy night. We're in a narrow flagstone alley, and rainbow-colored puddles line the center.

She walks all the way to the corner and stops, turning to look up at the façade of a newish building.

"This is new construction," I say, looking up with her.

The stucco exterior is painted white, and French doors covered with large green shutters line the first level down the block.

"Lara told me he had it torn down," she says softly. "It was right here until it burned. Then it stood here empty for another several years. Then Mark got permission from the city to have it torn down. I have no idea what it is now."

My eyes roam the length and height of the massive structure.

"What was it before?" We're both speaking in hushed tones.

At first I was only following her lead, but with every word, I understand this is a massive window she's opening to me. She's allowing me inside a sacred space in her past.

"It was a theater. It was the hottest burlesque show in the French Quarter, and Lara was the rising star." She says the words as if she's reading them from a program or a bulletin board.

"What were you?"

For the beat of two hearts, she blinks, looking up at some distant memory. "I was nothing."

CHAPTER 5: CONFRONTATION

Molly

Joshua stands beside me trying to understand. His immediate response is to argue, but he doesn't know this history.

I wasn't supposed to be in this club. I was underage, a child. Lara found me where I'd been left on the sidewalk in an alley. I'd been told to sit there and be quiet and wait. My mother would be back to pick me up in an hour, after she'd gone shopping or run her errands…

I was only eleven years old, and as the sun traveled lower in the sky, as the foot traffic grew thinner and the shadows grew taller, I played with a tiny, wooden nesting doll I kept in my pocket. It was the smallest of the set, and I thought she was so cute to be so tiny and still have so much detail.

My stomach growled, and my eyes grew heavy. A breeze blew damp, metallic air in my face, and I wanted to go home. I wanted supper and a bath and my mom.

No one ever came for me.

I sat on the wet flagstone in that dirty alley and waited and waited…

Until Lara found me crying and took me inside to live with her.

"I should have gone to school." My voice is quiet. "I should have gone into foster care."

"Why didn't you?" Joshua is close, but he's giving me space to remember this.

"No one cared," I say with a shrug, glancing up to

meet his eyes.

"Lara cared."

My lips tighten, and I nod. "I guess to her, I was something she'd lost. I became her family. She said she'd take care of me."

The only problem was neither of us were strong enough to fight the demons in this place.

"Did she?"

"She tried. When it got to be too much we left with a friend... We moved to Paris."

"France?" Surprise is in his voice.

I've never told Joshua this much about myself. I don't really know why. So many nights we lay in each other's arms looking at the light play across the walls. I could have told him then.

I never wanted to until now.

"Yep, France. From there we moved to Nice, to a beautiful villa right beside the Mediterranean Sea."

"It sounds amazing."

Nodding, I can't help thinking about my hidden scars. "It was."

His warm hand covers my upper arm. "Then why do you sound sad?"

Reaching up, I cover the back of his hand with mine. Our eyes meet, and understanding, concern... love radiates toward me.

We're interrupted by the click of heels on flagstone. It's a man's shoes, and alarm flashes in my chest. I spin quickly on guard to face the sound, but I can't see anyone in the shadows. The crowd of revelers bursts through the top of the intersection, where Bourbon meets Orleans Street.

Whoever was hiding there, watching us, is lost as a group of men and women wander up the alley in our direction.

"Tujague's is this way!" A girl shouts, pointing as they bustle past us.

My eyes are fixed on the place where they came, where the footsteps retreated. Who was standing in the shadows listening to us?

It could have been anyone, I suppose. A drunk tourist who lost his way or a homeless person. Still, that sound of footsteps…

"What now?" Joshua slides his hand down to lace his fingers with mine.

I'm still searching the shadows. "We could go to Oz… see if Dean's still there." It's the direction the footsteps retreated.

"Lead the way."

Joshua holds my hand, but I'm tense as we walk the few blocks towards Bourbon Street. I constantly scan the dark, arched doorways and fenced courtyards for any signs of a lone male.

I see nothing.

I don't even know what I'm looking for or why.

Why would someone be watching us? Who would even know I was here?

"You never answered my question." Joshua's voice is calm, reassuring in the eerie night.

"Sorry." I give his hand a squeeze. "What did you ask me?"

"You said you lived on the beach in Nice. In an enormous villa. I'm pretty sure that would qualify as paradise."

He's waiting to know why I wasn't happy there. The story is too long for this cold night. "I guess we carry paradise inside us after all."

Or not.

The alley ends, and the mass of tourists blasts toward us, snatching the breath from my lungs.

Pulling away from the noise, I step behind Joshua's shoulder. "I think we should go to Lara's now."

His phone is in his hand, and he grins as he punches up the Uber app. "I thought you might say that. Come on."

"Where have you been?" Lara meets me with a hug and a kiss on the porch of their small house in the garden district. "I've been waiting for you to call."

"I had to run an errand." I step inside, allowing her to greet Josh.

"Joshua?" Her voice goes high. "My goodness, I wouldn't have recognized you. You're huge!"

"That's what she said," he teases.

"Seriously, though." She follows us inside, closing the door. "You're so grown up!"

"Stop embarrassing Joshua." I pause in the living room, in front of a small pack and play with a baby's walking toy beside it.

"What is this errand you had to run? You haven't been in the city in a year!"

I'm about to make something up when Joshua nearly makes my heart stop.

"We stopped by the scene of the crime." He gives Lara a mischievous wink, and my throat goes dry.

Lara frowns. "What does that mean?"

"Your wedding! We stopped by the cathedral. Remember? You weren't supposed to get married in the square without a permit..."

Mark emerges from the kitchen holding their baby daughter Jillian on his hip. "You went to Jackson Square?"

Roland is right behind him. "I wouldn't be caught dead in the Quarter tonight."

"You work in the Quarter." It's out before I can stop

it, snarky as ever.

Roland stops and narrows his eyes at me. "Hey, Shortcake. What's new in bitch?"

My lips twist. I hadn't really meant to start off sparring with Roland, but oh well. "What's new in retirement?"

"You wish I'd retired. I bet I'm doing more than you."

"Enough, you two." Lara passes between us to take the baby from Mark. "Watch what Jillian can do." Chubby legs start pumping as Lara leans in close, rubbing her nose against the little girl's. "Show Aunt Molly how you can walk! Okay, Jilly? Okay?"

She sits on the floor with Jillian standing in front of her facing me. "Walk to Aunt Molly!"

"Wait! I'm not ready for this." I mean those words in so many ways. I have never been around babies, and Jillian has only seen me a handful of times, none that she can remember.

"Just hold out your hands," Lara whispers to me.

Bending my knees, I hold my hands toward her, but the baby only looks at me with round eyes.

"Walk to Aunt Molly!" Lara repeats in an even higher voice, but Jillian turns and walks into Lara's chest, hiding her face against her mother's neck.

"She's smart," Roland says from behind me, and I give him a look.

"Jillian!" Lara complains.

Joshua laughs and goes to Lara. "Let me try." He touches her little shoulder, and of course, she grins up at him. Little flirt.

"I don't do babies," I grumble, heading toward the kitchen. "Can I fix a drink?"

"I'll help." Mark follows me into the open, modern kitchen. It's really nice with stainless steel fixtures and

49

gray quartz counter tops.

"I really like your place." I wait at the bar while he takes out a bottle of wine and three beers.

"Thanks. We've been slowly fixing it up ourselves on the weekends." He sets the drinks on the counter and digs in the drawers for a corkscrew.

I fumble with something to say. Lara and I met Mark when he was only a member of the set crew at the theater. It was so long ago, before all the bad stuff happened. Then when we ran, I'm pretty sure Lara thought she'd never see him again.

I never knew the whole story.

"How do you like working here? Being a cop in New Orleans?" I trace my fingernail along a line in the counter.

"I'm a detective."

"Still, this place is pretty rough."

"It is." His blue eyes flicker to mine, and I remember a very brief time when I was really young and I had a crush on this handsome man. "Why did you go back there?"

The question draws me up short. "What do you mean? Go back where?"

"You went back to the theater... or where it used to be. Why?"

"I didn't know I was so easy to read."

"You're not. That's why I'm asking." He guides the corkscrew into the wine bottle.

"I couldn't do it the last time I was here... when it was still standing."

"It was a burned-out husk. It might have made you feel better seeing it that way."

Pain twists in my heart. "I don't think so. I didn't feel better seeing it as a whole new thing."

"It's not anything at the moment."

The cork is out, and he takes down two crystal wine glasses. "Pinot Gris?"

"Sure." I watch as he pours the pale yellow liquid, thinking about that old place and how many memories it held, good and horrible.

"As dark as those memories are, Lara couldn't see it that way either," he muses. "It was on the top of my list when I joined the NOPD. Gavin was dead. Guy was dead. No one fought us tearing it down."

He hands me the glass and tilts a beer bottle toward it. "Cheers."

I take a sip of the dry wine, thinking. If Lara is basically my sister, then Mark is like my older brother. "Why did Lara want me to come here?" I watch his eyes as he drinks the beer, scanning for any signs of deception.

"She did it for me." He lowers the beer, leveling his gaze on me. "I asked her to."

I almost choke on my sip of wine. "Why would you do that?"

"I wanted to see you face to face." We face each other, and his expression is grave. "I think you're doing it again."

Setting my glass down a little too hard, I step back, my walls shooting into position. "I don't know what you're talking about. Doing what?"

He only watches me, but I'm finished here. Mark is a cop, not my brother, and the last thing I'm going to do is confide in him. I'm headed for the living room when he stops me in my tracks.

"When you ran the second time, when you left Nice, I went to visit Freddie Lovell in Paris."

Skipping back through the years, I remember the wealthy Frenchman who helped us escape New Orleans. "Why would you do that?"

"I was angry. I was trying to find answers, and I thought he might have them."

"Freddie doesn't know anything. He's just a nice man who wanted to help us."

Mark closes the space between us, stopping right in front of me. "He said you'd wake up screaming in the night. Are you still screaming?"

My eyes fly to his. "I've got Joshua now."

"And I can tell he knows absolutely nothing." The muscle in Mark's jaw moves. "How are you fighting the demons now, Molly? Are you still doing it?"

My chest is on fire, and I've got to get out of this fucking house. Turning on my heel, I leave Mark standing in the kitchen. "Joshua, we need to go now. Dean might be looking for us."

I'm breathing hard and my eyes are clouded. I only barely register him holding Jillian against his chest, bouncing her with one large hand on her back.

"Trust me," he laughs. "Dean is not looking for us."

"Who's Dean?" Lara's eyes go from Josh to me.

"Joshua's cousin came with us. We really need to go. I'm so tired. Jetlag."

"You're going the wrong way for jetlag." Roland taunts me from where he's sitting on the couch with his arms crossed. "It's eleven here, which is only eight in Seattle. You could lie and say you're hungry."

My stomach is tight as a fist, and I couldn't eat a thing. "Fuck off, Roland. Maybe I just want to be alone with my boyfriend."

Joshua's eyebrows shoot up, but Lara's the one who speaks. "You know, pretty soon we'll have to start a swear jar. Jilly will be old enough to repeat everything we say."

It's her perfect mother way of telling me not to say *fuck* in front of her baby. Her goddamn perfect baby and her goddamn perfect husband and her goddamn perfect life in this goddamn city where she never has to worry about a goddamn thing.

"Joshua, I need to go." My voice trembles. The rage in my chest is only barely contained.

He hands off the baby and stands, coming to where I'm in front of the door. "We'll check in with you guys tomorrow," he says in his easy way.

Lara is on her feet, heading toward us, but I turn the handle and charge out onto the porch. I've had enough for one night. I want to get far away from here and do something to forget.

Only my method of forgetting isn't available at this time.

I'll have to figure out another way.

CHAPTER 6: LET ME IN

Joshua

"We're not going to find him." I do my best not to crash into Molly, to hold steady in the swaying mass of men dressed only in masks and Mardi-Gras-colored speedos.

Neon lights flash through the smoke filling the air around us. Every few minutes the hiss of the smoke machine blasts through the driving house music, and I can barely hear a word over the noise of the 808.

From Lara's I ordered an Uber, and we retraced our steps right back to where we almost started tonight before my girl got cold feet. Now we're in Oz at the bar. I've got a Guinness, and Molly's doing shots. Layers of beads are around our necks, and we haven't even seen a parade.

"They're not allowed to call it a hand grenade," she says, wrinkling her cute little nose after tossing back her third neon-green concoction. "Only Tropical Isle has those."

She tries to catch the bartender's eye, and I'm rammed by another wave of men dancing. "I think you've had enough." I brace my hands on either side of her.

"I think you're overdressed." Her eyes narrow with her smile, and she circles a finger around the button on my shirt. "Everyone else is in speedos."

Smiling down at her, I catch that finger and bring it to my lips. "Everyone else is gay."

Supposedly we came here to find Dean, but I haven't seen her look around the room once. She's buzzing, and I'm curious.

Since we arrived in the city, Molly's been on edge. Our moment in front of the old theater gave me hope she might open up at last, but whatever Mark said in the kitchen drove her out of Lara's house and right back in her shell...

Or it did until her third faux hand-grenade shot.

"Let's call it." I catch her waist, drawing her closer before shot number four can be ordered.

I hope if we get back to the room, she might start talking again. I want her to tell me what's going on behind those blue eyes.

"Patience, grasshopper." She places her palm on my chest. "Men come and go all night here. He's probably in the back making friends."

"If that's the case, he's even less interested in seeing us."

"Who's less interested?" The loud male voice causes Molly to stiffen in my arms. "Too late short stack. I've already seen you're drunk."

"I am not drunk." Molly's control snaps in place as she frowns at the man joining us at the bar. "Why are you here? I thought you wouldn't be caught dead in the Quarter tonight."

He signals the bartender, and they exchange a brief chat. The big guy pours Roland a vodka on the rocks. Another hiss of the machine, another layer of smoke falls around us, and the neon lights along with the patrons go wild at the start of an Abba song.

"Maybe I'm horny," he quips, taking a sip of the clear liquor.

"You're spying on me."

He leans back and exhales impatiently. "Lara's

worried about you. She's afraid you've fallen back into… old habits."

"Of course, this is about Lara. You don't give a shit about me."

I'm waiting for him to argue with her, but he doesn't. He only lifts the glass and takes another sip of vodka.

"Whatever." Molly pushes her hands against the bar. "You're ready to go?"

She looks up at me, and I know that look. She's pretending not to care, but this guy just shoved his thumb in an old wound. I don't know what it's about or why, but it hasn't created any warm feelings in me toward him.

I'm about to jump to my girl's defense when a voice I know well chimes in happily. "Well, look what the cat dragged in!" Dean dances up in nothing but a purple, green, and gold speedo, and I explode with a laugh.

Shit, I needed that.

"What the fuck are you wearing?" I hold back his sweaty torso as he tries to loop an arm around my neck. "Get off me."

"It's like the Mardi Gras Zissou society! Some guy in the back is handing them out."

Molly sees him, and she actually laughs, too. I'm relieved. I don't know why the fuck I worry about her. She's tough as nails.

I guess I am in love with her.

"You look amazing!" She grabs her empty shot glass and holds it in the air as a salute. "To Mardi Gras!"

Roland turns to see what the commotion is all about, and Dean steps back as if shocked. "Hell-ooo! Who do we have here?"

"Roland Desjardin." Molly's nemesis holds out a polished hand toward my dazzled cousin. "You must be the person we're looking for."

"God, I hope so!" Dean pushes through us, putting himself directly in front of Roland. "Dean Andrews. How do I know you?"

"I'm not sure you do. At least not as well as you're going to."

I've got to hand it to him. Roland's smooth.

Molly steps to me, holding the front of my jacket. "That's something I've never seen before. Let's get out of here. Leave them to it."

It's what I've wanted her to say all night. I tap Roland on the arm. "Go easy on my cousin."

"Never," Roland says at the same time Dean cries, "Don't you dare!"

I shake my head, leading her out as Molly calls over my shoulder to them, "No glove, no love!"

My hands are on her waist, and I grin as speedo-clad men around us shout the same motto back at her. She's high-fiving a million gay angels on the way out the door, and I shake my head.

Outside, the rain has stopped. Two blocks walking away from the party, and it's still a roar behind us. Our hotel in sight, but I'm not quite ready to go up to our room. Instead I stop, turning her back to the wall and covering her with my body.

"What is it?" She blinks up at me, and I put my thumb along her hairline, smoothing a silver lock behind her ear.

"I like you this way. You're more playful than I've ever seen you."

Her lips tighten, but she doesn't smile. "Am I? I think you're more serious now. I think it's because of me."

"It's because I need to be." Dipping my chin, I catch her eye. "I want to kiss you."

She catches my cheeks fast and rises on her tiptoes, pulling my mouth to hers. It's not what I expected, but shit, I'm there. Our lips part, and her tongue finds mine. I lean closer, pulling her to me and curling my tongue against hers, inhaling her scent of peonies and fresh rain.

She exhales a little noise and pulls back, sliding her fingers along my jaw.

We're both breathing fast, and I'm still holding her close to me. "What's going on here?"

"What do you mean?"

"I mean what's going on with you? Are you okay? We don't have to stay here if you'd rather go back to Seattle."

"No, we can stay… We should stay." Her gaze goes over my shoulder, and her irritation returns. "These people drive me crazy is all."

I catch her face, bringing her back to me. "Hey, kiss me again."

Her eyes blink to mine, and her lip goes between her teeth. "Okay."

I lean down, nudging her lips apart with mine. She leans into me, following the movements of my mouth, curling her nails against my cheek. Her breath comes faster, and her lips pull mine, tongues tasting.

It's citrus and too-sweet alcohol, and her breasts rise and fall against my chest. Her body sways against mine, and I can't fight biology. Leaning closer, I know she feels what I want, the hardness in my jeans, because her fingers go to my waist.

Her mouth moves lower, kissing my neck, dropping to the center of my chest. I realize a second after I hear the clink of metal she's unfastening my belt, lowering to her knees. My arm is against the brick wall where she was standing, and I rest my forehead against it.

Shit, I want her mouth around my cock.

I remember how it feels.

The first time Molly blew me, my knees gave out. This girl gives killer head. It took me a solid minute to come back from that orgasm.

The second time... Well, it was about the same.

By the third time, I realized something else was going on besides her blowing my mind. She used it to keep me away, to satisfy me so I'd let her retreat behind those walls.

So I stopped it.

Fuck, it'd be so easy to give into what's about to happen right now. My stomach is tight, and with a groan, I catch her under the arms before she has my fly down.

"What?" Her eyes are round with surprise.

"Come here." My voice is thick as I lift her, kissing her again briefly. "Don't do that. I want you here with me."

"I am here with you." She smiles, but I'm not buying it.

"Then don't pull away."

Her eyes close and she steps forward, wrapping her body in my arms. "Will you hold me?"

"I'll hold you forever." She's so close, and my erection aches. Damn whoever hurt my little bird. "Let me in, Molly."

Stepping out of my arms, she takes my hand. "Let's go to the room."

Chapter 7: A Visitor

Molly

Joshua's eyes are heated as he stands with his back to the closed door of our hotel room. He looks at me like I'm a steak dinner, and he's ravenous, his erection a tempting lump in his jeans.

It's thrilling and hot and sends tingles through my stomach.

I'm loose and relaxed from the alcohol, but contrary to what Roland said, I'm not drunk. Standing at the window, I open the blinds so I'm silhouetted by the streetlight.

I slip off my sweater then quickly unfasten my jeans, taking my panties off with them. When I straighten, I'm left in only a push-up bra. I arch my back, knowing how much he loves this profile.

Our eyes meet, and his burn my skin.

I slide a finger from my lips to the center of my breasts and lower, desire thick in my voice. "Like what you see?"

"Yes." Lust is heavy in his.

"Take off your shirt."

He unbuttons the top three buttons then grabs the back and pulls it over his head. His dark hair is a sexy mess, and the dim light deepens the shadows on his torso, the ripples of muscle when he moves. He's delicious, and I'm so wet.

I thought it would bother me as his body grew more muscular, bigger with every passing month.

It didn't.

It made me want him more.

He's gorgeous — my big, strong man with the heart I can't resist just below the surface.

Stepping carefully across the room, I stop in front of him, tracing my fingers lightly up the lines in his arms. I touch his stomach and feel him tense.

"What would you like me to do?"

Large hands cover my waist then slide down to my bare ass. "Trust me."

"I trust you more than anyone in my life."

Our voices are hushed, and I rise on tiptoes, stretching to meet his mouth. He leans down and kisses me, parting my lips and sweeping his tongue inside, curling and claiming me. I'm so hot, my core aches for him.

I've never ached for anyone.

I didn't think I could.

"Come." My fingers curl in the waist of his jeans, pulling him with me as I walk backwards. The mattress hits my calves, and I climb onto it. I'm in the center of the king-sized bed on my knees, waiting.

He pauses long enough to shove his jeans down, to allow his erection to spring free. It's thick and pointing straight at me, a clear drop on the tip.

He climbs up, crossing to me on his knees, and I stop him, pushing him into a sitting position. I want to straddle his lap. I want to ride him until he groans, low and deep, curling my toes. I want to come all over him as he fills me, hot and wet.

It takes less than a second to position him under me and drop with a deep sigh onto his straining cock. "Yes…"

"Molly…" He catches my waist, and that sound in his voice clenches my stomach.

He wants me here with him, and I want him to

know he's the only man I want to be with.

Holding his broad shoulders, I rise up on my knees, letting his cock slide all the way to the edge, then dropping down, sheathing him, balls deep inside me.

"Oh, yeah," he groans, and I do it again, rising high and dropping low, feeling every ridge of him as he massages me in the most erotic way.

I cup his cheeks with my hands and kiss his mouth as I move. I taste him slow and easy, like he's the most delicious forbidden fruit in the garden. Because he is. He's something I shouldn't want, yet my body craves.

Every hard muscle, every sharp edge heightens my desire.

My clit slides against his pelvis, and flashes of orgasm snake up my thighs. I ride him faster, irresistible pressure tightening low in my pelvis, blooming through my legs. My movements are more focused, faster... deeper... It tightens until I think it's too much to stand.

And then it breaks.

"Oh, yes," I gasp, my head falling back as I'm taken by the crashing wave of pleasure.

Joshua's mouth covers my breasts as my body breaks. He teases and bites my tingling nipples, and my insides break into another wave orgasm.

Then he comes with a shout, pulsing and holding me as my nails tighten against his skin.

I fall forward, hugging his warm body, my hair spilling around us. His lips touch my neck, my shoulder, tasting and biting, scuffing my sensitive skin with his beard. Then he kisses me again as his arms circle my waist. We drift down together, sated and happy.

We're sweaty and panting and joined by invisible bonds that grow tighter every time we connect this way. It's quietly terrifying, because I know time is running out.

He wants more.

He wants me to let him in, and I have to make a decision.

The room is dark, and my cheek is on his chest. I can hear his heart beating steadily, slowing with his breath.

"That's how I want you to be." His deep voice vibrates against my skin. "Here with me."

I trace a finger along his stomach. "I'm always with you."

"Not always."

I can't answer, because it's true.

One time I came close to telling him everything, right after Gavin was killed. I was healing and vulnerable, and I remembered how I felt thinking Gavin might have killed him.

I wanted to let Joshua in, and I almost told him why I'd gone after Gavin, what I knew about Dennis, what Brittanie had told me, and what I was planning to do.

Then he'd said he couldn't believe he'd thought Gavin was a friend. He was so angry. He thought he knew the guy…

"I could never be around someone who hurt others intentionally," he'd said. "I wouldn't even want them in my life."

It hit me in the stomach like a medicine ball, and just like that, I retreated back behind my walls.

He doesn't press for more, and I wait, listening until I know he's asleep. I wait for the minutes to pass, tracing my finger along his arm, following the lines to his shoulder as his sleep deepens.

"Joshua," I whisper. He doesn't respond. "I wish I could give you what you want."

He only breathes heavily, fast asleep.

Moving out of his arms, I linger to kiss his scruffy

cheek before I leave the bed and go into the bathroom, shutting the door silently.

Inside, I use the toilet, run some water on a cloth, and clean myself. I do my best not to make loud noises.

I need this time to think about what happens now.

Lara doesn't know about Dennis, but she's suspicious.

Mark knows about Esterhaus. He also knows about what happened to me, what happened to Lara, and even though he's a cop, he walked away from my vigilante justice once before.

He thought it was the last time.

When Lara shot Gavin, it was easily excused as self-defense, and technically it was. She was protecting me from being killed. When Gavin's illegal sex ring was uncovered, the authorities were even less concerned with punishing us.

Joshua knows about that incident in Seattle, and it was somewhat easy for him to understand. Maybe he didn't completely understand my need to infiltrate Gavin's crime ring, but in the end, he let it go.

He doesn't know about Dennis.

He doesn't know what happened here.

He doesn't know what's behind my scars.

At some point, I've got to tell him something.

I shut off the bathroom light before opening the door, and I'm momentarily blinded in the darkness. Feeling my way to the bed, I kick his shirt on the floor. I pick it up and use it to cover my naked body, leaving the buttons undone.

The blinds are still open, and with a heavy heart, I walk over to the window to look out. Foot traffic is nonstop at this time of year with all the tourists in the city. I stand for a little while watching them, wondering what it must be like to have a normal, easy, uncomplicated life.

No fear of the hammer of justice waiting just around the corner.

I'm about to pull the string to shut them out when I notice something.

My heart jumps, then flies like a hummingbird in my chest. The shadow on the ground doesn't move, and I follow it with my eyes up the pavement to the wall, to the man in the suit, leaning against it, lighting a cigar.

The light from the match illuminates his features just long enough for me to recognize him. He inhales, and his chin lifts as he surveys the hotel, looking up and around the perimeter.

My lips part, and I'm breathing fast.

How did he find me? What does he want?

I remember tonight at the theater, the sound of shoes on pavement. Was it him?

A noise from the bed makes me jump, and I clutch my mouth to silence my squeal. I'm frozen in place, waiting, but Joshua doesn't wake up.

Reaching down, I grab my jeans off the floor and quickly pull them over my hips. I fasten the center three buttons on Joshua's shirt and shove the tail into my pants, then I snatch his blazer off the back of the chair. It's too big for me, but I'm not worried about fashion. I'm worried about getting down there before the man disappears.

I'm pushing an arm into the sleeve when I spot a sheet of paper on the floor. It's been shoved under our door, and I drop the blazer to go and pick it up.

Myshka,

I was surprised to cross paths with you this evening. I didn't want to cause problems, so I did not speak. Still, I would like to see you again if you are able. I will be at The Napoleon House tomorrow afternoon. Perhaps we might bump into each other during happy hour.

My best wishes,
S. Volodya

Joshua makes a noise from the bed, and I crumple the paper in my hand. I pick up his blazer and return it to the chair before dashing to the window again. It only takes a moment to see he's gone. My shoulders drop, and I look to the door once more.

I'm sure he gave the note to the front desk clerk and had him deliver it. I'm certain he already knows my room number, but he wouldn't risk coming up here and encountering hotel security.

He doesn't need to.

He knows I'll meet him at the Napoleon House tomorrow.

I unfasten my jeans and slip them off again, going to the bed and climbing in beside Joshua. Curling my chest against his back, I wrap my arm around his waist and kiss his shoulder. He makes a noise in his sleep and covers my hand with his.

My eyes close, and my mind is far away, years ago, on the other side of the globe…

Chapter 8: Education

Seven years ago

Molly

The tree with the pink flowers hides the moonlight from the path, but I know my way in the dark. My chest burns, driving me faster until I'm at the top of the wooden staircase leading down to the pebble beach below.

Celeste the housekeeper had bragged about it the first day. *Our beach has sand mixed in with the stones, very unusual*, she said.

Then she looked at me too long, her black eyes examining mine, searching for clues. *What is wrong with this small girl? Why are her blue eyes vacant and haunted? Why was she sent here?*

They all watched me, and I had to get out. I had to get away from that house and that bed and the walls closing in on me.

My feet thump on the weathered steps leading down to the shoreline, and I pick up speed as I descend. Terror drives me on.

Every night the men return.

They surround me on that couch in that room far away… that room under the theater stage. The noise of dancing feet *click-clacks* above us, and I move closer to the man I think will protect me. He smiles down at me, green eyes glittering, and hands me a glass of clear liquid.

"Drink this," he says, and the light glints off his

gold pinky ring.

I don't question him. I take the cup and sip the sweet liquid. It tastes like sugar, but when it's gone, salty vinegar remains in my mouth.

The shapes grow hazy as they move around me. Large hands touch my legs, but I feel sluggish. I'm so tired. I need to close my eyes and sleep…

Until I wake up screaming.

My throat is tight, and the pebbles are under my feet. They're soft and feel good as I step on them, and the tightness grows stronger in my chest. It's filtering down into my arms and legs. I hear the noise of the ocean, but the moon is hiding behind a cloud. I keep pushing forward, faster and faster until I feel water on my feet.

Dropping to my knees, I fumble with hasty fingers at my waist, searching for the blade hidden there.

The moon emerges as I pull it from its sheath, as I place it against my skin, glowing white in the night.

Under the full moon, the world is black and white, stark truth, no shades of gray.

I drag the razor across my arm, and the blood bubbles up thick and black.

"Yes," I cry out, my voice trembling and broken.

I can breathe.

The blood flows, taking the darkness with it.

I move to my other arm, repeating the process, releasing the demons.

I shudder and cry, tears coating my cheeks. I cry until my throat aches, until my voice is raw. I cry as their evil leaves my body.

Warm blood drips down my arms, and I lean forward, allowing it to run into the salt water. It will float away on the waves. The sea will carry them from me. The rippling breakers repeat, repeat, falling over,

over, washing and churning, cleansing me of the past.

I put my palms against the sea floor under the waves, and I wait for the peace to come. I wait for the blood to take the pain into the ocean.

The ocean will carry it away…

The scent of frying ham and cheese wafts into my bedroom, waking me. Celeste is making her usual, Quiche Lorraine for breakfast. My arms are bandaged, and I sit up, checking the sheets for any sign of blood. There is none.

I'm very good at tending my wounds now. Lara has no idea I even leave the house at night. Last week she commented on how well I seem to be sleeping now that we're here, outside the noise of the city.

As if Paris were the problem.

Throwing the sheets aside, I go to the dresser and pull out a long-sleeved navy tee and a pair of tan cargo pants. They're capri length, but they'll still get wet when I walk along the shore. Nails click on the stone floor, and I lean down to scoop up my little dog.

"Hi, Pierre!" My voice is high, and he licks my face repeatedly.

He doesn't understand why I lock him in the kennel some nights, but like a good little boy, he doesn't whine or bark. He knows when I come back I'll be better.

I'll be free from the demons for a little while.

"Where you headed?" Lara's voice is different this morning.

I know she's sad being here. I know she dreams of Mark every night. I hear her say his name sometimes, but it's quiet. She thinks no one knows.

I don't mention it.

"Pierre needs to go for a walk. I'll be back in time for breakfast."

I don't wait for her reply. We set off down the stone path toward the wooden staircase. I'm at the shoreline in no time, walking along the pebbled sand, checking for any signs of blood.

Not that it would matter.

No one could ever trace them back to me.

Pierre and I walk for a while in the direction of town. Freddie's villa is away from the city, so our beach is essentially private. Several large estates are between us and the curve of rock that separates us from the tourists.

I'm about to turn back when a confident male voice stops me. "You're a guest of the Lovells'." His accent isn't French.

"I'm sorry?" I turn and face him.

He's an older man, tall and slim, with fair hair and small eyes set high under a low brow. He doesn't smile.

"What is your name?" It's a command I find myself answering.

"Molly. What's yours?"

"Most people call me Stas."

Pierre dances around my feet, and I bend down to pick him up. He wiggles against the fresh wounds inside my upper arms, and I wince, putting him down again.

"Why don't you hold your dog?" His gaze is piercing, and he looks to my arms then to my face as if he knows.

"I don't want him to get me dirty," I lie.

Stas's lips purse, but his eyes remain soft. He takes a step closer, lowering his voice, even though we're the only ones on this beach. "I was unable to sleep last night, so I took a walk along the shore."

My throat grows tighter with every word. My stomach is sick, because now I know he knows. It's no longer my secret. I'm certain panic is visible crossing my face, but he doesn't stop.

"Why do you do this to yourself?" He taps my arm.

"I don't know what you're talking about. I don't even know who you are." The words race out of my silly mouth.

I should walk away from this interrogation. Nothing is making me answer his questions.

"My name is Stas Volodya. I own this estate, Rivage sur Mer. Claude Lovell is a friend of mine. I've known his family since his son was a boy. You can trust me."

My heart is beating so fast, I feel light-headed. "You sound like a Russian. Why would I trust a Russian?"

"Because you're brave." His blue eyes fix on mine. "Because courage is the first quality of a warrior."

"I'm not brave." I swallow the knot in my throat. "And I'm definitely not a warrior."

"You are wrong." He straightens and tilts his head to the side. "You're brave because you are still here."

I don't answer him. I'm trying to understand how this man encountered me last night on the beach and saw straight through me.

"What if I teach you a better way to release the pain?"

Water breaks on the sand, and I don't leave. I can't find words to say, but I don't leave.

He nods, and takes my silence as consent.

The sun is high above our heads, and I'm sitting on the pebbled shore with my legs crossed. Tiny rocks press against my ankles uncomfortably, but I ignore them, using the pain to deepen my concentration.

Focus on the beat of my pulse against the stones…

Stas sits on the shore in front of me, mirroring my pose. "Inhale deeply and feel the air leaving your body as you exhale."

I do as he says. As before, his eyes fix on my face, watching me. "I'll ask you again. Why do you do this? Did you lose someone?"

I finish the exhale and answer. "No."

"Then why?"

I take another deep breath and close my eyes, feeling it expand in my belly... My insides are tight with concentration. Or maybe with the persistence of his questions, his intense gaze.

I'm caught like a mouse... Only, I came here willingly.

Perhaps something deep inside me knows I have to find a way to stop the cutting before it's too late. Before I slice too deep and the blood doesn't stop.

"Trust takes time." His voice is calm, and I open my eyes. "What would you like to know about me?"

My brow furrows, and I think about his question.

He'll let me ask questions first, then he'll expect me to answer his.

Perhaps I'll play this game.

I look up in the direction of his large estate. It's bigger than ours... or Freddie's... And I think about the way Stas carries himself, his formality. "Are you a soldier?"

"I was a general."

"Did you go to war?"

His smile is almost imperceptible. "Not that kind of a general."

Only the noise of the waves breaking fills the air around us as I try to understand what other kind of general there could be. I can't think of anything.

"How do you own this villa? Are you super rich?"

"Yes."

Again, a pause, and I think of what I've heard about

super rich Russians… Actually, I thought all Russians were dirt poor and stood in line for hours just to buy rock-hard bread. Then I remember hearing about the Russian mafia. "Did you make your money being a bad man?"

He watches me, that ghost smile still on his lips. "In the old days, doctors would bleed their patients to get the sickness out."

His eyes flicker to my arms, and my heart beats faster. "Did it work?"

"If they were lucky, they did not die. The body must be made stronger to fight whatever is hurting it, not weaker."

I turn this over in my mind. "Are you going to make me stronger?"

"Yes."

Large hands grip my neck, and I place my palms together in a prayer pose. Faster than a blink, I shove them up and through his arms, spinning my body as I go.

His hands fly off me, and I'm behind him now, one hand bracing the back of his head, one hand gripping his throat. My fingernails cut into the flesh around his Adam's apple, and I stop short of ripping through the skin.

"Tear out the larynx," I say, flattening my palm against Stas's neck and stepping back, shoulders straight.

He turns and faces me, three inches between us. His hands move so fast, I almost miss his fist swinging for my head.

But I don't miss it.

My arm goes up, and I block his move, using the momentum of his swing to power the rotation of my body as I drop my hands to the ground and kick my leg in a sweeping motion toward his face.

It's a roundhouse kick to the head, but I bend my knee and don't make contact. I follow through with the motion until I'm sitting on my butt on the beach.

"That blow would break your attacker's neck." Stas nods, a satisfied expression on his stern face. "You are little, but you are powerful, Myshka. Unless your attacker shoots first, you will not be conquered again."

We've trained here every day for six weeks, and the lines in my arms and stomach are proof of how strong my body has become. I'm fourteen now, and I'm a master of the open hand strike, the outside defense, the roundhouse kick, and several basic Jiu-Jitsu moves.

I know how to stay calm when I'm cornered and how to use my attacker's energy to strengthen my own strikes. I know how to walk away, how to sit and meditate, how to refocus my energy so the negative chi of my attacker doesn't enter my psyche.

We've worked on all these things, drilling day after day, until the horrors of my last year have morphed into steps along the path of my journey rather than boulders raining down on my head.

"Meditate. Refocus your mind." He steps back, and I know this is the sign he's leaving me for the day.

I also know he's leaving the villa and returning to the Ukraine at the end of the week. It's possible in only a few more days we might never see each other again.

"Stas?" I step forward quickly, my eyes growing hot.

He pauses and studies my face, but doesn't speak.

I hold back the tears. "What does *Myshka* mean?"

His shoulders relax and that microscopic smile appears. "It means *mouse*. What are you thinking, little mouse?"

"Last night when I slept, the men were back. They were around me like always, but I didn't fear them. I didn't wake up screaming. I didn't run away."

"They're in the past now. You've released them. They have no power."

My stomach tightens, and something inside me rejects that response. Anger burns in my chest, just like it had when I awoke last night in the dark room alone.

A different anger.

A righteous anger.

A need for justice.

"But they're still out there."

"Yes, but you are stronger now. You've learned what I wanted to teach you."

My eyes cast down to his hands. "I want you to teach me one more thing."

His head tilts to the side. "What is that?"

"Teach me to kill."

Chapter 9: Searching

Present day

Molly

The Napoleon House is jammed full of people like every other place in the French Quarter on the Sunday before Mardi Gras. Every weathered-wood table in the room is overflowing with people eating muffulettas or fruit and cheese boards or bowls of gumbo or fried oyster poboys.

Patrons standing around the polished, dark-wood bar have glasses of wine or beer or the signature Pimm's cup cocktail. The walls are plain, gray concrete, either scrubbed clean or covered in chipped white paint. The floor is the original tiny white square tiles, and ancient photographs, newspaper articles, and parchments hang in frames on every open wall space.

Joshua's hand is on my waist as we enter, guiding me with the crowd through the small space as we look for a table.

He leans down and speaks in my ear. "Cool place. We're going to have a hard time finding a table."

I put my hand over his. "We don't have to stay. Let's just have a drink."

Leading him to the far end of the bar, we nestle into an open spot and wait for service. Before the bartender arrives, Dean leads Roland through the arched doorway.

"I love New Orleans," he cries, and my eyebrow arches when I see his fingers are laced with my old frenemy's.

"Interesting choice," Roland says, glancing down at me. "What the devil made you want to come here during Mardi Gras?"

"Joshua's never been before."

He only huffs and looks around. "Come back another weekend."

The bartender finally arrives, and Joshua orders two beers and a Pimm's cup for Roland. I'm sticking to tonic.

"What else have you seen today?" Dean leans against the bar facing Joshua. Roland and I are on the outside of the pair.

"We walked down to Café du Monde and had beignets and coffee." Joshua's warm hand rests on my waist as I scan the crowded room.

So many men and women block my view. I'm straining my eyes for Stas's fair hair and lowered brow. I haven't seen him since the day we said goodbye in Nice, but I know he'll be dressed in a suit. I know he'll stand with perfect posture, always alert, but always appearing at ease.

I realize the eyes of the group are on me, and I quickly add, "It's a good thing they serve them all day. We slept until one. What did you do?"

Dean's eyes gleam. "Let's just say I'm very relaxed… and stretched out." He starts to laugh, and Roland lifts his glass.

My eyebrows rise, but Joshua sips his beer. "I don't need to know everything you do. You're a big boy now."

"Speaking of big boys—" Dean continues, but my breath catches.

Blue eyes lock on mine, and I'm not listening anymore.

Stretching up on my toes, I kiss Joshua's cheek before whispering in his ear. "I'll be right back."

The crowd grows thicker with every passing

minute, but I manage to weave my way through the bodies. I'm glad it's so crowded. Otherwise, I'd never be able to slip away like this.

"Excuse me." My hands are up, and I roll through another clump of tourists before spilling out in front of my old mentor.

He straightens in front of the bar and smiles down at me. Affection blooms warm and fizzy in my chest, and my throat aches with tears I won't cry.

"Hello, Stas." I might be able to fight the tears, but I'm definitely grinning like an idiot.

"You look very good, Myshka." He nods slightly, formally. "So grown up and beautiful. It's good to see you."

"You look good, too." I clasp my hands, then I put them on my hips. I have no idea what to do with them. I want to hug him, but I don't think he'd like it. "It's good to see you, as well. What brings you to the States?"

"I came to meet a man. In my haste, I didn't consider the time of year." He makes a face and shrugs. "Let me buy you a drink."

"I'm just having tonic." He motions to the bartender and asks for my beverage.

When he turns back, I feel fourteen again. I wave around the room. "Mardi Gras is always crazy."

"Do you live here now?"

The roar of the crowd grows louder as the "Mardi Gras Mambo" blasts through the loudspeakers hanging in the four corners of the room. Everyone begins to sway in time with the music, and I shout No, but shake my head so he understands me. I glance over my shoulder in the direction of my group. So far, no one seems to miss me.

"You're here with that young man?" Stas asks once the noise dies down.

I nod, taking the clear sparkling beverage. "We've been seeing each other about a year."

"And you look happy." It's not a question. "Do you still have the necklace I gave you?"

Remembering that day, the last time I saw him, makes me smile. "Yes, and I keep it in a safe place when I'm not wearing it."

He nods. "So you've worn it."

"I have."

Placing his elbow on the bar, I watch as he pinches his lips between his finger and thumb. My mind flies to the last time I saw him, standing on the beach...

"Will you be a victim again, Myshka?"

"No."

"How will you not be a victim?"

"I'll use what you've taught me."

In my hands is a hard, black case with a gold chain coiled inside on a black velvet cushion.

"Its core is titanium... unbreakable."

Stas taught me to fight, to use that piece of jewelry as a stealth weapon. It never occurred to me he didn't think I would.

He should have known I would.

Stubbornness rises in my chest, and I change the subject. "What man?"

His eyes flicker to mine. "Sorry?"

"You said you're here to meet a man. Is it Freddie? His dad?"

"Oh." He waves his hand dismissively. "No, no. It's nothing for you to worry about."

I know nothing of this man's life outside of the time we spent together in Nice. I only know he found me when I was broken, and he fixed me, as much as someone like me can be fixed.

"But you helped me." I place my hand on his forearm. "I want to help you."

His eyes warm like they used to, and he pats my hand. "You would not have liked me as a young man. I was very selfish. I was not careful with the ones I loved, and I lost them. This man might help me find them... or know what happened."

"Was it your family? Here in New Orleans?" He takes a sip of his beverage, and I chew my lip, thinking. "My sister is married to a police detective. He might be able to help. What's the man's name?"

Stas studies my face. "This is not a matter for the police."

The gravity in his tone makes me pause. "I don't have to tell Mark who it's for... or I can try and find him on my own. I have ways of finding people."

He tilts his head side to side and exhales a chuckle. "I see your knowledge has surpassed mine."

"You'd be amazed what you can find on the internet." I'm proud that I've impressed him, and I take a sip of my drink, arching an eyebrow. "Don't worry. I'll be discreet. Tell me his name."

His gaze lifts over my head, scanning the room as he leans close to my face. "Reese Landry."

"Got it." I nod. "How can I find you?"

"I'll find you, Myshka." Leaning back, he smiles. "Your young man is here."

I look over my shoulder to see Joshua making his way toward us. When I turn back, Stas has already disappeared in the crowd. He's across the room, exiting through one of the arched doorways.

His beverage sits unfinished on the bar.

"Hey, you never came back." Joshua is with me,

pulling me close. "Did you know that guy?"

"Funny thing." I glance over my shoulder again in the direction Stas disappeared. "I did know him... But he's just an old friend. Nothing to worry about."

They're the same words Stas said to me.

Joshua's brow lowers. "You're meeting strange men in bars and telling me not to worry about it?"

"That came out wrong. I just meant—"

"You know what? Save it, Molly."

He's angry, and I'm stuck. I can't tell Joshua who Stas is—I'm not even completely clear on who Stas is, other than some rich Russian I met in Nice seven years ago—and I just promised I wouldn't share why he's here.

"Joshua..." I put my hand on his waist. "Don't be mad. You know I used to live in New Orleans."

"When you were thirteen. When something bad happened to you." His eyes flash, and as much as it complicates everything, I kind of love this protective side of him. "That guy looks dangerous."

"Well... I mean, he probably is. But he's a friend."

The muscle in Joshua's jaw moves, and he turns on his heel, heading back to where Roland and Dean stand facing each other at the bar. I follow chewing my lip and feeling like shit.

"I have to get to work," Roland straightens as we approach. "It's Bacchanalia at the piano bar. You all should come by tonight."

"You're going now?" Dean sounds like a puppy.

"It's better to go in early. Beat the crowd."

"I need to see Lara," I say quietly.

Roland's dark eyes move from him to me then up to Josh. "Why don't you boys come with me now?"

I'm not sure why he's helping me, but I don't argue. Joshua looks at me briefly then nods. "We can tag along.

Do they serve food?'

"Some of the best Creole in New Orleans." Roland grins. "Although if you're really looking for something good, you should try Petit Monjou. They have the best—"

"Three-fer sandwich!" I say it with him, putting my hand on Josh's shoulder. "It's really good. You'll be addicted."

He faces me, voice lowered. "You're going to Lara's?"

"She wanted me to come here and talk." I exhale deeply. "I need to listen to what's on her mind."

Blinking up, our eyes meet, and I hate that I still see anger simmering in his. I put my palm against his cheek. "I'll come to Roland's place as soon as I'm done."

He holds my wrist and kisses my palm before leaving with the guys. I watch his cute ass as they make their way out wondering how I've gone from keeping one big secret to two.

My luck only seems to go bad when I come to this city.

CHAPTER 10: A NEW NAME

Joshua

Last night the windows were open, and the walls down. We were so close to making real progress... Today, we're right back to where we started.

She's hiding again, keeping secrets from me, shutting me out. I'm so tired of the secrets and the lies.

"You're angry with her?" Roland hops down from the stage and stops at the table, where I sit across from Dean. A quarter slice is left of a muffuletta wheel on the table where we've all shared a late lunch. I'm nursing a Guinness, and my cousin has a cherry-red hurricane in front of him while he posts pictures on his phone.

When I don't answer Roland laughs. "Get used to that feeling."

"You were shitty to her last night. You hurt her." As frustrated as I am with Molly, I remember the way she looked at Roland, the break in her voice, and the way he stonewalled.

"My loyalty is to Lara. Not the brat."

"Loyalty?" I sit forward, arms propped on my knees. "You act like you're still living on the street. That's the kind of bullshit the runaways around Seattle say. You have a house, a job..."

His sits heavily in the chair, studying the tips of his fingers. "I'm not sure you ever fully lose those feelings. Molly was a luxury we couldn't afford back then."

"She's not a luxury, she's a person."

"And in those days, it was every man for himself—"

"And your loyalty was to Lara." I finish his

sentence, anger tightening my throat.

Roland shrugs. "Lara and I share a history I can never ignore. Her mother took care of me when I couldn't take care of myself."

"It looks like Lara's found a way to move on. Maybe it's time you did the same."

"Has Molly found a way to move on?"

He's got me there. "I don't know. I hope so. I hope I've given her that."

"Maybe you should ask her. In the meantime, stay out of what you don't understand."

I understand more than he thinks. "Just so you know…" I level my gaze on him. "My loyalty is to Molly."

At that he laughs, dark eyes clashing with mine. "You're braver than I would be."

Dean finally looks up from his phone to join our conversation. "I like Molly. She's a cool chick. Tough girl."

"She had to be." Roland pushes out of his chair and starts back for the stage. "We all did."

"Tell me about it." My insides ache to know her story. I've reached the point where I can't be kept outside much longer.

"It's not my story to tell."

That answer almost makes me shout. I'm about to toss a chair and leave when a smiling red-headed woman strides into the room. "Well, this is a good looking bunch of men. Any of you dancers? I've lost one of my backups, and I could sure use a hand tonight."

Dean is back to posting pictures on his phone, and Roland is running scales to warm up his fingers. I realize her hazel eyes are on me, and I step back, almost knocking over the chair.

"No."

"Oh, please?" She rushes to me, clasping her hands together at her chest. "It would be doing me a huge favor, and you have the perfect excuse. It's Mardi Gras!"

"I'm not a dancer." I hold up a hand, doing my best to keep hers back.

"He's lying," Dean looks up, grinning at the lady. "He's a great dancer. At least he was."

"Seriously, it'll be a lot of fun," she continues. "You'll wear a mask, so no one will really know it's you. It has a headpiece, horns... Women go wild for it, makes them horny."

"I'm not on the market."

She quickly adds, "It also includes all the drinks and food for the night—on the house!"

"Do it, cousin!" Dean sits up, smiling big. "You'll have fun, and it'll take your mind off all this shit."

"Here." The lady holds out a tall, skinny glass of clear liquid to me. "Try this and see how you feel."

"What is it?" I sniff the liquid and smell a lot of alcohol.

"House recipe."

Roland looks over his shoulder from the where he sits behind the piano and mouths the word *Everclear*.

"Shit," I grumble, but I take the skinny glass and shoot it. I'm just in the mood for something as bananas as this. It's been a while since I've cut loose and partied with the nightlife.

Another shot is in my hand just as fast, and a beefy guy in a bronze speedo and shimmering body paint walks across the foyer from where we're sitting. He's carrying a satyr face mask.

"Is that—" I'm about to back out, but Dean grabs my arm and starts laughing.

"Too late! I want a horny goat mask, too!" he cries. "This is going to be awesome."

* * *

Molly

Lara is on the couch with Jillian asleep in her arms. The little girl has grown since I've been in Seattle, but she's still a baby. She still sleeps on her mother's stomach sucking on chubby fingers content as can be.

"I'm sorry if you felt ambushed last night." Lara's voice is low and soothing, not disturbing her daughter's sleep. "It wasn't supposed to be that way."

"Really?" I can't help a laugh. "How was it supposed to be? You called me here, made up an excuse about wanting to catch up, and really it was for Mark to cross-examine me."

Mark's heels click on the hollow wood as he walks from the kitchen to the living room where we sit. He places a glass of wine on the end table beside his wife and another in front of me. He's holding a bottle of beer.

"You know Mark cares about you," she argues gently. "He got a call that worried him. We're both only worried about you. I don't want you to get caught."

A knot is in my throat, and I'm even less interested in having this conversation now than I was last night. "I don't know what you're talking about. Joshua and I have been working with runaways. We've been looking at property and focused on the halfway house. We're doing good."

"You said you were doing good before." Lara's voice is quiet, non-confrontational. "You were getting rid of the bad guys."

I feel the heat trying to bloom behind my ears and spread across my chest. If I turn red or get flustered, how the hell am I going to keep up the charade? This is when Stas would tell me I need to excuse myself, go somewhere alone and refocus.

"I'm starting to get a headache. We stayed out pretty late last night."

I haven't touched my wine, and Mark stands just as quickly as I do. "Hang on. We're not trying to scare you off. You can trust us, Mol."

Passing a hand back and forth across my forehead, I actually do laugh at that. "You're not trying to scare me off? You're a cop, and your wife is quizzing me about an unexplained murder in Seattle."

Lara's voice rises from where she's still sitting on the couch. "We never said anything about an unexplained murder."

Fuck! My face is hot now. I just fucking stepped into their trap. "What else would it be?" I try to dodge. "You brought up the bad guys thing before and doing good. What was this call if not something like that?"

I look at Mark, and he shrugs. "You're right. Hendricks called me from Seattle because they had an unusual murder recently—no clues, crime scene scrubbed clean. He sent me the pictures…" His voice trails off, but steel blue eyes meet mine. "I've seen that pattern on a victim's neck before, Molly. Small bruises in the shape of chain links."

I'm out of my seat and heading for the door. "Okay, well, I just wanted to stop by and see if there was any other reason you wanted me to come here. Seems I was wrong. This was an ambush, start to finish."

"It was not!" Lara's voice goes higher, and Jillian lets out a little fussy cry.

Her mother shushes her and rubs her back. I keep moving to the door, stopping only as I'm about to open it.

"Just hang on." Mark's voice grows louder. "We do

want to talk to you, know how you're doing, what's new in your life. It seems you and Joshua are getting serious."

I stop, remembering my conversation with Stas. As much as I want to get out of here, I also want to help my friend, and talking to Mark would save me a lot of time. I also think about my other concerns, my need to control the flow of information.

"Josh and I are getting serious." I put my back to the door and hold the handle. "We're talking about more… Whatever that means."

"Have you told him anything?" Lara's voice is soft again, and our eyes meet.

"No, and I'm not going to."

She chews her bottom lip and doesn't say what I know she's thinking. I can't keep this from him forever.

Or can I?

"There's something else." I clear my throat and turn to Mark. "Have you ever heard of a man, an older man named Reese Landry?"

The entire mood of the room changes. It's like I threw a bucket of cold water right in his face.

Mark takes a step back, his expression going from shock to control so fast if I'd blinked, I would've missed it. "What…" He clears his throat. "Why would you ask me that?"

My brows rise, and I get the distinct impression I've inadvertently kicked open a huge can of worms. I've never seen Mark so thrown off-balance, not even when Lara shot Gavin in the back of the head, and he was stuck trying to figure out how to convince his cop friends in Seattle the mother of his baby shouldn't go to prison.

It helped that I was lying on the floor in one corner with strangle marks all around my neck and Joshua was out cold in the other.

Lara answers me as if nothing just happened. "You remember Landry, Molly. He was that cop who worked with Gavin. The one who hid their crimes and kept everything off the books. He buried evidence and kept those men from going to jail."

"I don't..." I shake my head. Now I'm the one flustered. I don't want Stas to be involved with someone like that, even if I've always worried it was possible. "I don't remember any of that."

My stomach is tight, and I try to remember exactly what Stas said. He's looking for this man... Did he call Landry his friend? My heart beats faster, and I try to remember. I don't think he did... He said he was careless and lost someone and Landry might know where he or she is. That's all.

"How do you know Landry?" Mark studies me like I'm a ticking time bomb.

"Someone asked about him." I shake my head, trying to turn this around. "If he's a criminal, a crooked cop, why don't you arrest him?"

Mark's dark brow pulls together. "Someone you know asked about him? Do they have reason to believe he might still be alive?"

"What does that mean?" The tension knotting my chest clicks tighter. "You think he's dead?"

He doesn't answer. He picks up his drink and exchanges a glance with Lara.

"He was a bad man." Lara's voice is conclusive, like she's speaking to a child and this is the end of the story. "If someone you know is looking for him, they're also bad. You should steer clear of whoever it is."

It's like a match to the dynamite buried in my chest. "You're actually saying that to me?" My voice rises louder. "All this time, and you're still treating me like a child? Keeping me in the dark? Like you don't remember how it ended last time?"

Last time, when I lived in the theater surrounded by rapists and abusers. My insides are crumbling, but I'll be damned if I cry. I never had the chance to protect myself. I never had a way to stay safe because no one ever told me anything.

"What are you so afraid of?" My eyes fly from Lara to Mark. "Stop acting like I don't understand or can't handle the truth."

Lara shifts her fussy baby to her other shoulder and exhales a resigned sigh. "Landry threatened Jillian last year, when Gavin was still alive. He had surveillance tapes of everything that happened in the theater when we lived there. He had a recording of what I did... to Guy."

I remember the video of Lara and the man who raped her. The man who raped me. The green-eyed fox who gave me the glass of Rohypnol, so I wouldn't fight the men who took turns hurting me.

The men I've systematically hunted down, one by one.

"This Landry is one of them?" My voice wavers. "There's still one left?"

"Landry didn't participate in the sex club," Mark's deep voice adds gravity to the room. "He did, however, keep the authorities away."

"So there's one left."

"I don't think so." He's unfazed by the intent growing inside me — if he even recognizes it. "I went to his house, to try and get the videos away from him."

He hesitates, and I jump in. "What happened?"

"Shots were fired..."

Lara lets out a deep sigh. "Landry disappeared. We haven't seen or heard from him since."

94

As we've been talking, I've slowly returned to the living room. Now I drop slowly to the couch. "So he could be in hiding." Stas's words enter my mind.

Mark cuts in. "I need to know who's looking for him and if they have reason to believe he's still alive."

"I don't know." It's the most I can say without violating my word to my friend.

Finding the control I've spent years perfecting, I smooth my palms down the front of my legs and push to a standing position. "I'll let you know what I find out."

Crossing quickly to the door, I'm ready to return to my hotel room and see if I can get any answers. "Molly," Mark's hand lands on my shoulder as I'm about to go.

I look up at his worried eyes. "These men are very dangerous. If you find out anything, let me help you."

My lips press together and I don't want to make yet another promise I can't keep. "I'll be in touch." It's the best I can do before I push out the door.

I don't call an Uber. I jog down the block to where the streetcar line curves onto St. Charles Avenue. I need fresh air and time to think.

Hopping into the green car, I drop my money in the slot and make my way to a wooden bench. I sit by the window and let the humid breeze blow in my face and try to figure out what the fuck is going on around here, and who I can trust.

I've always felt like I could trust Stas.

At least I feel like I can trust him not to hurt me. It wouldn't make sense, considering all he's taught me and how much time we spent together.

I know I can trust Joshua, but this is so far outside the realm of possibilities. It aches in my chest when I think of how he'd react to all of this.

At the same time, I long for him. I want him to put his strong arms around me and give me strength, let me hide for a little while.

I used to meditate through these overwhelming emotions.

Now I turn to Josh.

If he's not at the hotel, I know he's with Roland. I'll change clothes and meet them at the piano bar. He was angry with me before, but I'll smooth things over.

I'll give him something. I just have to figure out what.

CHAPTER 11: DESIRE

Molly

No one is in our room when I arrive at the hotel. I go to the window and look out in case Stas is there waiting. No one is there. I walk around the room looking for signs of a note, but there's nothing.

Stas didn't say when he'd contact me again, and for now, all I can do is wait. Wait, and I walk to the bedside table. There's a little notepad with a pen, and I pick it up, carefully writing the name *Reese Landry*.

It isn't my regular list, but the act of writing it down gives me a sense of calm, as if I'm putting the wheels in motion, focusing my intent.

I wonder if the person Stas lost was somehow caught up in Gavin's world of corruption. I wonder if he might help me dispose of this one remaining villain. If Stas and I are on the same side in this, it gives me a huge advantage.

Either way, I have something more immediate pressing on my mind right now. I have to find Joshua. After last night, I don't want to take steps backward. I meant it when I said I want to give him what he wants.

I pick up his pillow and hug it to my chest, taking a deep breath of juniper and citrus. It only makes me long for him more, and I quickly discard my jeans and shirt, grabbing a swishy black skirt and long-sleeved silk blouse with buttons up the front. The deep blue color makes my eyes glow, and I take a second to powder my nose and touch up my eyes.

I hope he thinks I'm pretty. I want him to forgive

me, be patient with me, until I can give him what he wants… as much as possible.

A knot forms in my throat when I think about it. I can't imagine my life without Joshua in it. I'm being honest when I tell Lara I don't care if I'm caught. I'm not afraid of going to jail. I feel justified in what I do. I'm fighting on the side of right.

Still, if I have a weakness, it's him.

And now I've added a new name to my hit list.

It's going to start again.

The club housing Roland's piano bar is overflowing with revelers, and it's crowded and sweaty inside every room. The structure is actually three different bars — a huge indoor area, the smaller piano bar where Roland works, and a more mellow outdoor patio space, complete with water fountains, twinkle lights, and tons of tropical greenery.

Bacchanalia is in full swing in all three, following the spectacle of the Bacchus parade earlier tonight. Jungle drums beat out a hypnotic rhythm, and everyone dances in time as if they're a bunch of… Romans, I guess.

I hesitate at the entrance. Large, unpredictable crowds like this set off every alarm bell and phobia lurking in my damaged psyche. If anything bad could happen, it would happen in a situation just like this. Hot, too crowded, sexually charged. Still, I have two things keeping me going — Stas taught me to protect myself and Joshua is in here somewhere.

As I slowly venture into the mob, writhing sweaty men and women immediately engulf me. The team of drummers never stops at the front of the bar, and men dressed as Satyrs, wearing horned masks, tiny speedos, and bronze body paint move through the crowd.

Two make their way to where I'm standing, dancing and dry humping over-eager men and women around me. A woman beside behind me shrieks as one sidles up to her, dirty dancing to the beat of the drums.

I'm momentarily caught in their swaying, their hips thrusting in time, his pelvis scooping deeply behind her ass, but I keep moving farther away.

When I look up, a tall one is staring right at me. He's at the back wall, and the intensity of his gaze tightens my throat. My heart beats faster, and I can't seem to breathe properly.

He slowly makes his way through the revelers to me, eyes holding mine, heated and predatory. My skin hums with electricity, and my lips part. I should back away, but I can't seem to move. I'm frozen in place by his gaze.

The drums grow louder and the crowd grows thicker. The noise is hypnotic, but I have to move, go to the piano bar where Roland, Dean, and Joshua should be. I want Joshua…

Breaking his spell, I turn and push to the smaller room, only to find it's equally crowded and the stage is empty. The pianos aren't playing, and I don't see Dean or Roland anywhere. I look for Lena, the night manager, but I can't even find her in this mob.

I keep pushing until I'm in the arched doorway again. Just a short distance away is the exit, but the tall Satyr is back. He followed me, and now he's between me and the door. He comes closer, not letting me get away this time.

Heat and sex are thick in the air around us. His skin is covered in the shiny bronze makeup that matches the tiny scrap of fabric covering his cock. He doesn't speak as he takes my hand.

"I'm sorry." I shake my head. "I'm not looking for a

date."

My voice is lost in the noise of the drums, and his large hand tightens around my smaller one. I start to pull it away, but he pulls me to him roughly. My nerves are flying, and I'm about to spin into one of the self-defense moves Stas taught me, when I inhale sharply and my nose fills with a familiar scent.

Juniper...

"Joshua?" My eyes widen, and his lips curl with a smile.

The horned mask still covers his face, but I recognize his gray eyes burning with lust from behind the brown fur.

"Yes." The word escapes on a hot breath.

Fear and panic melt quickly into desire, and I let him pull me to the dark hallway, deeper into the recesses of the building. I'm hot and my panties grow wetter as he leads me through a narrow door into an empty courtyard with a fountain.

It's dark, and even with the loud, hypnotic drums we can hear the constant trickle of water. It's overwhelmed by the sound of our pants, my moans as he kisses me, our mouths colliding, his tongue finding mine.

"Joshua," I whisper. "I want you inside me..."

My heart is flying in my chest, and I'm about to beg when he turns me at once, ripping my skirt over my ass and tearing my thong aside with a low growl.

"Yes!" I grip the lattice wall in front of me and arch my back for him to enter.

His heat was at my back and I strain for his lips. He steps closer, pushing my thighs apart, the fine hair on his legs tickling my sensitive skin.

"Oh, God." My voice trembles at the sensation.

His kiss is consuming, demanding, and with a hard

thrust, he drives his cock into my wet heat, lifting me onto my toes. Our mouths break apart as we moan loudly.

We're completely hidden in a cove of wisteria, and he fucks me hard. His chest is against my back and he bites and sucks at my neck. My nipples are tight, and I want this. I want him to take me, own me.

The drums grow louder, more intense, fast and pulsing in time with our movements. Long fingers circle my thighs, gathering my skirt and finding the place between my legs. He caresses me, circling fast. I cry out, my body vibrating with the beat of the drums, the sharp invasion of his cock.

My hands brace against the wall, my knuckles white as I clutch the wooden slats. My entire focus is on Joshua, the noise of the drums, his fingers circling my clit, his iron rod driving deeper, harder, impaling me, claiming me.

I'm feverish as I start to come. My core muscles clench, gripping and pulling as my knees go liquid.

"Joshua," I gasp. "Yes, yes…"

My screams are lost in the mêlée, but his hand covers my mouth. I open it, and a long finger dips inside. I suck it, and he fucks me harder. The upward motion of his thrusts are the only thing keeping me on my feet.

His body arches forward, and he growls in my ear. "Mine." It's possessive and primal, and I break into more spasms around him as another orgasm races through me. "Yes. You're mine."

Releasing the lattice, I reach behind my shoulder to hold his neck. His hands slide up the inside of my shirt, palming my breasts and pulling my nipples. I come again, and I hear him groan loudly. His thighs quiver as the waves of orgasm take us both.

"Say it," he breathes, kissing my neck, biting my skin, pulsing deep inside, filling me. "Say you're mine."

"I'm yours."

No hesitation.

He slips out and turns me, pressing my back against the wall, my breasts against his chest as he kisses me again, long and hard, deep and possessive, his tongue claiming mine, our bodies molding together. My arms tighten around his neck, holding myself to him.

I want him. I want it all, everything he has to give me. It's how I only want us to be.

He pulls up, and I feel the smack of our lips parting. He looks around as if remembering to make sure we're alone, and I see him panting. I stretch up to kiss his strong neck, running my tongue along the salty sweat there. He leans down, pressing his forehead to mine, and our eyes meet, gazes entwining. It's so good. My breath is calmer, and I feel warmth spill onto my inner thighs.

"Your come is on my legs," I say.

His eyes flare, and he kisses me again, tongue stroking mine. "I got you dirty." He breathes, dropping lower to kiss and bite my chin.

My stomach is warm and tight. "I'm your dirty girl."

"You're always my girl."

I'm so close to him, secure against his body, and that damn fear creeps in. "What if I'm more than just dirty?"

His warm hands cup my cheeks, and his thumb tugs on my bottom lip. Our hearts beat in time, and his eyes are so full of emotion. I'm excited and afraid and vibrating with everything we just shared.

He takes a step back, holding my hand. "Let's get cleaned up."

CHAPTER 12: A CRACK

Joshua

The drums are still going, but I want to get us out of here. I want to get us to a quiet place where we can talk.

Reaching down, I adjust the minuscule piece of leather covering my junk. I'm practically naked in this getup. Taking her hand, I lead her to the supply closet where I left my jeans and shirt then to the empty kitchen area. It's after midnight so it's cleaned and closed.

"I wish I had something to clean myself." Her voice is quiet.

"Here." I grab a dry washcloth off a hook and take it to the sink.

She's right behind me, and I hand it over then go to where I left my jeans. I hate to smear my clothes with bronze body paint, but Lena said it would wash out. I don't have another option. I'm sure as hell not walking down the street in a speedo loincloth.

When I check on Molly, she's finishing up, wiping the damp cloth against her inner thighs. Our eyes meet, and her cheeks flush pink.

She blinks quickly and smiles. "My heart's still beating so fast."

I feel like a jerk. I didn't consider how being stalked by a dude dressed up like a goat or Satyr or whatever the hell I was might trigger bad memories for her. "I'm sorry. I wasn't thinking…"

She tosses the cloth in a bin labeled *dirty*, then does a little sashay to where I'm buttoning my shirt. Her lips curl with her grin, and she clutches the waist of my jeans. "You mauled me."

"I guess I got caught up in the moment."

She rises on tiptoes to kiss my lips, and of course, I kiss her back. My hands go to her waist, and I hold her against me.

"I recognized your scent."

"Is that a good thing?"

"Yes." She buries her nose in my neck and takes a deep breath. "You smell amazing… like Joshua."

Leaning down, I catch her face and kiss her again, deeper. Our tongues curl and caress, my thumbs trace down her warm cheeks, and my insides pull like she's a magnet and I'm steel. It's intense, coming from deep in me.

She exhales a little moan, and I'm ready to take her again. I want to spend the rest of the night in her arms. I'm thinking of all the ways to make her mine when her stomach growls loudly.

She pulls back quick then snorts a laugh and covers her face with her hand. "That killed the moment."

It makes me laugh. "Let's get you some food."

"Oh! I know just the place." She pulls me, then pauses. "If it's still open. Hurry!"

I follow her out the back door, which puts us on the opposite block, away from the madness of Bourbon Street. She heads toward the river then we double back and cross Bourbon again, higher than the action.

"Where are you taking me?" The sky is dark with no moon, and shiny purple, green, and gold beads hang from the street signs and lamps.

"Petit Monjou! It's one more block." She walks faster, and I grin, watching her long hair sway down her back to the top of her short black skirt…

"You've got my handprints on your ass."

"What?" She twists, looking over her shoulder at

the large bronze handprints on her backside. She glances at my hands. "Think they'll know it was you?"

I check out my hands and arms. The bronze body paint is still there, although it's smeared off in most places. "They'd better."

"Come on! They're going to close."

"Those are my handprints." I tell a couple passing, their arms clasped around each other.

The guy looks up, and then shouts. "Yeah, they are!"

Molly is already at the end of the block. "Slow down." I hustle to catch up to her. "You're moving fast to be so hungry."

She lets out a little whoop, and when I look up, I see a two-block-long line leading to a tiny door.

"They're still open!" She's excited, unlike me.

"How is this a good thing?"

"Be patient." She holds my arm, bouncing on her tiptoes and looking over the heads of the million people in front of us. "It's worth it. Trust me."

The line actually moves nonstop, and when we get to the front, I see why. White paper-wrapped sandwiches are stacked beside a register, and it's cash only. The guy shoves a skinny roll in your hand, and you pay. No choices.

"Eight bucks for a mystery sandwich?" I dig in my pocket for a twenty.

She holds my arm. "We can split one if you want."

"Not with the way your stomach's growling. I've seen you eat."

She claps her hands. "Yay!"

Whatever anger I'd felt earlier is far away. We've gotten back to where we were last night, close, playful, open.

The food's paid for, and we start walking to our

hotel. Molly doesn't wait, she's ripping into her sandwich and taking huge bites as I grin, watching her.

"Oh... Oh my gosh!" She's making similar noises to the ones she made just a little while ago when I was buried inside her.

I squint an eye at her. "That sounds pretty good."

"Try it." She stops on the street and holds it up to me.

I take a moment, examining what looks like fried fish, shrimp, and oysters in pink sauce on French bread. She gives it a little shake, and I take a bite. It's like an explosion of tangy spices, flaky seafood, and perfectly crisp, warm bread.

"Holy shit," I manage around my full mouth. "That's good."

"I know, right?" Her eyes are round as she nods. I lean in for another bite, but she jerks it away. "You've got your own!"

Laughing, I shake my head as she continues stuffing her face. "You're going to throw up eating that fast."

"No, I won't."

"The voice of experience?"

We're only a few blocks from our hotel now, and I slow my pace. I want to go inside, but I don't want to lose this moment. Molly crumples the sandwich wrapper, and I look over at her.

"I'm pretty sure that was a record."

She tosses it in the trash. "I was starving! I'd only had those beignets today."

Catching her around the waist, I pull her to me. "Kiss me."

She stretches up, and our lips meet. It's a brief kiss, but I want to keep her here in this moment. "How did it go with Lara?"

She shrugs, her hands resting on my chest. "Better

than last time. This time she really did want to talk."

"Is everything okay?" He eyes dart to mine, and I see something there. *Fear?* "What did she say?"

Her bottom lip disappears between her teeth for a moment. "She said it looks like we're getting serious."

"Oh, well." My shoulders relax, and I give her a squeeze before catching her hand and starting toward our place. "We are."

She doesn't answer, but I feel the unspoken words heavy in the air. "Anything else?"

She shrugs. "We sort of argued again."

"About us?"

"About how they still treat me like a child."

We're in the lobby of the hotel, and I steer us toward the neon-purple-lighted bar. It's not crowded, and we pick a round booth in the back where we have some privacy. "Want a drink?"

"Wine, I guess."

I walk to the bar and order a Guinness and a rosé, putting it on our room to speed the process. When I slide across the white vinyl beside her, her mind is far away. I put my hand over the back of hers and watch it turn over. I cover her palm with mine, lacing our fingers, and our eyes meet.

"Remember how in old movies they would say, 'A penny for your thoughts'?"

Her nose wrinkles, and she nods. "I wonder what that would be in today's dollars."

I slide a lock of silver hair behind her ear. "Five bucks for your thoughts."

She shakes her head. "Overpriced."

"I have a feeling your thoughts are very valuable."

A little sigh, a touch on my forearm. Her voice is sad again. "What do you want to know?"

"Everything."

107

That gets me a grin. "Where does everything start?"

"I don't know." My eyes go to her slim arms covered in silky blue sleeves. "Would you tell me about your scars?"

"Diving right in." She takes a sip of her wine, and her eyes don't meet mine.

Our hands are still clasped, and I give hers a little squeeze. "I can handle it."

"Yes, but can I." She fiddles with the stem of her wine glass. "It's been a long time since I've gone back there."

A group at a table across the room explodes with laughter, and I notice her wince. Sliding out, I stand, giving her hand a gentle tug. "Bring your glass. Let's take this upstairs."

Relief mixed with gratitude crosses her face, and we go out into the foyer. It's lined with French doors and potted palms. The walls are painted white, and the floors are large Spanish tiles. Our room is on the second level, and it only takes a minute to catch the elevator.

"I feel like I see both sides of you here," I say, leaning against the wall as we rise. "In Seattle, you're an independent woman, but here…"

"I'm a kid who can't take care of herself," she grumbles, taking a drink.

"They love you a lot, at least Lara and Mark do."

"I guess. They're pretty distracted."

The bell dings, and I lead her out into the hallway thinking about my conversation earlier with Roland, his question to me.

Has she found a way to move on? I want to know. I want her to tell me.

Inside our room, I put my phone on the table and toe off my shoes. I pull my tee over my head and frown at the bronze paint all over the inside. "Give me a second to get this shit off me."

"Need some help?" She puts her glass down and unbuttons her shirt.

"Don't even." I cross the room to her and catch her wrists, kissing her lips briefly. "Two minutes. I want to pick up where we left off downstairs."

She giggles softly, and I kiss her again, heading to the shower and feeling like I've lost my freakin mind. But I know if she gets in the shower with me, we'll end up having sex in the shower, sex in the bed, then we'll both fall asleep, and it'll be another opportunity missed.

Steam rises, and the shower is hot as fuck. Still, I move fast, using the bar of soap directly on my skin to get the paint off me. As promised, I'm done and stepping into the room with a towel around my waist in two minutes.

Molly's standing by the window in that black lace bra and skirt with my handprints on her ass. Her blue shirt is draped over the chair, and it has handprints all over it as well.

"I'll see if we can get these dry cleaned."

"Okay." Her voice is soft, and when she turns to the side, the profile of her in that lace push up bra and skirt has me momentarily forgetting why I'm not taking it off and covering those perfect tits with my mouth.

Momentarily.

Clearing my throat, I go to the dresser and take out my boxer briefs. I'm sporting a semi, but I pull them on and tuck it in, holding out my hand to her. "Here, let's talk."

She puts her wine glass on the desk and steps over our dirty clothes with her cute bare feet. Her toenails are painted black, and when she puts her hand in mine, I pull her to me for one more quick kiss before climbing into the bed.

"I thought you didn't want to—"

"Lay beside me." I pull back the blankets and fluff the pillows against the headboard.

Settling in, I help her get situated on the mattress, in the crook of my arm. Her side is against my bare chest, and at this angle, with the streetlight shining through the window and the small lamp on the desk casting a yellow glow, it's intimate, but I can still see her face.

"Is this better?" Our eyes meet, and I trace my thumb over her cheek.

The slightest nod, and my stomach is tight, anticipation radiating out, through my torso. "When was the first time you did it?"

She inhales deeply and blinks a few times. I'm holding my breath, afraid she's going to back out on me, but she answers my question. "I was almost fourteen."

"You were in Paris?"

She shakes her head. "I shared a bedroom with Lara in Paris. It was after we moved to Nice, and I was alone more. I'd have these dreams, and I'd wake up covered in sweat, panicking... I felt like too much was inside me. I had to get it out."

Her body is tense, and I slide my hand along her waist. "Too much?"

"Emotions." She clears her throat. "I had all these feelings, these hurts, but I had no memory of how I got them. It was the hardest thing. I would remember being surrounded, feeling trapped. I know after I woke up, I was in intense pain, but I couldn't remember why or how, only shadows."

My throat aches, and it hurts so much to ask. "You don't know how you were hurt?"

At once she pulls away, pushing to a sitting position and bending her knees in front of her. I do the same, sitting up beside her and taking her hand.

"It's okay. You're safe now."

She blinks several times, and when she speaks, her voice is so small. As long as I've known her, Molly has always been so strong, tough as nails. I want to pull her to me, give her my strength.

"Before we left New Orleans, when we were still in the theater, I met a man." She clears her throat again, and her chin drops. "I thought he was nice, like an uncle or something. I didn't know he was a monster."

My jaw clenches, and I hadn't considered my involuntary response to hearing something like this, the feelings rising in my chest that I have no way to control.

"He hurt you?"

She nods. "He had some friends…"

Reaching out, I catch her waist and pull her to me. Her arms go around my neck, and I hold her as her body trembles. I hold her through the fury blazing in my chest. I slide my hand up her back and thread my fingers in her hair. I hold her head as her forehead presses against my neck and she clutches my shoulder. I hold her in a way that every part of our bodies are touching — head to head, chest to chest.

My body is tense, and I know she can feel the rage coursing through me. Still, I have to be strong enough to carry this with her. My arms relax, and she sits back.

I touch her cheek. "You said you don't remember —"

"I know now he gave me Rohypnol."

"The date rape drug."

"I basically passed out… although, not entirely. Like I said, I have shadows of memory."

My muscles tremble, and I release her to get out of the bed. I walk to the window and put my hands on the back of my neck, breathing deeply for a moment, doing my best to get my emotions under control.

"Joshua?" A tremble is in her voice. "Are you okay?"

"Where is this motherfucker now?" My voice is a low growl I don't recognize. "Where is he?"

A rustle from the bed, and she quietly crosses the room to where I'm standing, breathing fast. Her arms encircle my waist, and she puts her cheek against my shoulder. Turning quickly, I gather her to me, my beautiful girl. For the first time in my life, I realize I could kill another human being.

"He's dead. Last year when Mark and Lara came to Seattle... I found out."

"When you were looking for Brisbee, or Gavin? Was he involved with this? Was that why you were trying to find him?"

Her head moves against my chest as she nods, and I smooth my hand down the back of her hair. "Then I'm even less sorry that fucker is dead."

I'm furious I thought he was a friend, even if it was only for a short time. My jaw is clenched, she's secure in my arms, and I remember why we even started down this dark road.

"You said you did it to get the feelings out." She nods against my chest again. I choose my words carefully. "Are you... Do you still feel like you need to do it?"

"No," she whispers, and my eyes slide shut.

A few times since we've been together, I remember her waking up with nightmares, but I've never seen evidence of her hurting herself. I feel like I would have, considering how often I've been naked with her in the last year — pretty much every night. Then I wince.

"Does being with me, sleeping with me, trigger any —"

"No!" She pulls back and meets my eyes, hers wide.

"I meant it when I said I trust you more than anyone."

Both of my hands cup her face, and I smooth her hair back. I place my thumbs on her cheeks and look deep into those blue eyes. "Thank you for telling me this, for trusting me."

Her eyes glisten, and I kiss them gently. A touch of salt is on my tongue, the tears of my angel.

"I need to tell you something more."

I pull back and her brow is furrowed. She chews her lip, and my chest tightens. "Okay."

"It's about why I don't hurt myself anymore... When we were at The Napoleon House earlier—"

My phone goes off, ringing and vibrating on the desk. I look over her shoulder to where it sits, but I'm not about to fucking answer the phone. "Just ignore that. What were you going to say?"

The ringing stops, and she clears her throat. "Okay." She takes a deep breath, but just as she's starting again, my phone goes off, ringing and vibrating.

"Dammit. Let me shut it off." I leave her standing at the window, furious at being interrupted at this critical time.

It stops ringing when I pick it up, and I'm about to power it off when it lights up with a text from Dean.

Josh, call me—911! 911!

I hit the call back, and Dean's in my ear at once. "Oh, shit, thank fuck!"

"What's going on?" I rub my palm over the back of my tense neck, fear trickling into my stomach.

"We've got to get back to Seattle right now. Your dad's had a massive heart attack. I've already called the airport. The pilot's filing his flight plans now. Is Molly with you?"

He doesn't even stop for a breath as he says the words so fast. My world tilts on its side, and I grip the desk to stay on my feet.

"What? I mean, yes. Yes!" Darkness clouds my vision, and my throat aches. "Molly's with me. We're on our way."

A noise is behind me, and Molly's hand is on my back. "What's wrong? What happened?"

"My dad..." My voice breaks. I'm reeling from the onslaught of emotion. "We've got to go back to Seattle... or I do. I'm sorry, I know you were here to see your sister—"

She immediately pulls out the suitcase. "Get dressed. I'll pack our things."

CHAPTER 13: A WEAKNESS

Molly

The hospital waiting room smells like ammonia cleaning spray and coffee, and my head is spinning.

Less than three hours ago, I was in Joshua's arms, about to tell him everything. He was so angry and it seemed like if he would ever understand, it was in that moment… The words were on the tip of my tongue, and he got the call.

I packed our things as fast as I could, not missing the fact that he was crumbling. I've only felt that helpless about Joshua one other time — when Gavin hit him in the head and I thought he was dead. It's a feeling I never want to have again.

He was already dealing with what I'd told him. I love him so much for it. I thought we'd have time to work through those feelings, take a breath and sort it out, but Dean's call changed everything.

The pilot of his father's small jet got us to Seattle in just under two hours, which is some kind of record. From SETAC, we raced to the hospital, making it just in time to learn his father was out of danger, but still in critical condition.

Now I'm pacing, arms crossed over my cramping stomach, waiting to see what happens next. Joshua is in the ICU with his dad, and Dean is with me here, sitting in a navy pleather chair and alternately rubbing his forehead or shoving his fingers in his hair.

I go over to him. Dean and I have only known each other a few days, but I'll try to comfort him over a man

I've never even seen. It's all shared human emotions, right?

"This is a really good hospital." I say it as if I know what I'm talking about. "Joshua said they got him here really fast. I think that's supposed to make a big difference."

Dean is on his feet at once, chewing the side of his finger. "It's not that. Uncle Walter is strong as an ox. It's Joshua I'm worried about. I don't want this to be a setback for him. He's been doing so well."

A flash hits my chest at this unexpected response. "What do you mean? What setback? Joshua's doing great."

Hazel eyes meet mine. "He was pretty messed up after he lost his mom. Now his dad is his only family... close family..." He exhales, shaking his head. "I don't want this to be too much for him."

My lip is between my teeth, and I'm chewing it like crazy. *He has you*, I want to say... *He has me*. Only, I feel so inadequate. I feel so starkly the distance all the things we've never said to each other has created. It's like a gulf keeping me from being able to comfort him.

So many times we got close. So many times he tried to open up to me, but I didn't want him to. I was afraid if he opened up to me, I would have to open up to him, and I wasn't ready to go there with him, take that chance.

Now I'm terrified.

I don't know what happened to his mom. *He lost her*. Did she have cancer? Did she run away? I don't know how he could have a setback. As long as I've known him, he's been teasing and happy and... better than me.

My eyes are hot, and I rub my forehead.

Control. I've got to get it together.

Stas. *Shit!* I left New Orleans without telling him a word, not that I knew how to contact him.

Reese Landry, the new name on my list.

All these thoughts are a cyclone in my mind when a noise across the room causes me to look up. Joshua is in the waiting area, heading in our direction.

"Oh!" I rush to him, pulling him into a hug. "Is your dad okay? Are you okay?"

His eyes are red-rimmed and he looks shaken. "Dad's okay, but I'm going to spend the night here. He's still critical."

"Of course! Do you want me to stay—"

"No, no. Sleep at the apartment." He slides his hands down the sides of my hair to my neck. "The Realtor texted me. Someone wants to look at that house. She's giving us a final chance to decide if we want it. Will you take a look tomorrow and decide?"

My insides are tight, and house hunting is the last thing on my mind. "But I've never bought a house. I don't know what to look for, what to do…"

"I can go with you." Dean steps up beside us, and Joshua gives him a tight smile. "I have a good idea what you need, and I can help her."

"Thanks, man." Joshua turns to me. "I like it. I just want to be sure you do."

"If you like it, I'll like it." My hands are on his wrists, and I hate seeing him like this. "Can I get you anything?"

He shakes his head. "I'm sorry about New Orleans."

"It's okay. I called Lara." I think about Stas and leaving him without a word. "It'll be okay." I'm saying it as much to me as to him.

He leans down and kisses me slowly. I'm holding his wrists, but he steps back. "I'll check in tomorrow."

He disappears through the double doors, away

from us, heading to his dad's bedside. Dean and I exchange a look, and he shrugs.

"I'll crash with friends. Just let me know about tomorrow." He shoves a hand in his pocket and starts for the exit.

I hesitate, trying to decide if I should stay a little longer or go like Joshua said. I haven't dealt with many family crises. I don't have much in the way of family.

Glancing at the clock, I see it's late. With a deep sigh, I know I've got business to do.

Flicking on the bedside lamp, I go to our suitcases waiting in the center of the room where the delivery service left them. I haul mine onto the bed and slip a tiny key from a pocket hidden in my waistband.

Using a private jet eliminates the worry of random bag checks, but I still don't want anyone going through my luggage. My pink gun is in its black holster, which I wrapped in a sweater and tucked in the shoe compartment.

I take it out and unwrap it, placing it on the table. The small sheet of paper from the notebook on the hotel nightstand drops to the floor.

Reese Landry is facing up at me. I scoop it off the floor and fold it in half, tearing it before depositing it in the trash.

I dig the black case out of the back of my closet. Joshua being away is helpful in this situation. I open the small lid and lift out the black velvet holding the gold chain and remove the sheet of yellowed paper to add a name.

~~Guy Hudson~~ *(LH)*
~~Robert Esterhaus~~ *(MD)*
~~Lewis Rain~~ *(heart attack)*

118

~~Gavin Hudson~~ (LH)
~~Dennis Langley~~ (MD)
Reese Landry

Nothing has changed. The emotions are still there, simmering just beneath the surface of my skin. I have to do this. I have to get them out of me. Until I know they're all gone, I can't stop. I don't have a choice…

The thoughts filter unbidden through my brain, and I don't understand why I feel the need to rationalize what I'm going to do this time. I'm on the side of justice. I'm Black Widow. Or Rogue…

Still my chest is tight like I need to cough. Like something is trying to hold me back this time. My jaw clenches. I know what's holding me back.

My weakness.

I'm worried how Joshua would respond if I told him what I've done. Would he call me a villain?

When we were in New Orleans, and I told him what happened, I saw in his eyes the rage I've felt for so long. I felt certain he would understand and be on my side. Now that we're back in Seattle, his words from before feel stronger. The old fear is back, and I'm not so sure he'd understand anymore.

Shoving the paper under the black velvet, I replace my gun then straighten the gold necklace. It's not something I can change now. This is who I am. It's what I have to do.

The case is closed, and I return it to the back of my closet. Stepping over to the large iMac, I pull out the black leather chair as I wait for it to come to life.

Taking a seat, I open my Tor browser, a special browser configured to protect a user's privacy and anonymity while searching the dark web.

A gray window appears. *Establishing a Tor circuit.*

Once it's up, I take a chance and simply type *Reese Landry* in the anonymous search bar and hit enter. Links to Facebook profiles appear, to white pages listings, then it turns into listings for Renee Landry.

"So that's it? You're a ghost?" My eyes are fixed on the glowing screen, and I hop over to my secure chat room.

I quickly create a new identity and type my query.

HG187: *Seeking info on ex-NOPD Reese Landry. Whereabouts unknown. Last active one year ago.*

Rising from the seat, I walk to the refrigerator and take out the bottle of rosé. It's half-full, and I give it a sniff. Still good.

When I return to the screen, I'm surprised to get a hit so fast.

MM50: *No info on RL; will check sources and let you know. Will send expense sheet.*

HG187: *Thanks, MM. No limits.*

MM50: *Understood. Back tomorrow.*

I rock back in my chair and sip my wine, wondering how and when I'll hear from Stas. I want to have information for him when he does reach out. Considering the timeline, it could be as soon as tomorrow.

He'll know I've left the city in a few hours if he doesn't know now. He'll start at the hotel, discovering we checked out suddenly, and depending on how much Dean talked, he'll find out why from either the desk clerk or the airport personnel. Or he could just track our movements once we left SETAC and scan the hospital records.

If it were me searching in New Orleans, I could turn on the innocent charm, drop a few *darlin'*s and have all the information much quicker.

That's not Stas's style.

He gave me my first introduction to tracking people over the Internet. I took it a step further once I discovered Tor browsers and the Dark Web. Desperation drove me to invest in Bitcoin, their preferred method of payment. Lucky for me, a Bitcoin was only a few dollars ten years ago. Perhaps less lucky was my lack of foresight. I only bought ten. Still, today it's enough to buy all the information I need for a long, long time.

Taking a deep breath, I close the browser and shut down my computer. I have to get some sleep if I'm going to meet the Realtor tomorrow, and my confused brain doesn't know if I'm on New Orleans or Seattle time.

I quickly brush my teeth before climbing into the big bed alone. I don't like sleeping alone. Probably because I rarely have. When I was young, I slept with Lara, then when we were in Nice, I had my little dog Pierre.

Now I'm lying in this big bed missing my oversized, handsy, personal heater. The thought makes me smile, and that tug is in my chest again. I miss him.

"Joshua," I whisper, tracing my finger along the seam of his pillow case.

Somehow I've got to find a solution to this puzzle, and I have to do it soon.

CHAPTER 14: OLD WOUNDS

Joshua

I'm drooling on my forearm when I wake up with a large, heavy hand on my head.

"Dad?" I sit up and the hand drops to the bedside.

Relief hits me like a tidal wave to the chest when he opens his eyes and smiles. "Hey, little man."

It's his old nickname for me, and I don't give a shit that he's using it—even if I am two inches and twenty pounds bigger than him now.

"How are you feeling?" My voice is strained.

"Like shit. How do I look?"

My eyes heat, and I laugh. "Like you had a heart attack."

"Damn thing. I didn't give it the weekend off."

I'm encouraged by his ability to joke, but I'm still pretty freaked out. "Have you been feeling bad? What happened?"

I need a reason. I need something to fix, even if that's not always how this type of thing works. The control freak in me is something new, something that came after we lost Mom.

"I don't know." He shakes his head. "I guess I've felt more tired lately? I just don't know."

I'm holding his hand when the door opens, and a pretty nurse with long, dark hair and coco skin enters the room.

"Well, look who's joined the party. Nice to have you with us again, Mr. Andrews."

"Mr. Andrews is my father. Call me Walter."

More relief filters through my veins, and I shake my hand. "Easy, Slick. I'm sure Najah isn't picking up your moves."

"I don't know." Najah's voice is monotone as she studies the machines, jotting notes on the clipboard of papers in her arms. "I heard Walter here is loaded."

"Never underestimate the power of software," Dad teases.

"Your vitals are good." She gives him a wink. "Your doctor will be right in to talk about what's next."

Dad and I look at each other after she leaves, and he presses his lips together. "So that happened."

"You scared the shit out of me."

He pats my hand, and nods. "I need you to do something for me after the doc comes in. You still have those trust documents I gave you a while back?"

A fist of pain socks me in the center of my chest. "I've got them. I don't think we need to dig all that out yet—"

"I want you to dig them out and bring them up here so we can take a look and be sure everything's how you want it."

"Everything will be how I want it when you walk out of this place." His hand is on mine, and I put my other hand on top of his, holding tight. "You're only sixty, dad."

"Fifty-eight. Get it right."

"Even more reason why you're going to be okay. We just need to figure out what went wrong and fix it."

I sound like a little kid pleading for a new bike, and the lines around my dad's eyes deepen as he smiles at me.

"I love you, Josh."

The door opens, and his doctor joins us in the room. "Let's take a look at these scans…"

Molly

"The bedrooms are small, but the common areas are spacious." Dean and I follow the navy-suited Peggy and her helmet of red hair through the three-bedroom home.

"It's got a lot of carpeting." Dean frowns, lifting an old drape and holding it out. "We should get an allowance for flooring."

"It's possible. I can check with the seller." She makes a note on her iPad. "However, a motivated buyer will take it as-is."

"But we've placed a bid, so it's ours to negotiate."

I'm relieved he's with me, because I wouldn't have a clue about all this stuff.

"Does this bathroom seem a bit outdated to you?" He looks at me pointedly.

"Oh, umm, well…" I see white sinks and a white toilet.

"There's carpet in the bathroom. And is this marble?" He runs his finger along the white and chocolate speckled counter top.

"I believe it is." Peg's voice is disappointed.

While my mind is arguing that even with carpet in the bathroom and Dalmatian counters, this house is way better than living on the street, my gut is in total agreement. It's an ugly bathroom.

He spins to face her, hands out. "I'm just saying, Margaret, if they're wanting one point five million for this place, it ought to be top of the line."

She narrows her eyes. "I prefer Peggy."

"Suit yourself, P." I follow him into the large kitchen area, and we both pause. "Now this is more like it. I love this backsplash and the oversized refrigerator would work very well for our purposes. Quartz countertops?"

"Yes, and Viking appliances."

I step over to the glass door to take in the balcony view overlooking the park. "This is a really nice."

I'm unsure if I'm supposed to say anything good at this point. Dean is playing some serious hard ball here, and I can't say I blame him with as much as they're asking for a three-bedroom house.

"I believe these are the selling points." Peggy looks down at her notes again. "The view, the renovated kitchen, and the huge two-car garage and parking area. These are all advantages for what you're hoping to do with the space. At least that's what Mr. Andrews said."

"I am also Mr. Andrews." Dean's voice is condescending, and the Realtor gives me a worried look.

"Oh... I'm sorry, I didn't realize you were..." She looks from him to me. "Who are you anyway? Joshua told me he wanted his girlfriend to see the place, and I didn't get the impression he was speaking euphemistically."

"I'm Joshua's girlfriend." My voice is quiet, and I'm doing my best not to laugh at Dean acting offended.

"Joshua is my first cousin. He and I will be working together on this venture. I'm the art therapist."

Peggy turns to me, ignoring Dean's flourish. "What do you think, Miss...?"

"Dixon." I look from Dean to Peggy, panicking slightly.

I see all the flaws Dean noted, but at the same time, it's a great space for six girls and one resident social worker. It's three bedrooms, three bathrooms, a loft space, a big living room, kitchen, and balcony.

"I like it very much." My voice is quiet, and I do my

best to ignore Dean's pointed glare. "I'd better talk it over with Joshua before I commit us to anything. I'm sure he'll want to hear what Dean thinks, and with his father in the hospital…"

"Of course. I had no idea when I texted. Please tell him I wish Mr. Andrews all the best, and I appreciate him acting on this so quickly."

"Do you have any idea how flexible the seller is on price?" I can't believe how confident I sound asking the question. It just came out of nowhere.

"Not very, but we can try."

"Thanks."

We make our way to the exit, and Dean and I leave Peggy behind to straighten and lock up. We're halfway down the block when he finally breaks.

"It's a good place. They're asking too much for it, but who isn't? Seattle is a hot market, and they can get it, I'm sure."

"Wow!" I turn to face him as we continue walking. "You were being a real hard ass back there. I can't believe you actually like the place."

"You can't just give them what they're asking, that's not how real estate works. They're asking an unrealistic top dollar amount, we offer a moderately low-ball amount, and then we meet somewhere in the middle."

Poking my lips out I nod, thinking about it. "I guess that sounds reasonable."

"Here, let's get some lunch."

I follow him inside the small bistro, and the hostess directs us to a dark wooden booth with leather cushions. The air is rich with the smell of coffee, and the menu has an assortment of organic options.

"This right here is why property values are through the roof," he muses, studying the menu. "I remember when a place like that would run you three hundred, four fifty tops."

We each order coffee and specialty sandwiches, and when the waitress leaves, Dean settles back in the booth to study me. I suddenly feel awkward, like he's checking me for outdated marble counter tops.

"So what's the deal with you and my cousin?"

A server comes and places our coffees in front of us. I'm glad to have something to do with my hands.

I'm not intimidated by this guy. I'm not intimidated by anyone, but I confess, I don't like being cross-examined.

Cupping my hands around the brown mug, I lean forward, placing my elbows on the table. "I care about Joshua very much."

Dean takes a sip. "He seems super interested in you." He's not smiling as he says the words.

"But?" My chest tightens, and I feel my defenses kicking in.

"You're keeping secrets. Who was that fellow you were talking to at The Napoleon House?"

Stas would say focus. Center your thoughts. Stay in control.

"He was just an old friend I hadn't seen in years. Everyone comes out for Mardi Gras."

He watches me, unconvinced. "It didn't seem like Roland knew who he was."

"How well do you know Roland?"

"Touché."

Glancing up, I see he's still not smiling. I don't want to be at odds with Dean, but I'm not going to give him more than I've given Joshua.

A young man hurriedly places our orders in front of us. I'm having the regular club sandwich, while Dean's having something with sprouts. Pulling a sweet potato fry from the stack, I swirl it in the homemade ketchup. I haven't been particularly hungry in the past twenty-four hours.

One topic in particular is burning on my mind, and while I'd like to hear it from Joshua, I'm not sure when he'll be in the mood to tell me with his dad so sick.

"What happened to Joshua's mom?"

A forkful of sprouts is in Dean's mouth, and he chews silently, holding up a finger for me to wait. I take the opportunity to try the sandwich. It's delicious, with smoky ham and sharp cheddar. The bacon is crispy, but there's too much mayo.

"I should've said hold the mayo," I mutter, using my knife to scrape it off.

Dean finally finishes chewing and pauses. "She went for her usual morning jog one day and never came back."

My heart plunges, and I set my sandwich on my plate. I'm really not hungry now. "Did they ever find her?"

"Eventually." He lifts his coffee cup, and I do the same. "They recovered her body in the lake… raped and murdered."

I don't even want my coffee anymore. "Oh, Dean." It escapes on a painful breath.

"It pretty much rocked the town. It almost destroyed Joshua. I think it did destroy his dad. Walter never really left the house again after that. He just holes up in that huge estate in Madison Park, writing software and being a hermit. He never got rid of her things, never even changed the décor."

My hands in my lap are clutched, wringing together. "I'm not hungry anymore."

We're quiet, Dean finishing his coffee. When I look up, his expression toward me is softer. "So you really do care for my cousin."

"How could I not? He's generous and kind…" And sexy and dirty. I don't say that part out loud. "I can't believe he manages to stay so positive."

"Trust me, he wasn't for many years. Your boy Joshua was on the fast track to self-destruction for a while."

I frown trying to imagine such a thing. "I would never have guessed… What changed? How did he get better?"

"Don't know. A year or so ago, he just seemed to pull himself out of it. Maybe he saw the light or had a dream or whatever happens to converts." Hazel eyes study my face. "Next thing I knew he was talking about you."

Guilt hits me like a sledgehammer, and I dig in my pocket for a twenty, dropping it on the table as I slide out of the booth. "I've got to head back to the apartment."

He picks up the twenty and holds it out to me. "I'll cover lunch."

"Really?" I slowly reach for the money.

"When I suggested it, I had ulterior motives. I wanted to feel you out and see if you were just into Joshua for his money."

"His money?" I almost laugh at the suggestion. "I didn't even know when we met. Nobody was more surprised than me when he said his dad was… or is some tech billionaire."

Dean waves a hand. "Don't worry. You passed the test." Picking up his phone, he pretends to be disinterested. "You're better than I expected. I hope you two are very happy together."

My lip is between my teeth again, and I'm starting to worry I might chew it off if something doesn't give around here soon. "Thanks."

I'm gone before he can realize my response wasn't entirely joyous.

He didn't state his expectations, and I'm afraid I might be worse than he expected if he knew the whole truth.

CHAPTER 15: Discovery

Joshua

Molly's not at the apartment when I arrive. I texted her, letting her know I was heading to our place, but she said she was still with Dean and the Realtor looking at the house.

Stepping inside, I see my suitcase in the middle of the room. Hers is open but not unpacked. The bed is unmade and a half-empty glass of wine is sitting beside the kitchen sink. It's comforting to see the signs of her here. After going through this with dad, the feelings I only just acknowledged in New Orleans feel stronger than ever.

First things first. I go to the closet and try to remember where the fuck I put those trust documents. Dad rewrote his will and reworked everything right after Mom died.

I think it was his version of being able to control something.

We both had the rug pulled out from under us that year, and we've never fully recovered.

Feeling around in the back of the space, my fingers detect the corners of a case. Grabbing hold, I drag it out into the light only to be confused by this small piece of luggage I've never seen before.

Is it Molly's? I've never seen her with it.

Placing it on the table, I locate a push-button that releases a cushion lock. The top opens slowly, and light gleams off the gold links of a necklace arranged neatly on black velvet. I have seen this before. Molly's worn it once or twice, but never when we were together.

I lift it carefully, and it's surprisingly light. It's bright yellow-gold, which makes me think it must be twenty-four karat. So few jewelers use twenty-four karat gold, it's easy to forget how yellow it is in the light.

A lump is under the velvet, and I move the cushion aside to see the edge of that pink gun. My lips tighten, and I realize this is Molly's personal case.

I'm not into invading her privacy.

Shoving the gun under the velvet, I put the necklace around it again. Just as I'm closing the lid, I notice a slip of paper has fallen out. I bend down to pick it up, and it opens easily. It's old and yellowed, and the handwriting looks like it was done by different people or in different times.

The writing at the top is like a young girl's. It's swirly and the vowels are rounded and larger. It's a list of some kind, and while I'm not interested in reading it, it's so short, I can't help seeing what it says.

~~Guy Hudson~~ *(LH)*
~~Robert Esterhaus~~ *(MD)*
~~Lewis Rain~~ *(heart attack)*
~~Gavin Hudson~~ *(LH)*
~~Dennis Langley~~ *(MD)*
Reese Landry

The final names are not a childish script. The handwriting is mature and recognizably Molly's. The ink is even fresh.

For several minutes, I stand, reading and rereading the list, trying to understand what it means... If it means what I think it means...

What the fuck is this?

I recognize the name *Gavin Hudson*, of course. *LH* is

in parentheses beside it... Is that Lara Hale?

Lara shot Gavin dead.

Did this Lewis Rain have a fatal heart attack?

I'm having difficulty swallowing as I zero in on the letters following Robert Esterhaus and Dennis Langley. The name Esterhaus was written a while ago judging by the handwriting, but Langley... and Reese Landry? These names are fresh.

Dennis Langley was recently crossed out.

MD is Molly Dixon.

I drop heavily into a chair and try to force my brain to start working again.

The apartment is so quiet, I can hear a drop of water falling in the sink. I can hear cars passing on the street below. This is Molly's black case, gold chain, and gun... and her list of names.

I force my lungs to breathe as a thought enters my mind. *Who are you?*

Have I been sleeping with a serial killer?

For a while, I can't seem to get my brain to focus. I can't move from this seat. I think of the man in the bar in New Orleans. Is he Reese Landry? Is he a potential victim?

Am I?

I reject that thought immediately. We've been together too long for it to make sense. If she were going to hurt me...

She already has.

For the second time since this girl has entered my life, I've learned something horrible about someone I considered a friend. First it was Gavin, now Molly.

Should I call the police?

No.

Should I force her to see a mental health professional?

Maybe…

"God!" I shout, my stomach churning and my fists tight.

What's so fucked up is I fucking know how she's feeling. I understand the rage that would drive her to make this list, to find who I'm confident, based on what I know, are the men who hurt her.

When we found out what happened to my mom, it was all I could do to not go on a rampage of my own. I drowned my fury in alcohol and drugs and going out and raves and sleeping with girls I didn't care about… And anything.

Anything.

I would have done anything to make the pain stop.

Would I have been brave enough to do this?

I think of the cutting and the story she told me. My feelings are chaotic. I've got to get to the bottom of this. Taking out my phone, I send her a text.

Need to see you now. Come home.

I hesitate over that last word, unsure if home is what I want to say. Fuck it. I hit send. Her reply comes almost immediately.

On my way.

* * *

Molly

Joshua's at the apartment. My heart jumps, and I pick up the pace, thinking about what Dean said, thinking about how I want to hold him, comfort him. I can't imagine him losing his mom that way, being lost and alone.

In that instant I decide never to tell him what I've done. It would be selfish. It's not going to change anything, and it could only potentially hurt him. My secret identity is best left a secret. Until I don't need it anymore.

Again, my phone buzzes, and I pull it out. It's a text from an unknown number.

Hope your friend's father is well. Call me at this number asap.

I call back at once. Stas's accented voice answers on the first ring. "I'm sorry we didn't say goodbye before you left."

"Me too." I'm reassured speaking to my old mentor. "His father had a massive heart attack, but I'm sure you know."

"I know, Myshka. Will he be okay?"

"I think so. I'm headed to find out now." The sound of music is in the background. "Are you still in New Orleans?"

"I'll be here until I find what I seek. I only wanted to know if you had any information."

"Hang on. Can I call you back in ten minutes?"

"Of course."

Hotwire Coffee Shop is a block away, and I take a quick detour. It's nearly empty this late in the day, so I order an Americano and take a seat at one of the computers in the back. A Tor browser is in the Launchpad, and I pull it up and quickly log into the chat room.

HG187: Checking in. Any word?

I wait, sipping my coffee and surveying the other patrons. One looks like a college student. One girl has a backpack and her own laptop. Another guy has a small suitcase beside him. I suppose he's a tourist, but who travels without a laptop now?

The screen blinks, and my heart jumps.

MM50: *Somebody's anxious.*

HG187: *Not anxious, just checking in.*

Nothing's worse than a cocky hacker who thinks you need him. If I hadn't been out of the loop for so long, I could find what I'm looking for myself. As it is, I don't have time to reestablish the connections, and I don't like keeping the same identity for too long in this underworld.

MM50: *Your friend is hiding in plain sight. How much for the 20?*

He's using police codes to ask how much I'll pay for Landry's location. I sit and think about it. Stas is looking for information only — or so he says. I'm looking for payback.

I'll pick up the tab on this one.

HG187: *Name your price.*

MM50: *5K in BTC or ETH. No LTC or other.*

Pulling out my phone, I check my Bitcoin balance. No sweat.

HG187: *Send transfer info. Will send 1/3 now 2/3 when*

verified.

A Western Union ID appears, and I open Coinbase. In less than two minutes I have an address in the older part of New Orleans, Uptown. Scrolling through my call log, I ring Stas and tell him what I know.

"I'm impressed, Myshka. So fast. I'm sure it cost you. Let me pay you back."

"Don't worry about it. I owed you."

His soft laughter fills my ear. "You owe me nothing. I saw a caged bird and set her free."

"Either way, if the address is bad, let me know. I can try again."

He thanks me, and I end the call just as I'm climbing the stairs to our apartment. Glancing at my phone, I realize it's been almost an hour since I texted with Joshua, and I jog the rest of the way to the door.

I'm breathless and speaking fast as I push through the door. "Sorry, I got a call right after we talked, and I had to stop off at a cyber café—"

No lights are on, and the fading sun sends in a yellow beam slicing through the picture window. In a glance, I see my suitcase unpacked on the foot of the bed, Joshua's is still standing inside the door, and the closet is open.

Joshua sits at the table, my black case in front of him, and the list in his hand.

"What have you done?" My heart is flying in my chest, and now I'm breathless for a different reason. "You've been digging in my stuff?"

"I was looking for my dad's will." His tone is icy, and my insides start to shiver.

Doing my best to remain calm, I walk slowly to where he's sitting. "How's your dad?"

"He's going to be okay. The doctor expects a full

139

recovery." As I get closer, Joshua stands abruptly, and I stop moving.

"Why were you digging—"

"He wanted to see his will. What the fuck is this?" His tone switches to full-on anger, and I try to swallow the painful knot in my throat.

"You weren't supposed to see that." My voice by contrast is quiet, small.

"No shit. What the fuck is it, Molly? A hit list?" He opens the paper and reads it off. "These guys are dead, and these notes are how they died. What does this mean?"

His tone is so violent, so betrayed. I can only do my best to deflect. "What do you think it means?" It's not a challenge. I'll agree with anything he says... short of the truth.

"Did you kill these men?"

I don't answer. I can't bear the hurt and disbelief in his voice. It tears at my insides.

"Does Lara know about this? Does Mark?" His voice breaks, and my hand covers my mouth.

"How..." He shakes his head. "How could you do this?"

"I wasn't going to tell you. You didn't need to know—"

"Didn't need to know? That I'm sleeping with a felon? A killer?"

"It's not like that, Joshua. These men... They're the same ones who hurt me. They took a little girl, and... and they..." My voice goes out. Pain is in my head, but I try to explain. "They were out there, in the world hurting others. I did what I had to do."

The list drops from his hand onto the table as he paces the kitchen. I step forward, quickly gathering my things, closing the case.

His arms are crossed over his chest, and he shakes his head. "This isn't a comic book, Molly, there are laws… You can't do things like this."

Anger blazes to life in my chest. It's the same fury I can't deny, and my voice rises to match his. "Yes, I can. If they can do the things they did, I can do this."

He stops, and our eyes lock. "What are you saying?"

"I have to. It's the only way." My eyes heat as I say the words, but I won't cry. "I have to do this to calm the rage, to keep the pain away."

His anger melts, and I watch his eyes flicker to my arms then back to my face. "We're working with the girls, the runaways. Help them with me. Find your peace that way."

A dry ache is in my throat. "When I'm with them, I only see how the system has failed, day after day… I just can't. It makes it harder to look away. Something has to be done. Justice has to be served, and I can do it. I can." I beat my hand against my chest.

"Okay, okay…" He holds out a hand, taking a step forward, his voice gentle. "Then let's get justice together. I can afford the lawyers. We can do this through the proper channels. Get the justice you need—"

"It won't work!" I'm practically shouting now. "I don't want a slap on the wrist for them, a public scolding and life in a cushy jail cell. I want them to pay. I want them to suffer. I want them to feel the pain I felt. I want them to look in my eyes and know it's me who's doing it."

We're both breathing fast. Joshua's eyes are locked on mine, and I watch as he tries to process what I'm saying. I watch his large frame, his broad shoulders rising and falling fast. I watch that muscle in his square jaw moving back and forth as he thinks.

Finally, his shoulders fall, and he shatters my heart.

"I can't be with you this way…" He shakes his head, putting both hands over his face. "I can't."

Tremors move from my stomach to my chest, and my voice is a broken whisper. "I've got to do this, Joshua."

"No."

"You can't tell me that."

"I just did. I won't let you put yourself in danger." Again, our eyes meet, and this time his are begging. "If you love me, you'll stop doing it."

"If you love me, you'll understand why I can't."

He takes another step closer. "I can't live knowing every time you go out, you might not come back."

The trembling grows harder, and I can't hold back the tears for long. "Then I'd better go."

Thankfully, my suitcase is packed on the bed. I put my smaller case inside and close it, not worrying about the few things I took out last night. I can buy another toothbrush.

Joshua is across the space the moment the wheels touch the floor. His warm hand closes over my forearm, and he holds me still. The heat from his body surrounds me.

"Molly…" His voice is rough, but I pull my arm away.

"Let me go Joshua."

"I can't."

"You don't have a choice."

I'm at the door, and he's standing beside the bed. When I look up, electricity flashes between us. My stomach collapses, and it hurts so bad.

"This life…" He pauses for breath. "What you're doing… Is it more important to you than us?"

My hand tightens on the door handle. "You can't understand how it feels. You can't know the pain inside me."

"If it's anything like I feel right now, I do."

Turning away, I go through the door. My insides are torn out and bleeding. My throat is aching and tight. I can't argue with him about something he can't understand, and I can't ask him to be something he's not.

Joshua is good. He's found a way out of the darkness.

I am not good, and I've never seen a way through this pain.

I have to go back to what I know. I have to finish what I've started.

Chapter 16: A Job

Joshua

A lead weight is crushing my chest. I try to inhale, and my ribs are like knives stabbing my insides.

She walked out.

For the last fucking twenty-four hours, it's been one hit after another, but the biggest hit of all I never saw coming. Molly is gone.

My phone rings, and I sit up quick, hoping... But it's my dad.

"Josh!" His voice is strong, happy. "I wanted to let you know I'm in the car headed home."

"Wait... What?" I'm on my feet grabbing my jacket. "Hang on, I'll drive you. I'm sorry—I just got sidetracked. Molly was—"

"I know, I know." He chuckles. "I was young once. I'm fine. The doc said I could go home, and I wanted to get out of that place as quick as I could."

"Dad, let me take you. Just wait."

"Too late. I'm already in the car. Enjoy your evening and come by the house when you get a chance. We'll go over those papers together."

The call disconnects, but I'm standing in the middle of an empty room. I want to be glad my dad's out of the woods, but with every heartbeat, pain radiates through my entire body. Dropping to sit on the bed again, I open the messenger app and send her a text.

Where will you go?

It doesn't take her long to reply.

New Orleans.
I hold the phone in both hands.

Will you stay with Lara?

No, I'll get a room somewhere.

We need to talk.

What's left to say?

Everything? My finger hovers over the call button, but I don't press it. I wait for her to respond.

You can't be a part of this, Joshua. I never wanted you to be a part of this. I'm sorry I hurt you, but I can't let you into what I do.

I'm not letting you go.

She doesn't reply, and I drop the phone on the bed beside me. Falling back, I pull her pillow to my chest and try to figure out what to do next.

I've never felt so helpless in my life.

* * *

Molly

Mardi Gras has ended when I arrive back in New Orleans, and the city is completely back to normal, as if nothing even happened, as if it wasn't flooded with a teeming, chaotic mob just days ago.

It took almost two days to get back here flying commercial. First, I had to wait for a nonstop flight, and I had to go through TSA to declare my firearm.

Now I'm settled in a newer hotel away from the French Quarter. It's quiet and closer to the river, surrounded by high rises in the Central Business District.

I've mapped the address, and now I'm just waiting to meet with Stas later this evening. My old mentor is the only person who knows I'm back in the city… besides Joshua.

The room is quiet, and looking out the window, I can't see the sun setting. I can only see the sky growing darker like the pain in my chest expanding with every heartbeat.

Since I left Seattle, I've been entirely focused on the logistics of getting here—finding the right plane ticket, finding this hotel, pushing what happened far to the back of my mind.

Dropping onto the bed, I have to face what I've done. My head is in my hands as the scene replays before me.

He gave me an ultimatum.

I walked away.

My arms are cold. My whole body is cold, and all I want is to curl into Joshua's strong embrace. My fingers tighten on my scalp, and I pull myself across the slate blue bedspread. I'm lying on my side curled in a ball, and for the first time in a long time, I allow the tears to fall.

As I allow my insides to break, the pain of separation radiates through my bones.

"I'm sorry…" It's a broken whisper. "I'm so sorry."

My phone buzzes from beside me on the bed. I don't want to look at the face. I'm not ready to talk to

Stas like this.

Still I lift the device and read the text. It's Joshua.

He hasn't stopped texting. It's the way we would talk, every time he thinks of a new argument, some new reason I'm making a mistake, he tells me.

Only he can't fix this.

He can't fix me.

Where are you?

New Orleans. My finger hovers over the blue arrow a beat before I hit send.

He answers at once. *Does Lara know you're there?*

No.

Roland?

Of course not.

I wait, but he's silent. The floating gray dots aren't there. I can see his face lined with worry. He thinks I'm in danger, but he doesn't know the extent of my training. He only knows what I know. The pain of saying goodbye is overwhelming. It aches all the way to my soul.

If you come back, I will help you.

You can't help with this, Joshua.

I miss you.

I can't text now.

I drop the phone and bury my face in my hands. Tears slick my cheeks, but I've got to stop them. I have got to get on top of this.

I've known Joshua is a weakness I can't afford for too long, but I couldn't walk away. When he speaks, when he laughs, when he smiles... even when I just imagine these things, it's like happy butterflies swirling in my stomach.

It's a feeling I'd only read about, and it's addictive as hell.

It only got worse as time passed. He would touch me sweetly, move my hair off my cheek. Come up behind me to hug my waist when I'd be making coffee or making lunch or washing dishes...

Then he started that thing where he'd hold my face and look into my eyes right before he'd kiss me. Or he'd cover my whole body with his and make love to me.

It became a form of healing I wouldn't have thought possible.

Now it's gone, and I'm torn and bleeding inside.

The butterflies are all crushed, their wings broken.

Just like me.

Pushing off the bed, I go to the bathroom to splash water on my face. I have to shower and dress for my meeting with Stas. I'll wash my hair and shave and get on with the fucking show.

My job now is to help Stas get the information he needs, or help him feel satisfied he's gotten what he needs, then I have my own business with Reese Landry. I've got to get a fucking grip on myself and *focus*.

An hour later, I'm smoothing my hands down my black Gucci dress. The gold chain is around my neck — not because I plan to use it, but because I want him to see I still have it. It's still in mint condition, only slightly used.

The elevator dings, and I step out into the lobby with its sky-high ceilings and massive white Corinthian columns. The décor is modern, geometric furniture with leather cushions, and tall windows with dark, straight lines. The bar is in a separate room, off to the side, through soaring French doors. Everything in this place is open and tall because it used to be a cotton warehouse. These old buildings sat empty for years until they were refurbished and put back in use as hotels or offices or apartments.

A few still sit empty, but they're becoming few and far between.

My friend is waiting with a tumbler of brown liquid in front of him at the bar. He's wearing a dark gray suit with a light blue shirt and tie, and he's sitting on one of the vintage wooden barstools around the shiny black counter. When I approach, he stands.

"Stas." I place my hand on his forearm.

He touches my shoulder lightly, kissing my cheek. "You look very well." His eyes flicker to the gift he gave me so long ago. "It looks stunning on you."

"I wanted you to see I have it." Being with Stas helps me push my feelings for Joshua to the background.

His presence forces my thoughts to realign with what I'm here to do. "Let me buy you a drink."

The bartender isn't busy, and he quickly places a tumbler of Sazerac in front of me. I don't really care for the flavor of absinthe and bitters mixed with Rye whiskey, but I drink it as we talk.

"It's been years since I've visited this city." He takes a slow sip of his scotch. "I was afraid of what I'd find since the flood."

"Some places bounced back quicker than others." I take another sip of my cocktail. It's very strong, and the absinthe makes my stomach feel queasy. "I can barely remember it."

"You were in the Quarter, yes?"

"Yeah, we drifted around, but mostly we stayed on high ground." Stas knows my story. "Like good little mice."

He finds this amusing. "Myshka, I already know you're were a survivor. You don't have to remind me."

"I wasn't surviving very well when you found me." My glass is empty, and I frown. I hadn't meant to drink it so fast on an empty stomach.

"Ahh, but I did find you." He signals the bartender, and faces me. "Now, will you go with me to the address of our friend?"

"Tonight?" I'm feeling a little off-balance, and the drink I just slammed back didn't help.

"No better time than the present."

He places cash on the black tray and stands, holding his hand out to me. I put my hand in his and hop off the barstool, following him out into the night. He hails a taxi, and I slide across the cracked leather seat.

He hops in beside me, slamming the door and giving the driver the address. We take off, three blocks west, then around the crescent on St. Charles Avenue.

"I'm sorry for the primitive mode of transportation." Stas's sneer is withering.

I shake my head and look out the window. Inside the cab smells like cigarettes smoke, sweat, and a hint of vomit. We stop and start, the driver slams his fist on the horn, and I fight the rising nausea.

"I can order a Lyft to take us back to the hotel." My voice is quiet.

Shit, I've never been so sensitive to a drive. It must be the temperature of the air combined with the stopping and starting, the smells in the car. Outside feels like the inside of a human mouth—a thought that turns my stomach again.

In three more jerky blocks, we've arrived, and he stops in front of a looming stone mansion.

Stas hands him cash again and helps me out of the vehicle, and a faint tremble moves through my stomach. I look up at the structure and do my best to swallow the bile. I need to pay attention to this transaction. I need to see the facial expressions. I'm watching Stas for his.

A gas lamp is at the entrance to the sidewalk. We pause, and Stas slips a hand in the pocket of his slacks. "We'll simply ask to speak to Mr. Landry."

"Do you know what you want to say?" I watch him in the flickering lamplight.

"I've known what I wanted to say for years."

It's a sentiment I can understand. I nod and take his arm as we walk the short distance up the flagstone walk. The door is wide and heavy with square inlays and a round iron knocker. Stas presses the white button for the doorbell.

I'm feeling slightly better by the time a shadow passes in front of the glass. A slow creak and the lock opens revealing a man in a white shirt and black suit.

"May I help you?" His eyes are level, and he scans our formal attire.

"We're here to see a Mr. Reese Landry."

The man bows his head slightly. "One moment please." He closes the door and leaves us standing on the doorstep.

Stas and I exchange a glance, and his hand goes to his side pocket. I know he carries a pistol, and in an unpredictable situation like this, I would expect him to be armed.

We don't have to wait long. This time a woman opens the door. She's dressed in jeans and a black sweater with a long jacket over it. She isn't tall, and her dark hair is styled in a shag that ends at the top of her shoulders.

"May I help you?" Black eyes survey us.

"I'm sorry," I speak up. "We were looking for a man named Reese Landry. My friend here is an acquaintance of his."

The woman studies me a moment. Her eyes crinkle with her smile, but it feels fake, her eyes don't soften. I'm immediately on guard.

"Oh, no." She acts empathetic, concerned. "My name is Renee. Renee Landry. I must have a similar address to this Reese Landry, but there's no one here by that name."

Stas cuts in as confused as I am. "You're saying this has happened before?"

"Once or twice." She studies him with the same keen eye she used on me. It feels as if she's memorizing our features.

"How odd." Following her lead, I study her face, doing my best to commit her features to memory.

Renee Landry has a slim nose, high cheekbones, and pale, ivory skin. Her jet-black hair matches her eyebrows, and she's elegantly dressed.

"We're so sorry to have bothered you." Stas does a little bow. "I don't suppose you might know where we could find Reese Landry?"

She tilts her head back and a light laugh escapes her thin red lips, past her straight white teeth. "I never thought of tracking him down. I should have done it before!"

"So you don't know the man we're looking for?" I say it again just to be sure.

Her dark eyes level on mine, as if she's accepting a challenge. "I have no idea where he is."

Only, that isn't what I asked her…

"We're so sorry to have troubled you." Stas takes my arm and we step away, not turning our backs on her.

"No trouble at all. I'm always happy to meet new people. What did you say your names are?"

"Maggie." I answer before Stas can say anything. "I'm Maggie Brown and this is my colleague Stan Winchester."

"Nice to meet you, Miss Brown, Mr. Winchester."

We're still backing away slowly. She watches as I take out my phone and touch the Lyft app, quickly ordering a car. "We'll just call a car. Sorry again."

Another step… one more, and she finally closes the door. I exhale a deep breath. My phone pings that the car is arriving, and I look up to see a gold Prius pulling up at the curb.

Stas returns my serious gaze. We're both on alert after that bizarre encounter.

Once I'm sure we're out of earshot, I murmur, "What the fuck was that?"

"I don't know…" His voice is equally thoughtful. "Head back to your hotel and rest, Myshka. I'll see what I can find out and call you tomorrow."

I don't argue with him. I know Stas very well. He is both able to take care of himself and adept at finding information the old fashioned way. Anyone would be a fool to think of his age as a handicap.

Whatever just happened here, it felt like a test, a hunting expedition. I intend to use more modern technology to find out what the hell Renee Landry is up to.

Stepping into the car, I lean back against the leather seat and say a quiet prayer of thanks the air conditioner is blowing strong. My stomach is worse with the adrenaline pumping in my veins, but the drive back to the hotel feels shorter, whether because the driver knows a superior route or the traffic has thinned after rush hour.

We're back at the hotel, and I go straight to my room on the fourth floor. My phone is in hand, and I'm careful, checking the halls and watching over my shoulder as I go to my door and enter.

A quick sweep verifies I'm alone. I go in the bathroom and push the shower curtain aside to be sure it's empty.

"You're being silly, Molly," I tell my reflection, but I'm bothered by how pale my face looks. "Fucking Sazerac."

Returning to the room, I grab the phone and order room service. It's after dinner, and all I've had to drink are cocktails. I'm hungry is all. In the bathroom, I run the faucet and proceed to wash my face, splashing warm water on my cheeks. It doesn't seem to help.

I switch to cool water, and take a washcloth from the rack, getting it as cold as possible before returning to the bed to lie down and press it to my face.

That's a little better.

My phone buzzes, and I answer quickly, thinking it's Stas with information. I'm wrong. It's Joshua.

"I was thinking about you." His voice is low and rich, warm water in my veins.

"Is everything okay?"

"I wanted to hear your voice."

Oh. Rolling to the side, I put the damp cloth on the nightstand, my hand under my cheek. "I just ordered dinner."

"What are you having?"

"A hamburger."

"What?" The shock in his voice makes me smile. "I expected a foot-long three-fer. What's this hamburger shit?"

"It's late. I just went the easy route. Tomorrow I'll walk to Mother's."

We're quiet a moment. I listen to his breath. If I close my eyes, it's like he's with me here in the bed.

"I closed on the house today. The girls have started moving in." He exhales, and I imagine him rolling onto his back. I imagine tracing my finger down the line in his arm. "You and Dean did a great job—we got an allowance to install new carpeting or wood floors."

"It was all Dean. I basically walked around with my eyes wide and my mouth closed."

"We were supposed to do this together." His voice is quiet, and my stomach cramps. "Helping these girls was our idea. You helped me think of it."

"I have a different idea of help."

It's quiet again. Then he breaks my heart. "Are you ever coming back?"

A tap on the door interrupts us. "The food's here. Hang on."

I check the peep-hole before opening. A young man with dark hair and a black uniform is outside with a large tray on his shoulder. I quickly unbolt the door and allow him to enter. Without a word, he places the tray on the desktop. Then I sign, and he's gone. Just as quickly, I lock the two locks and slide the bolt in place.

My hamburger is under a large silver cover, and it smells like a good burger… but my stomach tightens. Instead I take the glass of ginger ale and sip it.

"What are you having? Rosé?

"Hm…" I swallow quickly. "Ginger ale. I had a Sazerac earlier and it made me feel kind of sick."

"Who were you having drinks with?" A note of anger enters his voice, and I hate that I like it. I hate that I screwed up, but I love that he cares. "Just an old friend.

Nothing for you to worry about."

"That's what you said about the guy at The Napoleon House. Was it him?"

I'm not going there with him. "How's your dad?"

"Molly…"

My stomach is tight, and I take another sip of ginger ale. He sighs in my ear.

"My dad is much better. They let him go home."

"That's good! I'm so glad." I wish I could hug him.

"Now back to my question…"

And just like that, my hugging feelings are gone. "Have I ever told you you're stubborn?"

"We haven't told each other a lot of things. Like you're the most stubborn woman I know."

His words, the swirl of pain and longing in my chest makes me start to laugh.

"And the prettiest…" That smile I love so much is in his voice, and my eyes heat.

Our voices are back to soft, longing, missing. I look at the clock and realize it's still early for him.

"What will you do this afternoon?"

"I've got to go by the title office and sign off on some paperwork, then I might stop by and check on the girls."

"I'm sure Candi will be glad I'm not there." Not sure where that snarky comment came from — or the simmer of jealousy I'm feeling.

"Why?"

"Oh, seriously, Joshua. You are so clueless."

He starts to laugh. "I don't know how you do it. One minute I'm miserable, the next I'm scratching my head. What's going on with you two?"

I exhale deeply, not really feeling up to it. "We just got off on the wrong foot, I guess. She hates me."

"Come back and we can work on making things

right."

My eyes close, and I hug my arms over my stomach. "I need to go."

"Okay," he sighs. "Eat something, get some rest. Come back to me, Molly."

I can't even answer that. I hit end on my phone, and start to cry. The pain in my chest hurts so badly, and I don't think I can fight it. I don't know which is worse, being here, doing what I do, or being so far from him, on the other side of the country.

My throat tightens, and I cover my mouth with my hand.

"Oh, no," I whisper, jumping off the bed and dashing across the large room.

I almost don't make it before I drop to my knees quickly and vomit in the toilet.

CHAPTER 7: ADVICE

Joshua

My brain won't stop counting the days since Molly left Seattle. It hasn't even been a week, and I'm continuously scrolling through all the ways I screwed up, all the things I took for granted. Every morning when I wake up alone, when I make coffee, when I go out to breakfast...

Why didn't I memorize the scent of her hair? I don't even know what perfume she wore. It was like peonies and rain, soft and flowery, and it's quickly fading from her pillow. I hold it to my nose and inhale deeply, but I'm losing her. It twists in my gut.

This apartment is too fucking big without her. I go out, and when I come back, my eyes automatically search for her.

Before, she'd be here, her long hair twisted in a cute little bun on top of her head, working at her computer. How was I supposed to know she was tracking down her targets, the men who had victimized her?

How was I to know when I told her to stop, she'd walk out that door?

My phone rings, and I snatch it up, answering on the first ring. It's my dad on the line, and he sounds better than he has in weeks. I'm happy and miserable at the same time.

"Josh! When are you planning to get yourself up here with those papers?"

"Sorry, I've been tied up closing on the house and settling the final paperwork with the title company and closing out the house we've been leasing—"

"I know you've been busy." he laughs. "I've got steaks, and it's supposed to be a perfect sunset this evening. No rain, mid-seventies. Come up here, and we can have dinner together."

"Are you allowed to eat steak already?" I don't know much about heart attacks, but I remember that movie where Jack Nicholson had a heart attack, and he couldn't eat steak.

"No!" He bellows through the phone. "I'm eating like a squirrel. I eat the food my food eats, but I can watch you enjoy a good meal."

I laugh at him quoting one of our favorite television shows. "Okay, I'll be there at seven."

We disconnect, and I go to that damn closet that started the whole thing. Pulling the doors open, I don't dig this time. I grab the side of a large, cardboard box and slide it out. A blanket spills behind it, but I don't bother retrieving it.

I'm almost gun-shy digging in here, considering what it cost me last time. I find the heavy, fireproof box where I keep the important papers my parents are always riding me about. Inside are several hanging folders. My passport is in one of them, my birth certificate and social security cards, insurance policy... Finally I find the folder Dad's lawyer gave me after Mom died. I never even looked at it.

When all that shit went down, I was so messed up, I didn't even want to think about the idea of Dad's estate coming to me. I didn't want to look at these papers and think about what they meant. I couldn't give a shit about this list of assets I would get when I was left all alone. I shoved it all in this box and never thought about it again.

Now he's forcing me to look at it, and I'm fucking

alone again.

With a sigh, I set the folder on the table. I told Rebecca I'd stop by the new house today to sign off on the utilities. I'll return here after and take this with me before I head to his estate in Madison Park.

Scooping up my phone, I take off, locking up before I dash down the stairs and out to the street. The new house is ten blocks from my apartment. When Peggy showed it to me, it was one of the things I liked most. I had imagined Molly and me being able to walk over easily if there was ever a problem. Or we could easily hop over on the weekend, check on things, then go to breakfast together or something along those lines.

Walking there without her, to the house she inspired me to buy, twists the knife even deeper in my chest.

"Joshua!" Brittanie meets me at the door, and I follow her up the narrow staircase leading from the double garage to the main level.

The house is built into the side of a hill, and it has an amazing view from the balcony over the park and out to the lake. Boxes are everywhere, but they've already installed a huge flat screen television over the fireplace. It's blasting some reality show with a bunch of women drinking wine, and Candi passes through with her rainbow hair on top of her head.

"Hey, Josh! You alone? Where's Little Miss Sunshine?" Sarcasm drips from her tone, and I remember my phone chat with Molly yesterday.

"Molly had to go to New Orleans." The last thing I feel like is discussing what's happening between us. "Where's Rebecca?"

Candi stops and gives me the eye. "Why is Molly in New Orleans without you?"

I go to the kitchen where several papers are spread

out on the table. "Her sister lives there. You know that. We went for her wedding last year."

She stands a moment longer in the living room, studying me. I think the main reason Candi and Molly always butt heads is because they're both too smart for the hand life dealt them.

Finally, she gives up and continues to her room. "Rebecca had to run to the store. She'll be back in a minute."

The stuff on the table needs my signature and I see notes indicating the amount of deposits to have the water and electricity transferred into my name. I collect them and plan to call and give those guys my billing information.

"I really like my room," Brittanie says, joining me in the kitchen where I'm flipping through the pages and signing quickly.

I consider getting Rebecca her own bankcard. I should probably set up and fund a separate account for the house so she can buy groceries and shit. Maybe put a spending limit on the card? This is all new to me.

"What's that?" I look up at the young girl. She's small and shy, and she's always reminded me of one of those squirrels in the park. She'll venture out, but if I make a wrong move, she retreats again just as fast.

"My room? I'm the only one without a roommate, but Rebecca said it's because I study so late. The lamplight bothers Candi at night."

"Don't get used to it," I tease. "I'm hoping we can get six girls in here."

She puts her hand on her hip and cocks it to the side. "You're a really good guy, you know that Joshua Andrews?"

My chest tightens, because the last thing I've been feeling lately is good. "Not really. Molly showed me a way I could help you guys, and I've got the money to do it."

"Molly's good, too." She sets her box on the table. "She used to talk to me a lot about my past, ask me questions about where I lived before, my life on the street. I could tell she really cared."

"She did?" A frown pierces my brow. I think about what Molly said, how talking to these girls made her angrier because of how the system failed them.

"Yeah, especially when I first got here. We used to talk all the time."

I follow her into the living room, and the television has gone from reality silliness to the early evening news... more reality silliness, I think.

But my attention is caught by the name on the screen. The talking head is describing an ongoing police investigation.

"Still no suspects and no leads in the murder of Dennis Langley." A picture appears on the screen beside the anchor's head, and Brittanie gasps. She steps back so fast, she bumps smack into my chest.

"What is it?" I catch her upper arms. I recognize the name, but it never occurred to me...

"Um..." She looks around and quickly steps out of my hands. "I'm sorry. I have to go put my stuff away. I've gotta go."

The news anchor continues saying how Langley had a long history of criminal involvement, ranging from drug trafficking to sexual misconduct, and how police are considering the possibility of organized crime at work in the metropolitan area.

My stomach is tight as I listen. I know what happened to Dennis Langley, who did it, and why. The number for a tip line appears on the screen, and a sharp pain shoots through my temple. I've never been in a situation like this, but I know with cold certainty I'll be damned if I ever tell what I know.

Talk about the system failing. What would happen if Molly were revealed to be Dennis Langley's killer? Would she be prosecuted? Would she go to jail? How could she not?

The story ends, and I drop to the couch. I'm in love with a killer, and nothing I can do will change it. I'm also not afraid. I'll do anything I can to protect her.

Dad has the grill going out on the back patio when I arrive. I park on the street and jog up to the giant home where I grew up. He never left after Mom died. He never even redecorated. Pushing through the door, I see the same pictures in frames, the same flowers in baskets. A cleaning service comes once a week, so it's polished, vacuumed, and dusted. Still, he's the resident hermit. The king of this castle he never leaves, as if leaving will somehow change what happened.

As if he waits long enough, she might still come back.

He slides the glass door open and meets me in the dining room. "Joshua! Good to see you outside a hospital room."

Strong arms go around me in a hug. Dad's smaller than I am now, and I can see the tired lines around his eyes. But those eyes are full of life. It eases the pressure in my chest.

"Show me what you've got."

I place the folder on the table and for the first time, break the packing tape over the flap.

"You never even opened it?" He gives me an incredulous look, but I just shake my head.

"I don't care about this stuff, Dad. I just want you to be here."

"I know, son." He grips my shoulder. "But this is my life's work. I need to know it's in good hands, so it doesn't just… stop."

Part of me understands this. I appreciate the feeling of finality that came when we buried Mom. I remember staring at her name carved in stone and wondering why we do anything, what's the point of it all.

From what I could tell, it seemed my father's response to the situation was to dig even deeper, work even harder to leave some legacy behind. I simply wanted to cram as much living into my life as possible.

He spreads the papers on the table and carefully scans each page. "I remember putting this together like it was yesterday. I wanted to be sure you were taken care of with as little trouble as possible."

"You set up a trust." That much I do know. "Tom said if anything happened, it would pretty much take care of itself."

"Still, you have to make it happen."

Finally, he seems satisfied and slides the stack of paperwork together again. "You need to look over this and be sure nothing has been left out."

"I'm sure you guys were very thorough." Orange flames outside on the patio catch my eye. "I think the grill's ready."

He pats my shoulder again and smiles. "Come outside with me. It's a great evening."

I'm pleased by this new "life is good" attitude. It's a dramatic shift from before, and I consider if anything good comes from his health scare, maybe he'll come outside again.

The house is covered in plants and greenery, but the landscaping is small rocks and stone boxes containing shiny-leafed plants and palms. For a climate as wet as Seattle, it's the closest they could get to desert.

"Nothing like old-fashioned charcoal," Dad says, lifting the iron lid off the grill. He places two steaks over the flames and then closes it again. "That's premium, grass-fed buffalo all the way from Montana."

"You're cooking two steaks?" I shove my hands in the pockets of my jeans and pause beside where he's watching them cook.

"One for you to take home with you. I know you don't eat right."

"I don't know where you got that idea."

"Dean says you eat like a middle schooler."

"Dean eats like a fashion model." I pass dad and walk out into the backyard. "I mean that in the worst way possible."

"You think his eating disorder is back?"

Shit, I didn't mean to upset Dad. "No, no. I'm sorry. I just meant he's always on a cleanse of some sort... coffee enema."

"Don't be gross."

Shaking my head, I walk out into the backyard. The grass is green, and it stretches wide, all the way to the lake, where huge boulders form a wall against the water. Dad has an enviable, 360-degree view of the lake and mountains. It's a beautiful place... and I'd have had to move if I were him. I'm already thinking if Molly doesn't come back, I'll have to sell my apartment and get something different. Her ghost is everywhere.

I study the pale beige stucco walls around our family home, the terra-cotta Spanish tiles on the roof. My parents didn't build the house, but they were always proud of their achievement, finding this place before real estate prices exploded.

It's twilight, and the sky is lined with partial clouds. Their bellies are streaked with simmering red, salmon pink, and on top, they're soft purple. It's a beautiful night, and as I watch, the solar-powered lanterns around the house automatically begin to switch on.

Dad flips the switch, and the patio floods with yellow light. Then he waves to me. "Steaks are ready, come inside and cork the wine."

We sit out under the growing dusk at the stone patio table. Dad lights candles in hurricane jars, red, orange, and yellow.

"What do you think?" he says, sitting back and watching me.

"Nice," I say, pouring the Malbec into large globes.

He lifts the glass and holds it to me. "To family."

Nodding, I clink. "I couldn't agree more. To you being home and happy."

His expression tenses as I take a sip. "That's something I wanted to talk to you about."

Sitting straighter in my chair, I swallow back the fear. I should have known him inviting me here, insisting I bring all this paperwork... panic climbs the back of my neck as I brace for him to tell me the worst.

"What is it?" I manage to ask.

"How would you feel..." He clears his throat and shifts in his chair again, looking at the table then up to me again, nervously. "How would you feel if I started to date?"

"Jesus!" Air explodes from my lungs, and Dad is immediately backpedaling.

"I'm sorry... If it's too much for you or if you think I'm too old—"

"Dad! No." I hold out my hand and lean forward to rub my forehead. "You scared the shit out of me the way you set that up. I'm fine with you dating. I actually think that would be a good thing."

"You do?" He looks so relieved, I almost suggest we go inside and check his heart rate. We could check mine while we're at it.

"Yeah, I do. I've always worried about you being up here alone, living like a hermit. That can't be healthy."

He takes a deep breath and leans back in his chair. "Well, I'm not making any promises. I'm not as young as I used to be. I don't even know how to date anymore."

"It's not as hard as you think." I take a sip of the full-bodied wine. It has a dark fruit flavor and a smoky finish. "Good Malbec."

He nods. "I did a little research on the best varietal to go with the steaks."

"See? Women love shit like that." I take my knife and cut into the medium-rare steak on my plate. "You're a great cook, and you're loaded."

He nods, pushing his fork through the dark green salad he's having. "That's the only thing that worries me. I don't want to find someone who's only interested in money."

I groan as the explosion of rich, tangy meat fills my mouth. "This is good." Finishing, I nod, getting back to what he said. "Dean and I can help you. He uses those dating apps. Is that something you want to try?"

He takes another sip of wine and rips off a piece of ciabatta bread. "I don't know. I'm starting to feel like this is a ridiculous idea." A deep sigh. "Just... being in the hospital, talking to Najah..."

"Ahh, I get it." I give him a teasing wink. "You just needed a sexy nurse to get your motor running."

He chuckles. "There's so much carbon on this old engine..."

Leaning forward, I catch his hand and give it a squeeze. "Hey, you can do this. I think it's a great idea. Don't psych yourself out."

He nods and leans back, and for a little while we

have a comfortable silence. The candles cast a calming glow over the table, and frogs start up, making their unique sounds in the night.

"Speaking of ladies, where's your girl? Molly, is it? I'd hoped to meet her now that I'm out of the hospital. I thought you might bring her with you tonight."

"She's in New Orleans." It's as much as I want to tell anyone at this point.

"Right, she has family there... you went to a wedding there with her?"

Nodding, I place my utensils on the table, not really hungry anymore. I lift the wine bottle and refill my glass, giving Dad a little top-off.

I can feel Dad watching me, but I hope he doesn't press for more details. To my relief he doesn't. He only takes another bite of kale.

Still, my situation is heavy on my mind. It's been growing heavier with each passing day, and the news story about Dennis made it all too real for me. It's hard to be here, knowing she's so far away, putting herself in danger.

At the same time, she walked out on me.

"Hey, Dad?" Inquisitive blue eyes meet mine. My chest is tight, and I'm choosing my words carefully. "What would you have done if Mom were doing something... if she'd had a project or a hobby..." That's not right. "What would you have done if Mom were involved in something that could hurt her?"

His brow lines with concentration, and he thinks about it. I've always appreciated the way he takes every question seriously. It's why he's so successful in his work. Every problem is analyzed before he answers.

"I'd stop her."

His answer is so simple it pulls me up short. "What if she wouldn't let you?"

"I guess I'd have to convince her to let me."

"But how?"

He takes a deep breath and swirls the wine in his glass. "Showing someone how much you care is always a good place to start. Other than that, sometimes you just have to pull people away from the cliff."

"Wouldn't you be worried you might lose her? For not respecting her wishes?"

"Sounds like you might lose her anyway. What's the risk?"

My eyes go to my fist on the table, and I nod slowly. "Would you mind if I borrow your jet for a few days?"

He gives me a grin. "It's going to be yours anyway."

CHAPTER 18: VULNERABLE

Molly

The room phone rings so loud, I almost fall out of the bed.

My eyes are crusty from crying myself to sleep, and the room smells like the hamburger I never ate.

"Shit," I hiss, as the damn phone blasts again with that metallic ring. Snatching up the receiver, I answer too sharply. "What?"

"Good morning, Myshka, you weren't answering your mobile."

Clearing my throat, I soften my tone. "What? My phone didn't ring." I lift it up and see it's shut off. "I think the battery might have died."

"Will you meet me at Mother's for breakfast? Or should I say brunch?"

"Brunch?" I scrub my eyes and look at the clock. It's almost ten in the morning. I slept for twelve hours? "Of course! I'll shower and meet you there at ten thirty."

We disconnect, and I plug in my phone. Then I hurry to take the smelly hamburger and put it out in the hall. It's too bad, because it was supposed to be this great, gourmet thing. Also, I'm sure there are plenty of hungry people in this city who would love to eat it. I used to be one of them.

Still, after throwing up again last night, I simply crawled into bed to cry myself to sleep.

What a fucking little crybaby I've become! *Get it together, Molly!* Standing in the bathroom, I give myself a stern look before turning on the shower and doing my best to scrub off last night. One thing's for sure—no more Sazerac.

Mother's is not as crowded as it will be in one more hour, and Stas and I quickly find a seat. I don't tempt fate and only order a coffee and toast. My companion has a debris sandwich with a side of bread pudding.

He surveys my brunch with a frown. "Are you not feeling well?"

"I'm not sure." I say, carefully taking a bite of toast. "I think it was the Sazerac on an empty stomach, but I didn't eat dinner last night."

"Your stomach gets too empty, then it doesn't want to hold food."

Nodding, I sip my coffee. "I've heard that. Although, it never has been the case for me. I've always been able to eat whatever I want."

A waitress circles through the room refilling coffee. Stas takes a bite of his sandwich made from the tiny scraps of roast beef that fall off in the gravy, and my throat gets tight. The Debris Sandwich is my second-favorite sandwich in this city behind the Three-fer. Still, watching Stas devour it has a lump rising in my throat.

"I don't know." I push back from the table. "Maybe it's a stomach bug."

"Come." He stands, gathering his items and placing them in the white bag. "We'll walk outside. It's stuffy and crowded in here."

Outside on the street, we stroll in the direction of the Super Dome. A light breeze is blowing, and my stomach starts to calm.

"I've never thought of myself as a lightweight." I got a go-cup for my coffee. "I guess I'm sensitive to absinthe... or whiskey. What happened last night after I left?"

"I went back and examined the property. Something

172

about Renee Landry didn't seem right to me. Did you get the sense we had been lured there?"

Squinting my eyes, I think about his question. "Something was off with her. She seemed to be expecting us, but how?"

"That's what I wanted to try and discover."

"Did you?"

"No."

We've reached a little park off the main road, and he guides me to a bench where we can sit and he can finish his lunch. It's then I remember what I need to tell him.

"In all my running back and forth to Seattle, I wasn't able to tell you what Mark said." Placing my coffee in the trash, I join him on the green iron seat. "He shot Landry."

Stas's eyes widen. "Is he dead?"

"Don't know. He said they exchanged gunfire. Mark was hit and had to run, but when he went back, Landry was gone. He said he's been trying to find him, to find information ever since, but nothing."

My friend leans back and stares at the street in front of us. His eyes are narrowed and his gray brow furrows. "I heard he might be in hiding. Is it possible he's dead?"

"I guess anything is possible."

"See what you can find, and I'll return to my original source. If it's a cold case, then there it is. I'll accept this is the end of my quest."

The sadness in his voice touches my heart. I remember myself as a child, lost on the streets, starving. If someone had cared about me, had been trying to find me, I would want to know it. I would want them to find me even now.

"It can't be the end." I put my hand on his arm. "Let me go back and try again. I'll help you find them. I promise."

His old face lines more with his gentle smile. "You've a kind heart, Myshka. I'm sorry you had to live through what you did."

"I'm better now because of you."

"Are you?" His smile turns concerned. "I wonder."

"I am." Standing quickly, I brush my hand down the front of my jeans, feeling a flash of embarrassment. He doesn't need to worry about me.

"I'll be out of town for a few days, meeting with a friend. But don't worry, I'll be back next week."

"I'll let you know what I find out."

I walk quickly back to the hotel, feeling focused and determined to help Stas, when I'm caught in a small group of tourists on the sidewalk. They step side to side, and I'm growing frustrated when a man passes carrying a Lucky Dog.

The aroma of hot dog, sauerkraut, and onion hits me right in the face, and before I know it I have to dash to a nearby trash and throw up the small amount of toast and coffee I had this morning. I cough and close my eyes, wishing I could disappear right this minute.

A woman touches my arm and hands me a tissue. "Don't be embarrassed. I was the same way when I was expecting. How far along are you? You're so tiny, I expect what? Three weeks? Six? The nausea will pass."

I immediately dry heave over the trash, only now I'm reeling from the freight train of panic her words send slamming into my chest.

"Are you okay?" The lady rubs my back, and I take the tissue she offers.

"Thank you… I-I'm okay. I'm not pregnant." I blow my nose and toss the tissue in the trash, and her kindness turns to a scowl.

"Honestly, are you hung over? Young people these

days."

The lady walks off in a huff, but I stagger into the lobby freaking the fuck out. I'm not pregnant.

I am *not* pregnant.

I always take my pill.

Always.

I can't be pregnant.

Fuck fuck fuck fuck fuck.

I hurry up to my room, pacing the empty elevator with my arms crossed over my stomach. That woman is nuts. I uncross my arms and shake it off. I shake my shoulders, down to my hands. I move my head side to side.

What a ridiculous suggestion. As if I would be so irresponsible.

When I get to the room, I wash my mouth with water and brush my teeth. I make another vow never to drink Sazerac again, and I open my laptop and pull up my Tor browser.

I log into the chat room and send a query to **MM50**.

HG187: *Bad address. Sent to Renee Landry. Want to try again?*

Three hours pass with me searching all my old sites for any clues. I go into the NOPD database and scroll around, looking for answers. The last recorded mention of a Reese Landry is almost ten years go, around same time the theater burned to the ground.

He was the policeman on record who filed the report that Guy Hudson died in the fire.

He lied to protect Lara.

They all lied to protect her, and I never knew why.

I'm not angry, but no one ever lied for me. No one even cared... except Lara. She risked her life for me.

Memories of how angry I was flood my mind, how I treated her after we moved back here.

My nose is hot, and a tear rolls down my cheek. I angrily shove it away. Why the fuck am I crying so goddamn much? Fear hits me like a flash, and the woman on the street's words echo in my mind.

Flipping quickly over to Google, I search for symptoms of pregnancy. Even as I type it my insides recoil. That is not what is going on. I'm just sick. Hell, I might be PMSing. That's why I'm ridiculously emotional and sick.

Only... I've never been super emotional with my period before.

The list pops up, and I read it fast... Fatigue, nausea with or without vomiting, food aversions or cravings, headaches, mood swings... Tender, swollen breasts.

I look down at my breasts. They don't seem swollen. No one has touched them in a week, but I don't think they're tender...

My phone buzzes, and I turn it over. The words on the face squeeze my chest.

I miss the cleft in your chin.

Tears heat my eyes again, and anger heats my chest. I've got to *stop crying*. I've got to get it together. Picking up my phone, I walk to the bed, dropping down onto it, and texting Joshua back.

I'm taking good care of it. What are you doing?

Missing you, Rogue.

Again, my heart aches. He's got me around his finger. He has to know this, otherwise why would he keep torturing me this way?

Dean told me about your mom. I never got to say I'm sorry.

For several minutes it's quiet. He doesn't respond. I wonder if he will. I sort of threw that in out of the blue, but it's been on my mind. It was on my mind the night I was running up the stairs to see him. The night he found my list.

When she died I felt so helpless, so angry. I understand what you're going through. Let me help you. Let me in, Molly.

He's asked me that so many times. I was so close to saying yes... then I decided never to tell him. Then he found out. The only problem with him asking me to let him in is he'll also ask me to stop, and that's something I can't do right now.

Not until they've all paid for what they did.

Taking a deep breath, I reply with the truth.

Joshua... you know you're in my heart. I can't let you in this part of my life.

I won't hurt you.

My computer screen wakes up on its own, and my eyes fly to it. A reply is on the screen, and I drop the phone, going to see what it says.

MM50: The address provided was correct. What happened?

HG187: *Current occupant isn't my guy. Doesn't know him.*

MM50: *That's a lie.*

My throat goes dry, and I read the words over again.

HG187: *Strong words. Based on what?*

MM50: *Sorry. Will double-check and let you know.*

I back away from my laptop and sit on the foot of the bed staring at the screen. We're all supposed to be anonymous in this particular online world. Still, something about this user prickles the skin on the back of my neck. He… or she is too familiar.

I look around the room, checking the window, checking the door. Everything is locked. No one can get in here. Still, with Stas going out of town, I feel vulnerable. My heart beats faster, and for the first time in a long time, I consider reaching out to Lara and Mark.

CHAPTER 9: RETRIEVAL

Joshua

"You can use this card at any ATM or supermarket. It's just like a regular bank card." I hand the dark blue debit card to Rebecca.

"But it's got a limit on it, right?"

"Yeah, and I was able to set up which stores will accept it. I added Wal-Mart, Target, all the grocery stores, Amazon…"

Her eyes squint and she laughs. "It's like I'm your teenage daughter."

Leaning closer, I lower my voice. "It's just a security measure… in case you lose it or if, I don't know. I know living on the street can create bad habits, certain weaknesses…"

"Oh, I know. I was only teasing." She holds up a hand. "I'm aware of the potential issues in our arrangement here."

I feel bad having to take these measures, but as our lawyer said, we can't be naïve about this. We stroll from the kitchen into the now-furnished living room as we talk. The four girls are all on the couch together watching *Jeopardy!*

"The place looks really good." I push my hands in my back pockets, looking over the space, the pictures on the walls, the way the girls seem to be getting along. "Sure you'll be okay while I'm gone?"

"Yep! The girls have unpacked and are settling in well. Brittanie is getting ready to take the GED. Candi is job hunting. I'm filling out the paperwork to get Tess and Cindi enrolled in the public high school."

"You settled in your room?"

"It's great. The fact they were using it as a study makes it a little larger than the other rooms."

"But you don't have a real closet."

"I've already planned to hit an antiques store. Looking for an armoire or some type of wardrobe."

"Great, and you've got my number if you need anything." It's exactly how we envisioned it. "I shouldn't be longer than a week. Maybe not even that long." *Hopefully…*

Truth is, I have no idea what to expect when I get to New Orleans. I'm not even sure where Molly is staying—other than it's near Mother's, which I've learned is a restaurant on Poydras Street.

My phone vibrates. Dean has texted me.

Meet me at the Brew House. Must have coffee!

I shake my head and tell the women goodbye. I can walk to the coffee shop from here. The house is in a good, central location for not needing a car, even though I have one, a really nice Acura, in fact. I rarely get it out of the garage.

Dean walks up to the coffee shop at the same time as me. He's dressed in a maroon skinny suit, with pants that stop above his ankles and loafers with no socks.

"Look at us! We got here at the exact same time."

"It's a miracle." I deadpan.

"Don't be sarcastic." He grabs my arm as we enter together.

I guess it should bother me that a guy is hanging off my arm, but it doesn't. Dean has always been this way since we were kids. I don't even notice anymore.

"I like this blazer. Where did you get it?" He slides a

hand down my gray coat.

"I think it was Dad's. I've had it forever." I threw it on over a white tee and jeans.

"Oh! I talked to your dad this morning. Is he the most adorable thing or what? Did he tell you he wants to set up a profile on Mingle dot com?"

An unexpected wave of overprotectiveness moves through my chest. "Yeah, what did you say? We're going to have to watch out for him."

"I said we'd help him as soon as we got back." Hazel eyes level on me, and my eyebrows rise.

"As soon as we get back?"

"You didn't think you'd sneak off to New Orleans without me! Not when you're making your great romantic gesture... and especially not after you dragged me out of there on a moment's notice."

This is getting a little too dramatic for my plans. "First, it's not a big romantic gesture."

"You're going to reclaim the woman of your dreams, are you not?" He places a palm in the center of his chest.

"Order your coffee."

Dean gets a skinny soy butterscotch decaf Frappuccino, and I just get an Americano to go, shaking my head at his order. While we wait for his beverage, I try to regain control of my trip south.

"I'm going to talk to her. I'm not going down there to make some big scene or scare her off... Or piss her off."

"You can do what you want. I'm going down there to find that sexy hunk of man we left behind." His drink arrives, and he does a little shoulder shimmy. "Musicians are so hot."

We start walking in the direction of my warehouse apartment. "She doesn't want Roland to know she's there. They don't get along."

"I don't see why her name ever has to come up. Or yours for that matter."

Standing on the sidewalk in front of my place, I consider what he's suggesting. "I had hoped you'd be here to keep an eye on the house for me."

"You hired Rebecca for that."

"What about Dad? He's not completely out of the woods yet."

"Your dad is doing so well, he's horny."

That makes me wince. Up until now, I hadn't really thought through everything it would mean for my dad to start dating again.

"I think he's more lonely." It's my attempt to hold back the truth.

"He's horny. Let the man live."

I only have one potential barrier left. "The pilot is expecting us to be there in just a few hours. I called him this morning. He's already filed the flight plan."

"How long are we staying?"

"I don't know." Looking down, I rub the back of my neck. "I don't know if she'll be angry. I don't know if she'll even see me."

Dean puts his hand on my shoulder and squeezes. "She's going to think it's romantic."

"You don't know her as well as I do."

"So it could be a few days or it could be a week?"

I shrug. "Something like that."

"Let's go."

CHAPTER 20: REVEALED

Molly

Stas and I meet for dinner at Emeril's, a few blocks from the hotel toward the river.

The restaurant is shaped like a barrel with arched ceilings and a sort of woven effect on the inlays. Wood floors and matching tables and chairs are arranged throughout the space. I tell the hostess I'm meeting an older gentleman, and she immediately leads me past the exposed-brick wall to a small table in a more secluded corner.

As we pass through the elegant restaurant, I coolly take in all the guests, scanning every face for any sign of recognition or threat. I see none.

Stas has a tumbler of scotch in front of him, and he stands when I approach. "I'm glad you felt like joining me." We exchange a brief hug. "How are you feeling?"

"Better," I nod, sitting. "I took a nap, and it seemed to help."

A nap. I never nap, but I'm so tired all the time now.

The waiter takes my drink order, and I dare a glass of pinot gris. Once he's gone, Stas is immediately down to business.

"My train leaves this evening at ten. I'll only be gone two days. Were you able to uncover anything new?"

MM50's final text has been on my mind. I'd been waiting for him to send me another message, but nothing had arrived before I left the hotel. I glance around us. The nearby tables are empty, and no one is

183

close enough to overhear us.

"I searched police records, but nothing was out of the ordinary." Nothing I didn't already know. "I know fabricated police reports, because I know what really happened in certain situations." My dinner companion only nods, listening intently. "But after the theater burned, his trail goes cold."

Stas exhales deeply and relaxes back in his chair. "I'm afraid that's the end of the story."

"Not necessarily." His brow perks at that. "I have one last query out to see if anyone has verifiable information. As soon as I hear back, I'll let you know."

The waiter appears to take our orders. Everything on the menu is so rich and flavorful, I have the Iceberg Wedge salad. Stas gives me a disappointed face, but I only shake my head. I'm not taking any more chances. He orders the Andouille Crusted Gulf Drum, a white fish crusted with sausage and served with a Creole Meunière sauce.

Once the man is gone, my friend leans forward and speaks quietly. "I'm probably going on a fool's errand."

"It's worth it to be sure you've done all you can." I take another sip of wine, feeling more confident in my stomach's ability to keep it down.

"What will you do while I'm gone?" He takes a sip of his fresh scotch.

It's unlike him to be sentimental, but I trust him enough to talk. "I'll wait for word from my people, and I'll probably stroll around the city. Pass the time."

"You miss him. You should ask that young man to come here. I have a feeling he'd drop everything to be with you."

Not even Stas knows the extent of what I've done, and while I do trust him, I'm not involving him in my plans either. "He probably would... It's not a good idea for this errand."

He sighs and leans back. "I remember being your age, having so much time. Don't wait for time to catch up with you. Marry the boy, start a family. Don't end up a lonely old man like me."

I take another sip of wine. "I don't think I'd make a good mother."

"Nonsense. You'd make the best kind, the kind who knows the world, who knows what to beware of."

I exhale a short laugh, my fingers circling the stem of my glass. "A real mother bear?"

"Yes, that's it. Mother bear."

Our food arrives, and our conversation turns more mundane. I manage to finish my salad, but it had a creamy dressing I didn't expect... or I didn't read the menu closely. By the time we're done, night has fallen over the city.

"I'll walk you to your hotel. From there, I can take a cab to the train station."

We walk the six blocks in easy silence, the click of our heels mixing with the hum of traffic, the occasional blast of a horn. My hand is on Stas's arm, and when we arrive at the entrance, he stops.

"You have my number if you need me." Nodding, I give him a brief hug. "Think about what I said. Life is too short, Myshka."

I smile at his nostalgia, and nod before entering the hotel. It's dark, but it's not super late. Instead of going to my room, I walk to the other side of the lobby and look out toward the Quarter. So much time has passed, so many years. I'm keyed up, not ready for sleep, and I pull out my phone to call a Lyft.

A car is waiting at the curb, and I dash out to climb inside. Traffic is slow, stop and go at this time of the evening with the tourists flooding the high-traffic areas.

We slowly make our way around the crescent, following the bend of the river until we stop in front of the square.

I hop out quickly and wait for the cars to pass before crossing the busy street in front of the old cathedral. The lamps are burning, and the tall banana trees cast long shadows. The live oak branches sweep low, all the way to the ground almost, and I walk slowly up the middle of the large circle, toward the monument of Andrew Jackson on horseback.

I keep going, all the way to the wide alley in front of the church, but I take a left and bypass the entrance, the place where Lara and Mark exchanged vows in that brief little drive-by ceremony.

That's not fair—it was actually a beautiful ceremony, if technically illegal, since they didn't have a permit to use the grounds.

Pedestrians pass me in a steady stream, and I walk up the narrow block to the corner. The last time I was here, the place was exploding with Mardi Gras revelers. It almost feels like a lifetime ago. Stas had been here.

Standing on the corner, I look up at the white stucco façade, the green-shuttered French doors lining the side of the building all the way down the block. The ever-present rainbow puddles are dotted down the center of the road, and the mist in the air surrounds the gas lanterns with mystery.

This time I reach out and touch the wall with my bare hand. I wait, quietly listening, hearing the echoes of the music, the noise of the cheering. I would stand in the wings and watch them perform and dream of one day being a star. All those dreams were destroyed in one night. Less than a night. Only a few hours.

A breeze moves past me, sweeping my hair over my shoulder, and when I turn my face in the direction it moves, I catch the flicker of a shadow. My insides jolt, and I realize how vulnerable I am alone in this space. All the pedestrians have filtered away, heading toward the river or in the opposite direction, toward Bourbon Street.

Turning on my heel, I walk steadily in the direction I came, up the narrow alley following the side of the cathedral. My steps create a curious echo, almost like two steps landing just off-time. I stop, and the second steps aren't quick enough.

I'm definitely being followed.

Placing my hand on the wrought iron fence, I do as Stas taught me. I allow the fear to filter from my chest through my stomach, down my arms and legs, then out my fingers and toes until it's all gone.

Feel the fear, Myshka, then let it leave you. You're more powerful than any attacker now.

I don't have my necklace, but I have the moves he taught me. I have the ability to run, which is the first rule of self-defense: *Avoidance.*

Still, I don't run. I only take another step, continuing my progress toward Decatur Street, toward the masses of people clustered around the bars and restaurants along the river. The strange echo fades away, and I feel the presence receding. Whoever is following me is falling back, and I turn to look quickly over my shoulder.

It's too late. No one is there.

The Lyft I order for the ride back to the hotel is stuffy. Like every other car seems to be, the faint odor of cigarette smoke saturates the fabric of the seats, and the driver takes the curves a bit too sharply. A cold sweat breaks out on my upper lip, and as soon as he pulls up in front of my hotel, I bolt out and head for that same fucking garbage can.

One Iceberg Wedge in the trash.

Stepping back, I cover my mouth with my hand. My

insides are shaking, a different kind of panic filtering through my veins. I can't defend myself from what I'm starting to fear is happening inside me. I double back to the drugstore a few blocks over, and once I've got what I need, I hurry back to my hotel room.

In my room, I discard my dress and bra and pull on an oversized, long-sleeved tee that once was Joshua's. Sadly, I stole it so long ago, it no longer smells like him. I grab a hair tie and twist my long hair on top of my head in a messy bun. The cardboard box is in my hand, and I spend a minute reading the purple print over and over as if English isn't my native language.

Easy home pregnancy test.

Oh, fuck my life.

Heartburn stings at the base of my throat. I place the box on the counter in the bathroom and wash my mouth out. I grab my toothbrush and brush my teeth. Then I grab the floss and meticulously clean each one. Then I take out my makeup remover wipes and wipe my face clean. Then I return to the bedroom.

I tap the touchpad repeatedly to wake up my laptop. Once it's awake, I click on the icon for my Tor browser. It takes several minutes to fully load. A bottle of water is on the dresser by the large flat screen television, and I pick it up and twist off the cap.

One long drink, and I know it's time to stop procrastinating. I have to find out.

My stomach is so tight, it feels like my bottom ribs are a corset squeezing my lungs tighter and tighter the closer I get to that cardboard box on the counter in the bathroom.

No badass tricks are going to get me out of this one.

Picking it up again, I re-read the directions.

Point the absorbent tip downward. Place the absorbent tip in urine stream for at least five seconds until thoroughly wet…

Sitting on the toilet, I shove my panties off and kick them across the slick bathroom floor then I spread my knees wide, leaning forward so I can make sure I do it right.

It's so awkward.

Five seconds.

I count slowly in my mind.

One…

Two…

Three…

Four…

Five…

I take the damp thing away, setting it on the counter while I pull a handful of tissue. Reaching for the purple cap, my hand knocks the slick cardboard box. It slides across the counter like a hockey puck, landing out on the floor in front of the door leading to the hallway. I don't have time to worry about it. I have to wait five minutes before I'll have an answer, and my Tor browser is waiting.

MM50: *Further investigation reveals… the information I sent you is correct.*

The message has been sitting a while, but I hop on and type a reply.

HG187: *I'm telling you, we went there. It was a dead end.*

MM50: *Well, hello DB187. Nice to see you've returned. And you made it safely to your room.*

Ice filters through my veins when I read the reply. My fears from before are back, front and center in my mind.

HG187: *DB?*

MM50: *Let's not play games. You might remember me as Shutr.*

Shutr... I sound it out in my head. **Shooter**... I remember Shooter. **DB** is a reference to my old username, Doll Baby. I used it when I was searching for Esterhaus almost a decade ago.

Shooter had good intel—he led me to the Whitehorse Yukon Railway, which was ideal for my purposes, and he liked to be paid in Bitcoin or Ethereum, but never Litecoin.

He's good... which makes me nervous. How did he know I might not make it back to my room safely?

HG187: *I guess I'm not a very good ghost.*

MM50: *I hope you're a better runner.*

My pulse thunders in my ears, and I decide not to respond. The cold realization trickles through my veins. If he's already tracked me down to my last username, it's too late to hide my identity. If he knows that much, he knows my IP address, which will lead him straight here.

How fast?

I run to the bathroom to retrieve my underwear. I jerk them over my hips and my eyes fall to the counter. The fucking pregnancy test. Snatching up the white plastic wand, I hold the little window to the light. *Two lines*. What the hell does that mean?

Searching around, I grab a pair of black leggings out of my suitcase and step into them, pulling them over my hips as I bend down for the box. I scoop it off the floor just as a sharp explosion blasts through the door at the line of my cheekbone.

I spin away as splinters of wood shoot out around me into the room, and I feel the sting of air flying past my face. I'm not hit. I drop to the floor and crawl into the bathroom, covering my mouth with my hand to quiet my breathing.

My back is against the cool wall, my butt is on the floor, and I'm staring at my bare feet, my black-painted toenails when another sharp *Pop!* sounds just outside the door.

Someone's shooting their way into my room.

Someone's using a silencer.

Adrenaline floods my veins, and the fucking nausea is back. I can't vomit now. I remember my self-defense techniques. *Krav Maga for disarming an armed attacker…* With the gun pointing at my face, I'll duck out of the line of fire and dive forward as my hands go up to grab the weapon, then I twirl taking the gun out of the shooter's hand.

That's how it should go. I've practiced this but never had to use it.

My eyes are wide, and I breathe faster, building my internal momentum, preparing to engage…

Glancing down, the pregnancy test box is still in my hand. Just before I toss it aside, my eyes land on the diagram on the back. Large squares have writing underneath them.

One line means you're not pregnant.
Two lines means…

"Oh, fuck." My stomach pitches just as the door blasts open.

Krav Maga flies out the window as my thoughts scatter over what I've just learned, what this stick I'm holding in my hand is saying to me...

I crouch lower behind the door, my heart flying out of my chest. *You'd make a great mother, Myshka.* My eyes squeeze shut at the memory of Stas's words. *Oh, fuck...*

The intruder is in my room, looking all around, moving fast and quiet. I'm small in the corner of the bathroom, and this person is going to find me. I've got to think fast if I'm going to get out of this without getting shot.

I watch the reflection in the bathroom mirror. It's a small person dressed all in black carrying a large gun. A quick swipe over the head, and the mask is off. Dark hair falls around her face. *It's a woman...*

She turns slowly, and in that moment, our eyes lock in the mirror. White teeth appear with her sinister smile, and she raises her weapon, aiming right at my face. I'm still on the floor. My heart hammers against my ribs, and I'm at a complete disadvantage. The time to get in position is gone, and I can't take a chance at getting shot. Not now.

Ducking my head, I hold out my hand — the one with the pregnancy stick. "Wait!" I shout. "Don't shoot. Just wait... Please."

It's enough to stop her. She lowers the gun a fraction, studying me. "Why should I?"

"I know this is strange, but I'm begging you. Hear me out. Why are you here? Who do you work for?"

One thing I do know — neither of the assholes I killed would have anyone trying to avenge their murders.

"You're the bitch looking for Reese Landry. I'm looking for you." Her gun snaps back into place, aiming right at my head.

"Wait! You're right. I was looking for him. But I have reason to believe he might be dead."

"I have reason to believe you might be the person who killed him."

My voice goes louder. "NO! You're wrong! I promise you. You're wrong. If Reese Landry is dead, it wasn't me who did it. I just returned to the city for Mardi Gras. Before that, I was in Seattle, and before that I was in Canada."

The shooter's eyes narrow. "Then why were you with the old man? Why did the two of you go to Landry's address?"

"We're looking for information on my friend's family. That's all." I hear the creaking of the trigger, and I shout louder. "Please! You have to believe me. Please, don't shoot. I just found out I'm pregnant. See? It's on this stick here."

"I don't care what you just found out. I have orders—"

"But you're making a mistake. Just let me talk to your boss… Just don't… Please don't kill my baby." Tears burn my eyes as I realize how much I mean these words, from the bottom of my soul. "Please… This baby has the best dad. Please don't kill his child."

Joshua flashes across my mind, and my throat aches so bad.

The eyes of the woman holding the gun flare. She grinds her teeth, and I see the muscle in her jaw move. I see the frustration in her eyes as they dart from me to the stick in my hand and back. In the flicker of an eyelash, she lowers her gun.

I just start to breathe when her face distorts and she rushes at me, pulling something small and black from her belt.

Her hand flies high over her head, and I don't have time to duck before she slams it down against my temple.

My world goes black.

CHAPTER 21: CONFUSION

Joshua

Since the moment we touched down at the New Orleans Metropolitan Airport, I've been texting Molly. Tension builds in me every second she doesn't reply.

She always answers me, and our last exchange was good, not heated or angry. I can't help feeling like something is wrong.

"If you grip that phone any harder, you're going to break it." Dean is beside me in the cab, his keen eyes studying my behavior like always.

Forcing a chuckle, I relax my grip. "I didn't even realize."

"Don't try lying to me. What's going on? No word from Molly?"

My chin drops, and I'm facing a decision. How much to tell my cousin, and how much to keep to myself. If Molly is in real danger, I'm going to need some help navigating this city.

"I guess I'll go with you to Roland's place for now. I'll see if I can get a hotel room somewhere else."

"You sure will." Dean's eyebrow arches. "Last thing I need is you cock-blocking me on my sex holiday."

"Is that what this is?" I do my best to play along. "Remember the motto."

"You don't have to educate a gay man about safe sex. I just hope you're being careful."

I look out the window.

"That's what I thought. This is more than just Molly visiting her sister. You two had a fight."

"We didn't have a fight."

"So why the need for the romantic gesture? What did you do?"

My jaw clenches tighter, and I swallow the growl rising in my throat. "This is not a romantic gesture. I told you, I came here to talk to her."

"But she won't answer your texts."

She always did before... Choosing my words, I try to give him something that will satisfy him and make him cool it with the bloodhound routine.

"Molly's here on business... She's working on a project. It's something I don't want her to do —"

"Is she a spy?"

"No."

"A hacker?"

"No." My voice grows louder with every question.

"A high-class hooker? She's sexy enough. Have you seen that show *The Girlfriend Experience*? You'd never expect these pretty college students to do what they do. It's wild."

"What the fuck? No!" A glance forward and I see our driver is trying not to laugh. "Would you knock it off?"

"How can I? You're clearly upset by whatever's going on, and you've never been this cagey a day in your life."

"I've changed my mind. I'm not getting out at Roland's. Let's stick to our original plan. Don't tell him either of us are here. You came by yourself."

He glances out the window and makes a pouty face. "Lying really gets a relationship off on the wrong foot."

"Are you starting a relationship with this guy?"

"A boy can dream..."

I stay back as my cousin steps out into the drizzle. He pulls a metallic purple carry-on behind him and does a little wave before dashing up the narrow sidewalk into the vintage duplex. I've only been here once after the wedding, but I know this old, restored house is really nice.

"I guess…" I think about what I know at this point. "Take me to Mother's on Poydras."

Molly said she was going to eat at that restaurant in one of our conversations. She said she could walk to it. Sitting back and pinching my lips between my fingers, I can only hope there aren't too many hotels within walking distance.

I'm fucking wrong as I can be. Standing on the corner in front of the red-brick dive restaurant, I'm surrounded by mirrored-glass high-rises and boutique hotels.

"Fuck," I growl, taking out my phone and trying again.

Where are you staying? Please tell me.

I start walking slowly in the direction of the river, waiting… I walk a few blocks, crossing a wide, four lane highway with a grassy median. I make it all the way to the Riverwalk mall, and nothing.

No answer.

The truth is, I'm really worried. It's true I only came here to talk, but I didn't expect her not to answer my texts. Heck, it's only been a day since we last communicated.

Taking a chance, I call her. It rings and rings, but then her voicemail picks up. Standing on the top of the levee, I pinch the bridge of my nose and decide to just lay it out there.

"Hey, it's me. Look, I know you're possibly not

going to like this, but I'm here. In New Orleans. Please give me a call. I just wanted to see you, talk to you. I'm not going to make you do anything you don't want to do... Just... Just see me, Molly. Text me where you're staying."

I end the call and walk to one of the green benches facing the river. I lean forward and prop my arms on my thighs, my phone in my hands, and I stare at the face waiting.

Minutes pass. A skinny white bird picks its way carefully through the tall grasses on long legs. A riverboat with a large red paddle wheel and *River Queen* painted on the side drifts past. A long barge drifts past. Somewhere in the distance, I hear the sound of a brass band.

It's hot. Okay, it's probably not as hot as it normally gets in this city, but the rain has passed and the sun is bearing down on me. The air is thick, and I'm uncomfortable.

I'm sticky and worried and sick of sitting here with my phone in my hand.

"Oh, fuck it." I scroll through my contacts until I see Lara's name.

If Molly is avoiding my calls, she's mad I'm here. In that case it won't make much difference if I contact Lara and get some help. Alternatively, if she's in trouble, the longer I wait, the worse her situation could get.

That thought drives my finger forward, and I quickly hit the call button.

CHAPTER 22: BAIT

Molly

My head hurts like a mother when I open my eyes.

"Shit," I groan, turning slowly onto my side and blinking hard to clear my vision.

I'm on a cold, concrete floor in a small, dark room. The walls are cinder block painted a dark color—maroon or brown, I think. The light isn't strong enough for me to tell.

It smells like dust. Damp and dust. It's a wet, metallic scent that stings my nose. Not dirty or moldy, but definitely not clean… And my face is against the floor. Gross.

Placing my palm against the concrete, I push my body into a sitting position. The room tilts, and I grip my legs, holding my back against the wall until the dizziness passes.

I'm barefoot. I'm still in my black leggings and the oversized tee, with no bra. It appears the shooter knocked me out and brought me here. She must have had help. A woman that size couldn't carry me alone without being noticed, if she could've carried me at all. Only, I didn't see anyone else.

Like I had a chance to see anything. My brain was scrambling for any way to hold off the inevitable.

Slowly, I bend my legs and rest my hands on top of my knees. A shudder moves through my shoulders, and my stomach cramps. Looking up and around the space, I see I'm trapped, a prisoner in a dark basement, God only knows where.

Nobody knows where.

Stas is gone. Joshua is in Seattle. Lara and Mark don't even know I'm in the city... for however much longer I'm alive. I hiccup a breath.

No. Stop.

I steel myself against the onslaught of emotions.

I focus on my breathing.

I focus on the air moving in through my nose and out of my mouth.

I listen to the sound.

I feel the expansion of my lungs.

I *do not cry.*

Moving my fingers along my scalp, a large lump is above my temple. When I touch it, the pain is freaking unbelievable.

"Ouch!" I gasp, jerking my hand away.

I gingerly touch it again, checking for blood. I don't feel any, but I don't have a mirror. I can't check my pupils to see if they're dilated. I'm nauseated, but that's nothing new. I have no idea if I have a concussion.

Another shudder racks my body, and I hug my arms around my stomach trying to get warm. I'm not really cold, so I guess this is shock. Leaning forward, I rest my forehead on my knees again and do my best to hold it together. In my mind, I see that white stick with the purple cap... the picture on the box.

I'm pregnant.

How did this happen?

I always take my pill, faithfully, at the same time every day.

I try to think... Did I ever forget? No. The only thing I can remember is when I was sick — the sinus infection that went into my ears. I had to take antibiotics, and the dizziness kept me in bed. Of course, Joshua would join me, hugging me and trying to make me feel better.

Stubborn tears fill my eyes as the memories fill my mind. I'd be lying on my side with my hand over my face, and he'd slide in behind me, curling his body around mine. He'd kiss my neck and wrap an arm around my waist. He'd press his nose against my hairline and inhale then kiss me there, sending warm tingles through my body. It wasn't long before we'd be making love…

And that's how it happened.

At the time I wasn't feeling well, and it didn't occur to me. Now I remember people saying it, or maybe I read it somewhere, how antibiotics can interfere with birth control.

None of it matters now. All that matters is there's a little being inside me who belongs to Joshua… I mean, it belongs to me, too, but for whatever reason, I can only see his face when I think of it, his cocky, sexy smile. His smile is always so full of love for me.

I have Joshua's baby in my body…

My nose heats, and I sniff. I don't understand these feelings in my chest, in my heart. It's an ache echoing through my limbs with every heartbeat.

I'm already in love with this little person. I want this baby so much.

How did this happen to me?

I never wanted a baby…

But with my eyes closed, I can see a little boy or a little girl with Joshua's smile, running and laughing. I can see Joshua holding him or her, swinging his child around in his arms. I'm there with them, touching them, touching Joshua's arm, touching our baby's hair. It's like the most beautiful dream I didn't know was hiding in my heart.

Lifting my chin, I look at the corner of the ceiling, doing my best to stop my tears. My palm moves to my stomach, flat against my skin, and everything is changing. Without my control, without even my knowledge, it's like my view on the world has shifted overnight.

My life doesn't make sense this way.

I have to stop doing this.

Joshua wants me to stop. He wants to help me stop. I have to let him.

This little girl... or boy... needs me to stop chasing my demons. I don't even want to anymore. Life isn't about me now.

Like a wash of cool water through my veins, I understand so much. I understand Lara and how she started pulling away when she was expecting her daughter. When she told me it's not the same — finding these men doesn't give her joy anymore — I understand her now.

At the time I was furious. I felt like she was betraying me, betraying us. I believed she had become weak. I thought being a mother had robbed her of her strength.

Now I realize I was totally wrong. Being a mother changes the direction of that strength. It goes from being all about my own needs and demands to making a safe place for my baby, this tiny innocent. I only want her to be pure and happy and *safe*.

Oh, God, I need to tell Lara I'm sorry. I have to get out of here so I can tell her I understand now, and I'm so sorry.

Turning to the side, I lean my shoulder against the wall. A hollow ache creeps into my bones. I need Joshua. I need him to hold me. I want his strong arms around me.

If he knew...

I can't stop the tears leaking out of my eyes now,

because the truth hits me so hard. If Joshua knew about our baby, he'd be tearing the walls down to get to me. He'd do everything in his power to save us, to get us out of here.

Our family. I've never had one of those. He almost lost his…

Closing my eyes, I see his face in my mind. "Joshua," I whisper. "I love you so much. I'm going to protect our baby. I'm going to come home."

A metallic *clatch!* echoes behind me, and the bolt on the door slides open. The wood sticks, and whoever is out there bangs against it. It shakes, and with a loud push, it flies open, making me jump back.

An enormous man stomps into the room. He must be six foot two, and his head and neck are the same width down to his broad shoulders. He's bald, and his round stomach strains against his black tee.

"Get up." He speaks in a hoarse growl.

I don't move fast enough, and he bends down, grabbing my arm and jerking me to my feet like a rag doll. A cry escapes from my throat.

I'm too disoriented and weak to fight him. I'm starving from throwing up so much, and my mouth is like a desert.

"Walk." He steps to the side to let me exit the room ahead of him.

Reaching out, I hold the wall for support. My legs tremble, but he doesn't have time for my shit. He grabs my arm again and jerks me up again, pushing me forward as my feet stumble to keep up.

"Slow down, please," I beg, holding the wall, an approaching chair, anything in my path to stay on my feet.

The man doesn't even respond. He doesn't even look at me. He's built like a house, and he marches like a soldier. We head through another, larger room to a staircase leading up. The stairs are covered in worn gold carpet, and they're not the height of normal stairs. They're shorter, and he drags me up them.

At least the disgusting old carpet pads my shins crashing into the steps as I trip and try to find my feet. Cave Man doesn't seem to care if I'm falling more than climbing up the steps. He keeps moving until we reach a door. It's closed and he stops, tapping on it in a rhythm.

Another loud *clatch!* and it opens into a dark hallway at a back door. The door has one small window at the top center, and I can see bars through it. It doesn't look like it's been opened in years, but I make a mental note. *Escape.*

"Keep moving." I'm back to being shoved forward.

"I-I don't know where to go." Again, my arm is snatched into his meaty fist, and he drags me down a short hall into an open kitchen.

It's rustic and dark, with stainless fixtures and brown wood cabinets. A large island is in the center of the room, and assorted pots and pans hang from a rack over it. I notice a stovetop in the counter, and in a corner is a wooden block with knives in it.

I don't know that I'll have access to any of these items, but I note them. I'm aware the woman who broken into my room had a gun, but beggars can't be choosers.

We round a corner, and a large living area is to my right. It's rustic as well, with a stone fireplace and a burgundy leather sofa and chairs. A moose head is mounted on the wall. I've only ever seen a moose in Canada, which makes me wonder…

A few more steps, and we're at a closed wooden door. It's ornate with square panels carved down the length. The Neanderthal holding my arm knocks and waits for us to be summoned.

Inside, the room is dim with those green-shaded lamps on a dark wooden desk. A fire crackles in the fireplace, and a dark red Persian rug covers the floor. It feels soft on my bare feet.

A voice purrs from the leather chair across the desk from us. "Thank you, George."

I recognize her voice, but I'm not sure if I'm relieved or terrified as she turns the chair to face me. Dark eyes narrow on mine, and her elbows rest on the chair arms. Her fingers are steepled in front of her lips.

"We meet again." She says it almost like a joke, like she's quoting every super villain in comic book history. "How do you like your room, Maggie Brown? Or should I say Molly Dixon? Or Doll Baby… Or Hit Girl."

"You know who I am."

"I know everything."

Light glitters in her eyes, and she studies my appearance. I study hers in her navy suit and peach blouse. A thick strand of pearls is around her neck, and while she's not old, lines appear in the corners of her eyes and along the sides of her red-painted mouth when she speaks.

"Then you have me at a disadvantage. I don't know what I'm doing here."

"I'm looking for the man who killed my father."

My pulse ticks faster. "So he's dead. You're sure?"

"We recovered my father's body in the swamp a half mile from his home. He'd been shot and callously dumped by the river… mutilated by the wildlife." She rises from the chair and walks to a small table holding a crystal decanter of brown liquid. She pours two fingers into a tumbler and takes a sip.

"I-I'm sorry." It's a lie. I'm not. Sounds like that fucker got what he deserved. Still, my mind is on my baby. I've got to get out of here. "That must've been hard."

"We had to use dental records to identify him. His casket was closed at the funeral." Her voice is simmering fury on the last part.

I'm thinking, trying to figure out this woman. "I don't know who killed your father."

"Yet you came here with Stas Volodya, your mentor. The man who taught you how to kill. Why did you show up on my doorstep if you know nothing?"

"Because you brought me here." I realize now she gave me the address. "You're Shooter. Or is it Marksman?"

"You met Shooter last night." She shakes her head and takes another sip of whiskey. "She's one of the many hackers in my employ. If you want to use online tipsters, you'd better increase your price. I simply outbid you."

Anger flashes in my chest, but I'm not going to argue. I know better than to trust anyone I meet on the Internet. I didn't know I was being hacked.

"If you know I didn't do it, why do you care about me?"

"Oh, I don't care about you. You're the child of a whore who died on the street. Your mother was a sex slave until they wore her out. Who knows who your father was. Probably some drunk river rat." Her words slice into my heart. "You're nothing."

I'm blinking fast, taking in what she's saying. I've never known where I came from, and she seems to know it all...

"How do you know all of this? H-how..."

Thin red lips curl into a smile. "I inherited my father's records. I know everything he knew... *Everything.*"

Pain blossoms in my chest. The pain of knowing my bleak heritage. As fast as it rises, it changes. Like a muscle memory, I turn it into hatred, into burning need for revenge. If Renee Landry knows everything, then she's seen the videos. She knows what happened to me, and she knows what Lara did.

Swallowing the thickness in my throat, I decide to play dumb. "If you know everything, then you know I didn't know your father."

"You know enough to be useful to me." Her eyes level on mine. "For now."

My gaze is defiant. "What do you want?"

"It's simple. You're what we in the business like to call an incentive."

"I'm bait."

"I'm pretty sure I know what happened to my father. We ran ballistics." She returns to the leather desk chair and takes a seat. "I'll let the people in your circle know you're going down for my father's murder. We'll see who comes to save you... Or set the record straight."

The wooden door opens, and the woman from my hotel room, Shooter enters with Cave Man right behind her. "Get me what I need and put her back in her room."

The man grabs my arm again and drags me into the living area. My back is against a blank wall, and he shoves a copy of the *Times-Picayune* in my hands.

"What is this?" I look down at the newspaper, but he jerks it up, under my chin.

"Hold it there. Face forward."

Proof of life. I understand what they're doing, and for a moment, I consider resisting. They'll take a photo of me holding today's paper and send it... Where? To Stas, I'm sure, but... to Mark? Would she send it to the police station? Was she fishing?

My eyes circle the room, landing on what has to be

the front door. I've got to figure a way out of that basement. The camera flashes, and I'm momentarily blinded. The paper is snatched out of my hand, and Cave Man has me in his fist again.

Renee is behind me. "Don't waste time circulating that photo."

"How can you be so sure the right person will come for me?" I won't lie, I'm thinking what might happen if Joshua sees this.

She reads my mind. "Concerned about your... baby daddy?" She sniffs a laugh. "Why, that would be almost biblical. An eye for an eye. A father for a father."

"Don't you hurt him." My voice breaks, and I've given her what she wants.

She's close to my face now. "Hard to be a hit girl when you have so many weaknesses."

Meathead grabs my arm and drags me away, back down the stairs, back to the dungeon. He throws me on the floor and slams the door. The last noise is the bolt sliding in place.

"Oh, God," I whisper, pressing my hands over my eyes. "Please don't hurt him."

CHAPTER 23: TRACKING

Joshua

Mark stands in his kitchen typing quickly on his laptop. "Is she staying under her real name?"

My arms are crossed, and I watch over his shoulder. "Yeah. She said the hotel was near Mother's, within walking distance."

He connects with an online database and runs a check. Numbers fly by, and I hope this isn't a mistake. It's a strange, mixed up feeling to want her to be okay, but hope she's not. If she's just not answering my calls, I'm really putting the nails in my coffin doing this.

"Jillian's asleep." Lara glides into the room and goes straight to her husband. "What have you found?"

"Give me a few more seconds… and… She's at the Ace hotel on Carondelet. Looks like she hasn't checked out." Mark's eyes meet mine. "Do you want to head over and try to see her?"

"You have her room number?"

"I've got a badge."

I glance from him to Lara. Since I arrived and told them Molly is missing, they immediately went to work. I said I found her list, and Lara's face turned pale. She left the room with her little girl, and Mark asked if Molly was "still doing it."

I answered honestly, I'm not sure, and here we are. Here I am wondering how deep this web of crime and revenge runs. How far back into the past it stretches. At some point, I'll have to get the whole story.

Now is not the time. Scooping up my phone, I nod

to him. "Let's go."

The hotel is a tall, refurbished warehouse with twenty-foot ceilings and industrial accents. Exposed brick walls line the lobby, and the floors are scrubbed, dark wood. The front desk isn't busy when we arrive, and Mark goes straight to the attendant.

"We need the room number for Molly Dixon." He places his black leather wallet on the counter and subtly shows the badge.

I'm scanning the lobby for anyone acting suspicious. Two men are sitting on leather chairs near a palm. I watch them to see if they're watching us, but they never look up. One is reading a newspaper. The other is working on a computer.

"I've got it." Mark's voice is quiet, and I follow him to the elevators.

We ride up to the fourth floor, making our way quickly down the slate-blue hallway to a corner room.

"Hold up." He takes a knee, pulling a white handkerchief from his coat pocket. "Look at this. Don't touch."

"I don't see anything."

"Get closer." Mark steps back, scanning the hall around and pulling out his pistol.

I lean closer and see the *Do Not Disturb* sign hanging from the doorknob is hiding a crack along where the latch is located. Mark steps forward and gently leans into the door with his shoulder. The mechanism drops, taking the sign with it.

"Shit!" I hiss.

The door creaks open, and my stomach drops at the sight inside. Splinters of wood are on the floor, clothes are scattered everywhere.

"It's empty," I say quietly.

"Just be careful, and don't touch anything. It's all

evidence."

We step gingerly into the room. He continues toward the window, but I pause, looking into the bathroom. Her makeup remover is out, and a washcloth is on the sink. A white plastic stick with a purple cap is on the floor beside a bent cardboard box.

Leaning down, I see *Home Pregnancy Test* printed on the side. My stomach drops, and I swallow the sudden dryness in my throat. "What the fuck… Mark!"

He hustles back to where I'm standing. "What is it?"

"Look at this. Pick this up and tell me what it says."

Frowning, he steps to see what I'm looking at. I straighten and shove both hands into my hair. "Tell me she's not pregnant."

I have to get out of here. My chest is exploding, and I'm about to start breaking things. This is too much. We've reached the point where this is all fucking too much for me.

Mark's voice is grave. "Somebody's pregnant." Straightening, he sees my expression and grips my shoulders. He and I are about the same height and equally built. "Grab the reins. We're going to find her."

"I can't—"

"This might not even belong to Molly. Was she traveling with anyone? Are you sure she was alone here?"

I'm nodding as I answer him. "I think so… If she met anyone, it was the man at The Napoleon House, but he's older—"

"Who's the man at The Napoleon House?"

"I don't know." Shaking my head, I stagger out of the bathroom and collapse onto the bed. "She never told me his name. Just that he's an old friend. Someone she knew from before."

Mark follows me out. "Someone from before? I

know everyone she knew from before... What did he look like?"

My eyes snap to him. I hadn't considered the possibility he might know this guy. "Older. Silver-haired, very well-dressed. He looked possibly foreign."

"In New Orleans?" Mark shakes his head. "That could be anybody."

My elbows hit my knees, and I drop my face into my hands. "We've got to find her. If anything happens to her or..." Shit, my mind is still trying to catch up with this.

My baby?

My insides are churning, growing hotter and more desperate by the second. If anything happens to Molly or my baby...

My baby... my little boy or, *shit*. I force a breath. My baby girl?

The laptop across from me lights up, and Mark and I snap to attention.

He steps forward and examines the message on the screen. "Do you have gloves?"

I'm on my feet. "No. What does it say?"

"The username is *Vox3000*. It's asking if she got the information she needed."

The message floats on the black screen, and I reach forward to wake it, pausing before I touch it. "Are you worried about contaminating evidence?"

"I think we'll find what we need faster by taking it rather than leaving it behind."

"I agree." I carefully close the laptop and gather the power cord.

Mark scans the room one last time before we go. "This might come in handy."

He points at a white device just peeking out from under her black silk dress.

"Shit…" Panic steals my voice. "She wouldn't go anywhere without her phone."

"Still, there's no trace of blood. She wasn't hurt here."

We exchange a glance, and he hustles to the door. I'm right behind him, Molly's phone in my pocket and her laptop under my arm. Our only hope is in finding an address or hoping the old man calls her.

"You said it was an older guy with gray hair?" Lara paces the kitchen, bouncing her little girl on her hip and frowning as she thinks.

The toddler pulls a long strand of her mother's dark hair to her mouth, and I can't take my eyes off her. All I can think about is Molly kidnapped and pregnant. Molly and my baby.

I have to find her…

I have to find *them*.

"Josh?" Lara's soft voice brings me back to attention.

"Sorry, what?"

"Did you at least talk to the man? Did he possibly have a French accent?"

"I never talked to him." My chin drops, and I look at my helpless hands.

Mark is in the other room running a password hacker on Molly's laptop. We're sitting here waiting, hoping and praying he can get into it.

Lara frowns, and moves her daughter to her other hip. The little girls squirms, and Lara bends to put her down. "Go play, Jillian," she says softly.

The little girl stays beside her, pulling on her leg and whining. "I guess she can tell we're all stressed out." Lara opens a cabinet and takes down a bag of goldfish crackers.

I watch her being a mom, doing these domestic things, but Molly's list is heavy on my mind. I didn't need to be told what happened to Gavin. I was there, and it was awful. He was strangling Molly, and when I tried to help her, he knocked me out cold.

When I came to, I discovered Lara had shot him. It was unsettling but understandable... The other name is a mystery, and I can't stop thinking about what I read and trying to make it fit with what I know of this elegant woman married to a cop.

"On the list Molly had... your name was beside another man's."

Her blue eyes widen briefly before she squats down beside her daughter, turning her back to me. "I can't believe she kept a list." Her voice is casual, but I can tell she's worried. "What a great way to get us all locked up, Mol."

"Did you do it? Did you kill that man?"

She doesn't answer right away, and Mark yells from the other room. "I'm in!"

Forgetting my question, I'm on my feet, running to where he's sitting. Lara is right behind me.

"Okay, let me see if I can follow this chat."

I watch as he scrolls through the window. It's a conversation spanning more than a month of back and forth between users HG187 and MM50.

"It looks like Molly is HG187. This MM50 sent her an address here in town. Write it down."

"Here." I pull out my phone and snap a screenshot. "I've got it. Let's go."

Shoving my phone in my pocket, I take one step toward the door before Mark stops me. "Nope. It looks like that's a dead end. She comes back a few days later and says it was bad information."

Returning to where he sits, I look at the screen

again. "Does it have a different address?"

"Hang on…" Mark is scrolling, reading. "This person claims the address is correct, but Molly insists it isn't."

"I don't care, I'm going there."

"Wait," Mark reaches out to grip my arm. "If this address is connected to her disappearance, we'll tip them off if we show up without a reason."

"If it's connected, we don't have time to waste." Taking out my phone, I open the Lyft app and enter the address. "I won't give anything away. I'll just see who lives there and if I can find out anything."

"You don't even know what you're looking for."

"I'm looking for my family."

CHAPTER 24: SHOOTER

Molly

I've lost track of time in a room with no windows and no phone. It could be day or night, and I wouldn't know.

All I do is sleep. Whether it's the knot on my head or the pregnancy or the stress, I sit on the floor in the corner curled in a ball, doing my best to stay warm.

Last night I dreamed I was back in the theater again. I was very little, and I was cold and afraid. Lara was speaking to me. Her voice was soft in my ear and her arms were tight around me. She was giving me comfort, but I understand now I was giving her comfort as well.

She told me that old story about my mother being a beautiful dancer who fell in love with my father. He would sing to her, and she would go to him.

The story changed each time she told it, but the basics were the same. My father was poor and my mother was promised to another man. My mother left me with Lara until she could come back and get me...

I remember the night I shouted at her it was all a lie. I was hurt, and I'd stopped believing. Now I see how much she tried. I'm so ashamed. I was so ungrateful.

I don't believe in praying. Killers like me don't get to pray, but I close my eyes and speak the words very softly anyway. "Please let me tell her I'm sorry. Somehow..."

The loud metal *clatch* causes me to push into a sitting position. I don't know how long it's been since I've had a visitor. I'm so hungry, my stomach is a hollow ache. I've been rationing the gallon of water in the corner by the toilet. I have no idea how long I'll be here.

The door opens, and I'm shocked when Renee walks in. I pull the long sleeves of my shirt over my hands and wipe my eyes with them. At least I washed my face before they took me, otherwise, I'd have mascara smeared all over my cheeks.

She walks to the center of the room and turns as if inspecting the place. She looks at the walls, at the tiny toilet area in the corner, then she looks at me.

"Houses in New Orleans don't have basements." Her chin lifts, and her dark hair is tied in a small knot at the nape of her neck. It enhances the severity of her features. "We're below sea level. It's impossible to keep the water out. This is my father's secret room. It was a temporary holding cell, a place no one would look. Because no one looks for a basement in New Orleans."

I'm wiping the crust out of my eyes, trying to process her words. How do I respond to this?

"I know you're planning to kill me…"

"I won't have to kill you. No one will look for you here. You're already buried alive."

My head drops, and sickness fills my stomach. If her goal is to demoralize me, to steal my last bit of hope, she almost succeeds.

I inhale a shaky breath and do my best to keep my defiance alive. "Can I get a book?"

The woman actually laughs. "Of course. I'll send something down."

"Thank you." I'm so fucking hungry, I decide to push my luck. "And a sandwich would be nice. Or just some crackers."

She sniffs and goes to the door. "I'll see what I can do."

The door closes and that metal latch slides in place. I

turn to my side and fall against the wall. If I'm to be punished for what I've done, I guess I'm getting it now.

I don't know how much time has passed when the door opens again. I slept, and I don't care. She intends to leave me here to die. I guess I have to deal with it.

Pressing my back against the wall, I brace for the reappearance of Renee.

I'm disappointed.

A petite young woman with straight black hair enters the room carrying a tray with what looks like a club sandwich and a large book. She places it in front of me, and I hesitate, watching her.

"What's the catch?" My eyes flicker to her dark ones.

"No catch. Renee said to bring you a sandwich and a book."

My foot moves, and I scoot forward, scooping up the food. It's too thick for me to bite, and I drop the top bun to the side. I'll eat it next. I peel off the bacon and wolf it down. Salty, tangy, fatty goodness coats my tongue, and I let out a loud groan. "It's so good."

The woman stands back watching me. "You hadn't eaten when I picked you up." Her voice is small, quiet.

I realize it's Shooter, and I scoot back again, on my guard. Our eyes lock, but she's unarmed. She's not here to hurt me. Still, I watch her.

My hunger is momentarily abated, and I'm ready if she tries to hurt me. "Why are you doing this?"

She shrugs, stepping to the side and looking around my small prison. "We're the same. We're killers, hackers... I've watched you for years, tracked you. You're one of the best."

"Thank you." It's a tight reply. All my muscles are tense, ready to react.

"I consider myself one of the best."

I nod, taking another bite of food. "Noted."

She's more relaxed. Turning on her heels, she crosses her arms and faces me, frowning as if she's trying to figure out a complex problem. "Why did you do it?"

"Do what?"

"Why did you kill those men? They were lowlifes, criminals with no connections, no payoff." She takes another step, studying me. "You're clearly smart. Why take a chance like that? Why gamble your freedom for no reward? Are you an adrenaline junkie?"

"You want to know why I didn't just hack into a bank and steal a bunch of money. Move to Indonesia and live like a queen on an island in the south Pacific?"

"Basically, yes. You could do that."

My eyes move from my hands clasped in my lap up my arms where tiny silver scars stripe my skin. "Being a hacker didn't come first for me. I became a hacker so I could find the men who raped me when I was thirteen."

Shooter's arms move. She tightens them higher over her chest, but she doesn't interrupt me. She wants me to keep going, so I do.

"We ran away from New Orleans to escape our abusers. We ran all the way to France... but I couldn't escape what happened to me. I couldn't remember the details, but the feelings would bubble up. They would rise to the surface of my skin and burn until I let them out." Shooter is the first person I've spoken to so plainly about why I cut my skin. I never told Joshua. I never even told Stas...

"Killing helped you to stop?"

"Stas... the old man helped me stop. He taught me to meditate. He taught me to confront the feelings and name them, give them a place, and let them go. He taught me self-defense, so I would never be a victim again."

She's thinking about what I'm saying. Her heels make sharp clicking sounds as she paces the concrete floor. "But it wasn't enough. Meditation, self-defense, they weren't enough."

"I guess I'm not as enlightened as I ought to be. The only way I could stop feeling their hands on my skin, their breath on my neck, was to make them stop breathing altogether."

You could hear a pin drop it's so quiet in the room. It's not an uncomfortable silence. It's more a respectful silence. The silence of two people who kill for a living acknowledging their truths.

"My little sister was shot in the head at a bus stop. She was on her way to school, second grade, and some drug dealer wanted to send a message. Annie just happened to be in the way of his gun."

I bend my legs, placing my hands on top of my knees. Not everyone has a reason to carry a gun, to hunt down the people who wield ultimate power over the lives of the helpless.

We do.

"I'm sorry for your loss."

"It was a long time ago."

She goes to the door, and I wait as she slides the latch. "I didn't tell you congratulations on being a mom. I guess that adds a new layer of difficulty to your chosen profession. Or maybe it changes things."

My voice is quiet. "It changes everything. My quest for revenge doesn't matter anymore. The only thing that matters is my baby, my family."

"So you'll walk away?"

"If I get that chance."

She nods, and I think she's about to leave. Instead, she hesitates. "Is there anything you'd like? Anything you want to know?"

I didn't expect her to say this, and a thousand questions flood my mind at once. "Is anyone looking for me?"

"Not yet."

The door opens with a jerk, and she steps out.

"Wait," I call. "One more thing."

She puts a foot inside my room again. "What?"

My brow furrows, and I look down. "This might not be something you can tell me. If it's not, I understand. Renee said something... about my mother. She said she knows who she was." Swallowing the pain in my throat I continue. "If you could tell me who I really am... It's something I've always wanted to know. I'd like to know before..." I don't know how I want to finish that sentence.

Shooter thinks about my request. "I'll see what I can find out."

"Thank you."

"You're good, Hit Girl. Your story deserves a better ending than dying alone in an underground cell."

"Maybe I'll get one."

CHAPTER 25: STRATEGY

Joshua

The address leads to a private residence on St. Charles Avenue. At least I think it's private. It's an enormous stone mansion with round turrets and those gingerbread-type cutouts along the top. It's more like a castle with a large iron gate around the grounds.

The wide driveway is blocked, but I hop out of the Lyft at the curb. I walk up the narrow foot path leading to the front door with no impediments.

Okay… What am I going to say?

I have no idea.

Should I pretend to be a salesman of some sort? Should I make up some excuse like I'm lost? Shit, I don't know.

I only know this is the last place Molly came before she went missing, and I've got to try and find out if whoever lives here knows where she is.

Pressing the doorbell, I take a breath and hope for the best.

It opens quickly and a young woman with dark hair is in front of me. She's wearing black leggings and a black leather jacket over a white tee.

"What do you want?"

"Um, yeah." Not the greeting I expected for this place. "I'm sorry to bother you. I was looking for someone."

"They got a name?"

Clearing my throat, I stand a little straighter. I'm several inches taller than this girl, but she's not intimidated in the slightest. It has me curious.

"My name is Joshua. My girlfriend is… from out of town. She's not very good with directions. I think she might be lost."

The girl's eyes narrow on me. "Why didn't you go to the police?"

"I did. She has to be missing forty-eight hours for it to be a police matter. I don't want to wait that long… In case something happened to her."

"You said your name is Joshua?" Her head tilts to the side. "What does your girlfriend look like?"

"Sheryl, who is it?" A woman in a dark green pantsuit and a thick strand of pearls walks up quickly then freezes when she sees me. "Hello, how can we help you?"

For a second, I'm not sure what to do. For a moment, the younger girl, Sheryl, almost seemed to recognize me. This older woman is clearly defensive. Is it because she's hiding something?

"Hi. Sorry to bother you, I was just saying my girlfriend is visiting the city, and she's not very good with directions. I think she might be lost. Is it possible she stopped here?"

The woman's dark hair is tied in a tight little bun at the nape of her neck, and her features are very sharp. "Why would she stop here?"

I shrug and give her my best friendly smile. "I don't know. I'm just asking around. I'm worried about her. New Orleans can be a dangerous place."

She looks me up and down. "You say she's your girlfriend. What is your name?"

"Joshua." I hold out my hand. "I'm Joshua."

She doesn't shake it. "How do I know she isn't running from you, Joshua?"

I turn my hand so my palm is facing her. "Oh, she's

not. It's not like that."

The three of us size each other up, until the older woman breaks the silence. "I'm sorry. Your girlfriend didn't come here looking for directions."

She starts to go, but I try one last thing. "Would it be okay if I sort-of... checked the grounds?" It's a longshot, and the woman frowns. She's about to say no, but I hastily add, "You have a really nice estate here. She might be here and you don't know it."

"Are you suggesting your girlfriend is hiding in my bushes?"

"Oh, no, but maybe she dropped her phone... or she might have left something behind."

"Is she Cinderella?"

"No, but—"

"I'm sorry. I can't let you search the grounds." She goes inside and starts to close the door, but I step forward.

"Wait." Shooting out my hand, I catch the door before it closes. "You could walk me around the property... or if you're nervous, you could have one of your servants do it?"

"Why would I be nervous?" Her eyes are flinty, and it's almost like a challenge. I'm not sure what to make of this. "If you would kindly get off my property, Joshua. I don't want to have to call the police on you."

Her hand is on her hip, and she's scowling now. I start to back away, when my eyes lock with the younger girl's. Her chin lifts slightly and then lowers, almost like she's nodding yes very slowly. A knot forms in my throat, and I'm certain she's giving me a signal.

"I'm sorry for bothering you—" The door slams in my face, but I'm intrigued.

I walk down the path again as if I'm leaving, but when I get to the end, I step quickly into the large bushes along the iron fence and duck down to wait. Slipping out my phone, I turn my back to the house and do my best to keep it close to my body while I send Mark a text.

Might have a lead at last known address.

I put it away, holding my breath no one saw it. I know in the dark, a phone face is like a freaking spotlight. My only hope is I'm in the bushes near the street, behind a skinny lamp post.

What could the girl Sheryl be trying to tell me? Did she know my name? Is it because she knows Molly? My phone buzzes with a text, and I'm almost afraid to check it. I hold the side of my blazer open, around it and read Mark's reply.

Come back and we'll strategize a way inside.

I don't want to leave, but I know he's right. I can't just walk in the house. I can't break in without knowing Molly's here. What would I do once I got inside? Demand they lead me to a girl they've already claimed they don't know?

"Shit," I hiss, looking over my shoulder again toward the house before slipping around the hedge to the street. I walk a block in the opposite direction before tapping the Lyft app. A car will be here to get me in less than two minutes.

"Something's there," I say, pacing the dark wood floor of Mark and Lara's living room. "The older woman was bitchy, but the younger woman sort of signaled me."

"How?" Lara frowns at me.

"Like this." I do my head exactly the way Sheryl did hers—chin up slow then down slow.

Lara's eyebrows shoot up. "She did that? What had you said?"

"That's the thing..." Scrubbing my fingers along my brow. "I hadn't really asked a yes or no question. It was when I asked if I could check the property. The older woman threatened to call the police on me."

"You asked to check the property?" Mark does a little laugh.

"I figured I'd take a chance. All she could do was say no."

"It was a risky chance. If they have something to do with this, now they know we're looking for her. At their place."

Molly's phone rings, and Lara pulls it out of her pocket. She studies the face a moment then looks at Mark. "It's an unknown number, but look at the area code..."

He takes it from her and studies the face. "It's an international number." He swipes his finger across it. "Here we go..."

Holding it to his ear, he doesn't speak. He only makes a soft, grunting noise—I guess like he's imitating Molly.

Taking it down, he taps the speaker button.

"Myshka? Is that you?" The voice is an older man with a thick Russian accent.

Nodding, and I point at the phone, speaking in a voice barely audible. "The man from The Napoleon House."

Lara takes the phone. "Hello? Who is this?"

A pause, and we're all holding our breath. "I'm sorry. I think I dialed the wrong number..."

It's an old saying, an anachronism in this age of cell

227

phones and speed dialing.

Still, we go with it. "Are you trying to find Molly?" Lara asks. "Please don't hang up. This is her sister Lara."

Another long pause, but he doesn't hang up. "Lara. My name is Stas Volodya. I am a friend of your sister's."

"Yes! I've heard of you."

"I was not aware she spoke of me to anyone."

We exchange a glance. I can't tell if he sounds offended, and I worry Molly promised not to tell anyone about him.

"She actually didn't speak of you to me…" Lara makes a face at her odd choice of words. "I knew she had a friend who was an older gentleman. I assumed it must be you."

"I see." The tone of his voice isn't angry, but something is troubling him. "This might seem like a strange request. Would you mind if I came to your house? I have something I need to show you in person."

Lara answers quickly. "Does it have anything to do with Molly?"

"I'd rather not say over the phone."

Her eyes go to Mark's and he nods. "Yes, then, Mr. Volodya. Please come as soon as you can."

"The last time I spoke to her, I had to leave for a few days to visit a friend out of town." Stas Volodya stands in the middle of Lara and Mark's living room, dressed in a suit and vest, complete with tie. A polished wooden cane is in his hand. "She and I don't speak frequently on the telephone, but we do text least once every other day…"

Mark stands opposite the coffee table, his muscled arms crossed over his chest. "When is the last time you heard from her?"

Volodya turns and paces the small room. "We went

out to dinner the night before I left. It was early when she returned to her room. I went to my hotel to pack. My train was scheduled for a five a.m. departure."

My back is to the wall, and I mirror Mark's stance. My arms are crossed over my chest, and I'm not ready to trust this guy. I don't know his relation to Molly or if he's a true friend or simply a spy.

"So you've just arrived back in town?" I don't move from where I'm leaning, watching him.

His gray eyes flicker up to mine. "I actually cut my trip short by a few hours after I received a rather disturbing email."

Lara sits on the couch holding her sleeping daughter. At that, she scoots forward. "What did it say? Why were you disturbed?"

The older man takes out his phone and we watch as he touches the face several times. "You are a policeman, yes?" He turns to Mark once he has the phone how he wants it.

"I'm a police detective."

"I don't know what the difference is in the two. However, you have to agree this image is a bit alarming."

Mark's eyes go from Volodya's to his phone, and he uncrosses his arms to take the device. Examining the face, he looks to Volodya again quickly.

"Who sent this?"

"I don't know. It came from a gmail account with a name I did not recognize."

Lara is on her feet. "Let me see it."

I close the distance between us not wanting to be left out of the loop. "I need to see it."

Mark turns to the old man. "You have no idea who might have sent this?"

Lara lets out a little cry when she sees the image.

"Oh, no! Molly, no!" Her baby rouses and makes a little whining noise.

I take the phone and my heart plunges when I see the photograph of my girl. She's holding a copy of the city newspaper dated yesterday. She's dressed in one of my old, long-sleeved tees, her hair is messy, and she's not wearing makeup. A dark purple bruise is over her left eye, and she looks so pale and tired. My heart aches to see her so defeated. I want to gather her in my arms and carry her home.

"Quite the contrary," the old man says. "I think I know exactly who sent this."

"Who?" My voice is loud, and Volodya gives me a slight smile.

"You must be Joshua." He nods. "Whenever she mentions your name, I can tell she's very fond of you."

I don't have time to reminisce. "Who sent you this photo?"

"The image was attached to an email message that said I'm looking for the man who killed my father. Come to the last known address of Reese Landry. The last known address we had for Reese Landry is on St. Charles Avenue, a large stone mansion."

Turning, I sweep my blazer off the back of the chair. "I've been there. I was just there today!" My phone is in my hand, and I'm pulling up the app to get us over there now.

Mark holds both hands up. "Hang on. Slow it down a minute. How do you know that's the correct address? According to Molly's chat, she went to there, and it wasn't right."

The old man nods. "I was with her on that visit. The woman Renee Landry claimed to have no knowledge of who we sought. However, I'm convinced Reese Landry is her father. It's the only thing that makes sense."

"I'm not sure it's the only thing…" Mark puts his hands on his hips.

I'm infuriated at this waste of time. "If Stas thinks that's the place, we're going. The girl Sheryl signaled me when I was just there. It makes total sense now. Renee is lying, and Sheryl was trying to let me know!"

Lara sways side to side as she bounces her baby and nods quickly. "I think Joshua's right. Mark, you have to go there and make them let you in to search."

"Lara…" He flares his eyes at her, and I've had enough of secrets. I've had enough to last me a lifetime.

"What the fuck are you hiding? Why don't you want to go there?"

He glances at me. "As a police officer, I can't just go to someone's house and demand they let me inside to search for someone. I have to go to a judge and get a search warrant… there are laws about these things."

"Fuck the law! Molly is in danger, and she's carrying my baby. I'm going to get her."

The old man's head jerks back. "Molly's pregnant!"

My chin drops, and I look down at my hands. "I think so. We found a pregnancy test in her bathroom, and it was positive."

"Yes, yes," Stas says. "That makes sense now. She was having bouts of sickness. She actually vomited once when we were together. She thought it was the Sazerac she'd drunk on an empty stomach."

"I remember her saying something about feeling ill…" Fuck it. I don't need any more convincing. "Let's go."

I've already touched the app while Mark is still arguing laws and police procedure. "Tell you what," I say, stepping to him. "You stay here and do what you need to do to be in compliance with the law. I'm going to get my girl back. You can arrest me later."

His eyes flash, but I'm right back at him, ready to fight.

"Hey, hey!" Lara steps between us, putting her free hand on her husband's chest and the sleeping baby against me. "We're all on the same team here. There's no reason to fight."

Mark's jaw moves with the clenching of his teeth and so does mine... but we step back, taking a breath.

"I have a car," he says. "I'll follow you since you already ordered a Lyft."

I don't argue. I'm out the door with Stas behind me. He'd better hurry up, because now that I know she's in there, I'm not stopping until I walk out with her in my arms.

CHAPTER 26: RENEE

Molly

I think three days have passed.

Shooter has brought me two more meals since my first club sandwich. She brought me a wax crayon and a notebook after my second meal — at my request.

I asked for a pencil, but I guess that was too close to a weapon. Whatever.

She told me someone's looking for me, which is simultaneously thrilling and heartbreaking. Who is it?

The only person I know for sure Renee will contact is Stas. Joshua doesn't know where I am. Mark and Lara don't know — unless Renee contacts them. Would she? I suppose she might if she inherited her father's files… If she studied them all the way back to the beginning.

Of course, I would never tell her what I know about her father's shooting or who pulled the trigger. It's best if she thinks I don't know anything. And if that's the case, will she assume Lara and Mark are equally clueless?

I'm pretty sure Renee will have done her homework. We're all on the hook in this scenario.

Sometimes when I'm going crazy with boredom, I imagine Joshua somehow manages to track me to this house, and Renee tells him she doesn't know anything about me.

Alternatively, I imagine Stas comes here to find me, and she kills him. More likely, Stas will kill Renee, but still, he doesn't know I'm down here. He'd leave…

Would anyone let me out?

Would they all go away and let me die here?

My heart beats too fast when I have these thoughts, and it's difficult to breathe. I feel like I'm suffocating, and I get panicky.

The fucking door to this place is impenetrable. I'm in a concrete room underground with no windows and a door that's not only bolted but sticks.

I cross my legs and do another meditation ritual. I've gotten to where I do them a lot. I have to keep my hope alive. I can't fall into despair. I have to think of my baby.

When I'm not meditating, I sketch pictures of Joshua to calm my nerves. I draw his hands, large and strong. Joshua has beautiful hands with short fingernails and the lightest dusting of hair on the back...

Or I'll sketch his dark hair, his square forehead, his brow dropped low over his light gray eyes. If I take my time and do it right, it feels like he's looking at me, and my heart squeezes. His expression heats my eyes, and I trace my finger along his cheekbone. I miss him so much. I promise his drawing I'll never make him wonder.

I'll never leave again.

Once, I decided to try sketching a little girl with his eyes. I softened the shading on her baby cheeks, her rosebud lips, and I added her daddy's smile... I'm starting on her halo of blonde hair when a tear hits the page.

I'm dreaming again, praying I'll live to see her.

Praying in spite of all I've done, I might get another chance.

The loud slap of the bolt unlocking startles me. I don't know what time it is, but it feels too early for Sheryl to visit. I'm not hungry yet...

I lower the sketchpad as the sticky door shimmies

and finally blasts open with a loud noise.

"Fucking door," Sheryl growls, looking around the frame. "It must swell with the humidity."

She's dressed all in black. Her dark hair is in a high ponytail, and a butterfly tattoo is on the back of her neck. Her hands are empty, no food, nothing.

I'm confused. "What's going on?"

She enters the small room and puts her hands on her hips. "I just wanted to check on you. See how you're doing down here."

"Going crazy as usual… Trying to distract myself."

She nods, walking around the small space. "It's tough… I thought you might like to know… something is happening."

I swallow the tightness in my throat. "What does that mean?"

She shrugs. "My eyes outside have picked up movement. We might not see each other again."

A tremor is in my stomach. I'm not sure if it's happiness or dread. "Is Renee going to kill me?"

"I don't know." She takes a step to the side and crosses her arms as she studies the concrete. "She doesn't tell me her plans."

"I thought you were her girl."

"Renee's a meal ticket. A means to an end. I just follow the money."

"So you're a mercenary?"

"You say it like it's a bad thing." She tosses me a smile, but it doesn't encourage me. Mercenaries are only loyal to themselves. "Anyway, I might have found what you wanted. The intel on your mother."

Pushing against the floor, I stand on my still-bare feet. "Okay…"

"I found something about a girl who came to the city from somewhere in Tennessee. Some little small

235

town near Memphis. I couldn't find a reason why she moved here, but Gavin Hudson pimped her out several times. After a while, she went off the radar, disappeared. It all happened about the time you showed up, when someone named Lara took you in."

My heart had initially beaten faster with every word, but the more she speaks, the more I realize it's not my story she's telling.

"Thank you for that." I don't have the heart to tell her she just described our friend Evie's background. I'm pretty sure the tale she recited has nothing to do with my mother.

"No problem. I was bored with waiting, and I figured I'd want to know if it were me."

Glancing up, I frown at her. "Why are you helping me? What are you getting out of it?"

The slightest grin curls her lips, and she tilts her head side to side. "I have my reasons."

"Care to share?"

She stops pacing and faces me. "Have you ever seen the movie *The Princess Bride*?"

I nod. "Everybody has."

"I don't know about everybody, but do you remember the part where Wesley, the farm boy turned pirate, is taken to the Pit of Despair?" Again, I nod. "He asks The Albino why they're taking care of him, and The Albino says it's because Count Rugen likes his opponents to be cured before he breaks them."

"You've watched that movie a lot," I quip. "So you're the six-fingered man? You're keeping me well so you can break me? I'd like to see you try, bitch."

Shooter's chin lifts matching my cocky attitude with her own. "I did just fine in your hotel room."

"You did nothing in my hotel room. I didn't fight you because I didn't want to risk getting shot."

"But you admit I could've shot you." Her expression is smug.

My eyes narrow. "Not at all. Gun fights are unpredictable. Anything could happen, and I wasn't prepared to risk it with a baby onboard. I'll be glad to have a rematch once I'm sure my baby is safe."

She laughs. "I'll keep that in mind."

All my recent prayers and promises hit me in the stomach, and I shake my head. "No... if I get out of here, I'm retired. I'm not doing this anymore. I want a different life."

"But you're a killer."

"I'm a mother." Sliding down the wall, I sit on the floor with my legs bent. "I've laid my weapons down."

The sketchpad is beside me on the floor with my baby's innocent face staring at me. I trace a finger down her cheek, thinking when Shooter breaks the silence.

"So maybe I'll see you again on the deep web. A battle of wits is more my speed when it comes to you."

"What do you mean?"

We're interrupted by rapid popping noises from upstairs. We both instinctively duck at the sound of gunfire, and she holds up a finger in a quiet motion. "I'll see what's happening."

She's out the door, slamming it shut behind her, and I'm left looking at the empty space where she stood, waiting for the noise of the bolt to latch.

It never happens.

Another sharp pop sounds, and I'm on my feet, running to the door. My heart thuds in my chest, and I hesitate. I have no idea what's out there. Cave Man could be waiting to shove me back in here by my face— or worse.

It's a chance I've got to take. I won't be forgotten in this tomb. Grabbing the handle, I jerk it open. It unsticks with a loud blast, and I look out. No one is there. Voices echo from above, and I realize they must all be on the first floor dealing with whatever is happening.

Carefully, I creep across the larger basement room to the foot of the gold-carpeted stairs. The door at the top is closed, but I can't just run out there unarmed. Looking around, I don't see anything to use as a weapon, and even though I'm not a shooter, for the millionth time, I wish I had my little gun. It's locked in the safe in my hotel room along with my necklace.

My pulse is racing, and I reach for the handle.

I turn it slowly and give it the slightest push…

It doesn't budge.

"No!" I whisper-cry, trying again.

I give it another push, and it's locked.

"Fuck," I hiss, looking all around the cracks.

I see an old-fashioned little sliding bolt thingie holding the door shut. If I had a coat hanger, I'd have it open in ten seconds. I'm about to dash down the stairs and search for one, when I hear a voice that stops my heart.

"I'm not leaving without her." It's Joshua!

I want to cry. I want to scream to him *I'm down here!*

Just as fast, my stomach plunges. Renee has a gun, and she's a career criminal. Joshua is not. I've got to get out there and help him. I run down the stairs into the larger room and search. Oh, thank the baby Jesus in heaven and all the angels! I spot a wire hanger.

Snatching it up, I dash up the gross, sticky gold-carpeted stairs again, untwisting it and straightening it out. I form a small hook on one end and wedge it through the crack in the door, fiddling with the lock. I'm moving too fast. My hands tremble, and the metal hook slips off the bolt.

"Come on," I whisper taking deep breaths,

steadying my nerves.

I try again… and I hear Renee speaking. "Stas Volodya. I've been waiting for you."

I freeze, eyes wide as I look up through the crack. I'm at an angle where I can't see a thing, but I can hear their voices bouncing off the stone floor and walls.

"Once again you're standing between me and what I want." My old mentor's voice is calm and focused. It makes me smile.

"What you want? Oh, right. You want to know what happened to your precious wife and child." Her voice is sarcastic.

Fuck you, Renee.

"Where are they?" Stas's voice is a low growl.

"Maybe they're back in Russia. Maybe they're living it up on a Caribbean island. Maybe they're at the bottom of the Mississippi River. I don't know, and I don't give a shit."

Mark's voice comes next, and I sit back on the top step. Mark is here? "You inherited your father's computer, all his files. I think you know more than you claim."

"Go to a judge and get a search warrant. I'm not giving you anything, pig."

Stas's voice rises in volume. "Your father was a cheating, lying river rat…"

The hook catches on the latch, and I slide it apart. The door falls open with a loud squeak, and I fall out onto the stone floor. Shit!

"Molly!" Joshua starts for me, but another loud pop stops him.

I'm jerked off my feet by a meaty hand I recognize. Cave Man has me, and he starts for the basement when Renee stops him. "No! Bring her to me."

I'm roughly dragged across the kitchen where I

quickly take in what's happening. Renee has a gun pointed at Joshua, who is closest to the basement with his hands raised. Stas and Mark have their backs to the front door facing Renee, and Stas's small pistol is in his hand.

Renee turns the gun she had pointed on Joshua to me, shoving it hard under my chin. My teeth clench, and I close my eyes.

"Wait!" Joshua shouts. The panic in his voice squeezes my heart. "We'll give you what you want. Just let me have her."

"Isn't that adorable?" Renee's sarcastic voice is right in my ear.

Hate burns in my veins as she jerks my head by the back of my hair, shoving the gun harder against my jaw. My arms are pinned by the massive man at my back. Air explodes through my lips and nose, and I manage to grit out a *Fuck you*.

Her dark eyes slide my way only briefly. "Fuck you, too, bitch."

"You assholes have five seconds to tell me who killed my father or I blow her head off. Five, four, three, two—"

My eyes squeeze shut as my heart pounds in my chest. I'm breathing so fast, and I try to clear my mind. If this is the end, I want to be ready.

"I did it." The confession is loud, and my eyes fly open.

"I did it," they say again, and I realize both Mark and Stas are speaking.

They look at each other confused.

"You think this is a game?" Renee's fists my hair, jerking my head to the side and jamming the gun so hard against my neck, I let out an involuntary cry.

Mark speaks fast. "I went to his house in Algiers. I

240

met with him... I was trying to get his files, the video he has of my wife, and he pulled a gun on me. I was hit, but I know I shot him. I went back and saw the blood — "

"When was this?" Stas lowers his weapon and faces Mark. "I was at his house in Algiers. He wanted money in exchange for information, and I shot him."

"Stop this bullshit!" Renee screams. "I'll kill you all!"

Out of the corner of my eye, I see Joshua lowering slowly. He does something to his pants, and I catch a flash of pink.

"Molly, drop!" he shouts, and I go limp, bending my knees so fast, Cave Man's grip slips.

I hit the floor just as the popping of two guns sounds. Renee hits the floor, and I scramble away from her body. One black dot is in the center of her forehead and another is in the side of her neck. Another pop and Cave Man goes down. He's shouting and groaning, and I see his injury is in his shoulder. Blood is everywhere, and I'm crawling away when I'm scooped off my feet into Joshua's strong arms.

"Fuck, I thought I'd never see you again." He breathes into the side of my hair and I throw my arms around his neck, lifting my feet off the floor.

"Joshua!" My voice breaks.

His hands are under my butt, and I'm holding him, joy vibrating electric in my veins. It's so good. He's so good. I kiss the skin of his neck, breathing in his scent.

"Oh, Joshua," I whisper. Adrenaline is the only thing keeping me from crying like a baby.

Mark rushes toward the bodies when Shooter's voice shouts loud and clear, "Get out of here now."

He starts to argue. "But, I should — "

She steps between Mark and the bodies. "You should go back to your wife and daughter. I'll clean up this mess."

My cold body is pressed against Joshua's warm one, and I look from him to her. "You both shot her."

"Come." Stas speaks in a low, firm voice. "It will take us ten minutes to drive to your home. We'll report it from there."

Shooter nods, and Mark looks pained. Still, he backs away, going to the door. Joshua lowers me to my feet, taking my hand as I follow him out. I take one step on the gravel walk and let out a little cry.

"Come here." Relief, joy, love are all mixed together in his low voice. "Hop on my back."

I gladly jump up, wrapping my legs around his waist and my arms around his shoulders. I bury my nose in his neck and inhale another deep breath of juniper and citrus.

Warmth ripples from my beating heart to the tips of my toes, and I hug him closer.

It's so good to be home.

CHAPTER 27: SOMETHING NEW

Joshua

I'm buried deep in Molly's warm body. We're sitting in the middle of a king-sized bed, in a corner room overlooking the lights of New Orleans, and she's on her knees, straddling my lap.

We're sweaty and breathing hard, coming down from a mind-erasing orgasm, and she rises slightly, holding my cheeks and devouring my mouth. My hands tighten on her ass, and I follow her lead, hungry for all of her kisses.

It's hot and so fucking perfect. She's in my arms, and I only want to hold her and keep her safe here by my side. Our lips capture and pull, our tongues curl and taste. Her fingers slide into the sides of my hair, threading and grasping.

We kiss each other as if we've been separated for years instead of days. Our heads tilt, a whimper escapes in her breath, and it's like an electric shock through my pelvis. My cock pulses again, and she starts to laugh against my mouth.

"You feel so good," she says as her teeth bump against mine.

Her breasts are flat against my chest, and I wrap my arms tight around her waist. "You are the most amazing woman."

Our eyes meet, and it's like another little strike of lightning.

She smiles, and her voice is quiet. "You were willing to shoot someone for me."

My eyebrows rise, and I frown. "I did shoot someone—"

"Shh…" Slim fingers cover my mouth, stopping me. "You saved me. That's enough."

Pushing out my lips, I kiss those fingers. "I'd do anything for you. For the first time I felt like I understood how you must feel."

Her head tilts to the side. "You kept me from being hurt. You're my hero."

"You're having my baby."

Just saying the words fills my chest with the most incredible surge of joy. Molly's arms are around my shoulders, and she buries her face against my neck. "We're going to have a baby."

Her bare skin is smooth and warm under my palms. "It wouldn't have mattered. I'd do it again, baby or not. I'd do anything to keep you safe."

After carrying her out of that house, we went back to Mark and Lara's where Mark did as he said he would—he called police dispatch and reported shots fired and gave the address. As soon as he did it, he left us to return to the scene of the crime.

Molly left my arms to go straight into Lara's. She cried and apologized, which I didn't understand. Lara cried and hugged her and told her to stop apologizing. I gave them their time and Stas filled me in on what must've happened at Reese Landry's home that night.

Landry had been taunting the old man, hitting him up for millions of dollars in exchange for information on his missing family, until finally Stas went there to demand answers in person. Landry gave him a fake address, and between the time Stas followed up and the time he returned to Landry's home, Mark must've been there.

"When I went back, I knocked on the door, and he

started shooting. I returned fire, and when I went inside, he was on the floor, dead." He shook his head. "I didn't waste time counting bullet holes. I simply wrapped his head and dragged him out to the river. I figured the wild animals would take care of the rest."

"Sounds like they tried." I looked up and saw exhaustion in his old eyes.

"It's time to face the truth," he said with a heavy sigh. "My family is lost. No one knows what happened to them."

"It was your wife and child?"

He nodded. "A daughter."

I was turning it over in my mind when Mark returned and told us the matter was being treated as an internal hit. Evidence of Renee's involvement in criminal activities was left all over the house. On the computer screen were links to foreign bank accounts, and ties to money laundering schemes in the city.

"Whoever that girl was, she gave the police everything they needed for an airtight case." He held up a thumb drive. "She left this for me. She said it's the only copy. I guess we just have to trust her."

"What is it?" Stas asked.

"His files." The old man's eyes lit, and Mark nodded. "I'll keep searching, but it stays with me."

Lara led Molly into the room, and I smiled when I saw my girl holding Jillian. The baby was threading her fingers in Molly's hair and saying happy words like pretty, baby, and Molly…

It all made me want to take her somewhere private, make up for lost time, and make new plans for our future.

Now she's in my arms, and the world feels right.

I kiss the top of her shoulder, her collarbone. "You have to marry me now."

She laughs and pulls away. "Tickles."

"Say you will."

Our eyes meet, and she cups my cheeks. "You want to marry me? With all my baggage and checkered past?"

"I can't think of anything I want more."

Her brow relaxes, and when she smiles, she glows. "I want to be your wife."

"So that's a yes?"

She nods rapidly, adorably. "A very emphatic yes."

Catching her face in my hands, I kiss her again. I press my mouth to that line in her chin, I pull the skin along her jaw between my teeth. I kiss her ear and groan because I love her so much.

She moans and starts to move against me. I rock us back on the mattress so she's lying under me. I cover her body with mine. I cover her mouth with mine, and we kiss, long and full of love.

Then we start on round two.

The Ruby Slipper is packed at breakfast, and I'm texting with the pilot to get the jet ready for us to return to Seattle. The four of us are at a table with Jillian in a high chair. Lara is on one side of her and Molly is on the other, watching as Lara gives her goldfish crackers and sets up toys to keep her occupied.

"How do you know how to do all this?" Molly asks, wonder clear in her tone.

"Babies are actually very simple," Roland cuts in, and I look up to see Dean right behind him, hands shoved in his jean pockets. "It's the easiest time of a person's life."

The little girl squeals at him, and Molly sits back in her chair watching. "Right, because the man who will never have one knows everything about babies."

"Nice to see you too, Shortcake."

I'm ready to get annoyed when I see Molly's thoughtful expression. "I think we can declare a truce now." Roland glances down at her from where he's standing holding the baby. "Or not," Molly continues. "But the past is, well, past. And I'm ready for a better future. I'm starting a new life."

The wooden chair squeaks across the floor as he pulls it out, taking a seat across from her, still holding Jillian. "Well, look who's feeling optimistic. What happened to you? Find Jesus?"

"Oh, I hate that expression," Dean says, taking the seat across from me. "Was Jesus lost? Was he just waiting for you to find him?"

"I'm going to have a baby." She looks down at the table, waiting.

I'm ready to scoop her into my arms and tell her she has every reason to be optimistic. I intend to make her life unbelievably happy starting now…

"Oh my Goooood!" Dean cries, bouncing in his chair. "This is so exciting! Can I be the uncle? I know it's not technically right, but I've always wanted to be an uncle."

"Sure," Molly says, giving him a bright smile.

We're interrupted by the television overhead reporting the murder of Renee Landry, along with her shocking criminal ties… Roland's eyes meet Mark's, and Mark shifts in his seat.

"Was Renee Landry related to—"

"Yes," Lara says, taking Jillian. "It was all related. We found out she was his daughter."

"Did they ever say what became of… her father?"

"His body was recovered near the river," Molly says, glancing at Mark. "She told me they had to use dental records to identify him."

Dean shivers. "How gruesome! What happened?"

"Just some old local history," Roland answers quickly and signals the waitress.

We all place our orders, from apple-braised pork debris on buttermilk biscuits to cinnamon swirl pancakes. The table is loaded with food, and when we're done, my stomach aches from how full it is.

Dean hangs back with Lara, playing with the baby and discussing burlesque as an art form. Mark strolls ahead with Molly, Roland, and me.

"I've played it right up to the line many times," Mark's voice is quiet, thoughtful. "Still... I'd do it all again. I'd do whatever it took to keep Lara and Jillian safe."

We take a few more steps, and Molly speaks. "I think sometimes justice can't be so clean and neat, because the world is so messed up."

"Still," Mark continues. "I want a world of law and order for myself, for my daughter."

Molly's voice is quiet, but she takes his hand. "I agree."

"Okay," Roland finally says, watching them. "We'll start this over. Turn over a new leaf and hope for the best."

Relief shines from Molly's eyes. "Thank you."

CHAPTER 28: SOMETHING BLUE

Molly

The house in Seattle is even nicer than I remember when I visited it with Dean. The girls have set up their own rooms, and the furniture just seems to belong here, like the pieces were made for the space.

"It's so homey and welcoming." My eyes meet Joshua's where he's leaning against the wall. His arms are crossed and he's smiling at me in that way that curls my toes. I'm sure my cheeks are pink. "What?"

"I'm just happy to see you here finally. We had this idea together, and for a little while, I thought it might not happen."

"Molly!" Brittanie skips into the room, straight into a hug. "When did you get back?"

I give her a brief hug. "Just a few days ago. How do you like the place?"

"It's amazing!" She spins around, arms out. "I've never lived in a place this nice. I have my own room—"

"How did you manage that?" Joshua and I exchange a glance.

"Candi says I keep her awake studying, so for now..."

"It's just until we add more girls." Joshua's voice is kind, but he sounds so businesslike. He's a total boss. "I'll check in and see if Rebecca needs anything while we're here."

He leaves us alone, and I sit on the couch beside Brittanie. "I got my GED." She's so excited, her eyes sparkle. "I'm applying to colleges for the fall, and I've already heard back from two!"

I can't help feeling a little envious. I don't expect to ever go to college. "That's really amazing. Your determination is… remarkable."

Her chin drops. "I just want to be like you. You're a successful businesswoman, and you were an orphan like me… you were hurt."

"You've gone way past anything I've ever done."

Round eyes meet mine. "That's not true! You helped me… You and Joshua bought this house…"

"Joshua bought the house. I only looked at it."

"Still…" She looks in the direction he went. "I don't think he would have done this without you. You really care about us."

"I care about you…" Guilt is in my chest. "I was never very noble. I only wanted revenge for what happened to me, what happened to you…"

"What changed?"

I meet her curious eyes, and my answer makes me smile. "Becoming a mom. I want my baby's world to be better than the one I entered."

Her eyes widen. "Is it Joshua's?" Then she laughs as I nod. "Of course, it's Joshua's! Are you going to get married?"

I'm still nodding when Joshua returns to the room, followed by Candi.

Brittanie sees him and cries out. "Congratulations! I'm so excited. Have you decided where you'll get married yet?"

Candi's face goes red, and I'm about to say something. Joshua cuts me off. "We can get married down at the city hall for all I care."

"What's this?" Rebecca enters the room. "Have you two finally decided to tie the knot?"

"As a matter of fact..." I raise my eyebrows and give her an excited smile.

Candi stands back, shooting daggers at me with her eyes. Sadly, I'm not mature enough to say it doesn't make me feel super smug and happy. Still, I am trying to turn over a new leaf...

Joshua puts his arm around my waist and pulls me to his side. "We're even starting a family."

Sorry, Candi.

"Yes!" Brittanie is on her toes, bouncing. "It's going to be so cute. I can't wait for everything to happen."

Candi's voice is flat. "Congratulations, I guess."

She walks to the door and leaves just as Dean is walking in. "Oh, yes! Don't you think these new floors make all the difference in the world?"

My eyebrows shoot up. "That's what changed!" I step back, looking at the warm hardwoods and the bright tile in the kitchen. "It really makes a difference."

"It's my artistic eye." Dean carries a large notebook straight to where Joshua and I are standing. "Speaking of artistic eye. I saw this in your things. Did you draw these?"

He flips the pages quickly. My sketch of Joshua, the drawing of our baby I made from my imagination.

"They're not very good." I take the notebook out of his hand and try to close it.

Joshua stops me. "Let me see these. They're amazing!"

"No, I'm not—"

"Stop that now!" Dean waves a hand at me. "You've been going on about wanting to find a new career. I say you've got one right here in your hands!"

"What?" I look down at the notebook. "Drawing?"

"Art!" He waves a hand. "I've talked to Rebecca about adding an art therapy component to the services at the house here. You can help me. Go back to school, get your degree in art and psychology. Don't tell me you don't like the sound of that."

As he speaks, a feeling unfurls in my stomach I usually only get when Joshua tells me he loves me. "I think I do like the sound of that." Just as fast, I'm panicked and nervous. "But I can't go to college... I don't know anything about school. I dropped out—"

"I can help you get your GED!" Brittanie cries out at my side. "That would be amazing. It would be like I have a way to help you back! You already know all about computers and everything. It would be easy for you to take the courses online!"

"I don't know about easy..." I'm already getting cold feet.

Joshua's warm hand covers mine, and he smiles into my eyes. "I'll help you. You can do anything you want. I know it."

It's good enough for me. A new plan is born, the start of a new life. Gratitude swells in my chest like a happy balloon. Dean and Brittanie are immediately strategizing and charting out a course.

"Okay," I say softly, looking into the eyes of my future.

* * *

Three months later

The clouds roll back, and the sun electrifies the world with color.

After a brief shower this morning, it looks like we're going to have the perfect day for our wedding in the park.

"I could never get used to this weather," Lara says, helping me place the art-deco style sterling silver and marcasite headband across my head, just above the soft, braided coil of my hair pinned off my neck. "I thought it was going to rain all day."

"How's it looking out there?" I smooth my hands down the front of my sheer ivory dress, realizing it's a gesture I do every time I'm feeling uncertain.

Studying Intro to Psychology with Dean is getting in my head. I'm analyzing everything these days.

"Don't be worried." She smiles and places her hands on my upper arms. "It's everyone who knows us and loves us."

"Us *you* or us *me*?"

"Us, *us*." She laughs, handing me the enormous bouquet of Marsala roses and pale pink peonies, mixed with a few white roses. "This bouquet is incredible."

"Dean was over the moon helping me plan everything." I look down at my dress, at my thick middle. "He said it's a good thing I'm not showing yet. It would mess up the line of the dress."

"I hated this stage." She places a hand on my thickening middle. "I felt like I just looked frumpy. I was so happy when Jilly finally pooched on out."

My nose wrinkles, and I lean forward. "I wish I was showing."

"Sorry to interrupt..." Mark is at my side. "I have a call for you."

Frowning, I look up at him. "A call?"

He places a slim phone in my hands. "You'd better take it."

The device is in my hand and for a moment I study the name on the face, the seconds ticking past... I'm almost afraid to answer.

It's a call I've dreaded I might one day get, and now, of all days, my wedding day...

"Go on," Mark urges softly.

"Hello?"

"Miss Dixon?" The voice commands me through the line. "This is Chief Hendricks, Seattle PD." My breath disappears, and I can't speak. It doesn't matter because he doesn't stop. "You're good, Miss Dixon, very good. I have no evidence, but I have every reason to believe you're responsible for the death of Dennis Langley."

My lips part, but I still don't speak. I can't. My heart thuds in my chest so hard, I can barely think.

He exhales and continues. "I didn't expect a confession. I also don't plan to waste taxpayer money on the death of a child rapist and kiddie pornographer. I'm satisfied a dangerous criminal has been removed from our streets. But hear me now, Dixon..." If his pause is for effect, it works. "I don't tolerate vigilantes in my city. This ends here. You won't get this chance again."

My stomach is tight, and my breath strangles me in my throat. "I'm going to be a mother..." I don't finish that. It's not what he wants to hear. "It's over."

We're quiet for the space of several heartbeats, and when he speaks again, his voice is less forceful. "Best wishes."

The line disconnects, and I can't move. I'm just starting to breathe when Mark takes the phone from my hand. "It's over."

He places a warm hand on my shoulder, and when I blink up to his eyes, they're reassuring.

He had something to do with this, I know he did.

I place my hand over his and give it a squeeze. "Thank you."

"What are you girls whispering about?" Dean joins us in his pastel suit waving a hand. "It's time to walk down that aisle, Shortcake. Your daddy is waiting."

I squeeze my eyes shut, breathing slower, coming back to the present. My wedding is about to happen, and I was just given a pardon. Hope floods my insides, and I know I can do this. I can make this step forward.

Taking Dean's hand, I'm able to meet his playful tone. "Please don't call him *Daddy*."

He's referring to Stas, who agreed to come here and stand in as my father for the event. After everything went down in New Orleans, before Joshua and I came back here, my old mentor and I took a walk on the levee...Two orphaned souls, coming to grips with reality on the banks of the Mississippi.

"I'll never find my family, Myshka."

I'd never heard him sound this way, and I didn't know how to comfort him. Solidarity seemed like the best response.

"I'll never know who my mother was. I guess we both have to let go of that part of our lives."

He'd stood, looking out over the swirling currents stretching across the brown water before us. After a moment of silence, he turned to me.

"I don't see any reason why we can't have each other."

At first I was confused, then it all became simple. "You're right. We don't have to be orphans if we have each other."

From that moment forward, we became each other's unofficial, adopted family.

He's dressed in a pale gray suit when I go to take his arm. "You look very beautiful, Myshka. You remind me of Anastasia."

That makes me smile. "The lost Russian princess?"

"My lost Russian princess."

I give his arm a squeeze. "If it weren't for you, I wouldn't be here today. You saved me on that beach."

"You saved me on the banks of a river."

Leaning my cheek against his arm, I give him a squeeze as the music starts, and we walk around the partition separating "backstage" area from the rest of the wedding party.

When I see Joshua, my breath catches. I almost miss a step, and my adopted dad speaks in a low voice. "A good sign, Myshka. He should take your breath away."

Joshua does more than steal my breath. He owns my heart.

He looks like a sexy model, standing at the front of our group of friends, one hand in the pocket of his black tux. A lock of dark hair falls attractively over one eyebrow, and he glances up at me from under his brow. His gray eyes flood my body with heat.

"My hormones are working overtime," I whisper, and Stas chuckles.

"Sounds like a good match."

When we get to the front, he passes me to the man of my dreams, and the ceremony begins.

"I think that went well." Joshua's breath tickles the nape of my neck, and I let out a hum.

"How much longer do we have to stay?"

We're on the top floor of Columbia Tower, and the city is a gorgeous display of lights over the water below. Lara and Mark dance close by. Jillian is secure in Roland's arms, with Dean fussing over her little dress and her curls. He really will spoil our baby rotten...

We've decided not to find out the sex.

Brittanie, Tess, and Cindi are seated at a large table near a window. They're dressed in assorted pastel colors from being my bridesmaids along with Lara, my matron of honor. Rebecca catches my eye and lifts a glass. Candi sits beside her sulking. She would *not* be a bridesmaid, and I can't even be bothered with her mood.

Joshua's lips trace over my cheek before stopping at the side of my hair. "Are you saying you're sick of our guests?"

Stretching up on my toes, I let my lips graze the shell of his ear as I purr. "I'm saying you've had me hot and bothered since I walked down the aisle."

His grip tightens on my waist, and he pulls back. When our eyes meet, his are darkened with lust, and a flash of excitement moves through me. "Maybe we can find an empty room..."

"Absolutely beautiful ceremony." Joshua's dad walks up and pats him on the back.

I almost laugh through a groan at the frustrating cock block.

"Dad!" Joshua clears his throat. "Thanks, and I'm glad you could make it..."

The petite woman with the dark hair and cocoa skin beside his father gives me a wink. "What did we interrupt?"

"Nothing!" I lie quickly. "We were just talking about how great the view is from here."

"I don't think we've met." She extends a hand. "I'm Najah. I was your father-in-law's nurse after his heart attack."

"Oh, it's so nice to meet you! I remember Joshua saying his dad decided it might be time to start dating again after that hospital stay."

The older man coughs a laugh, and Joshua gives me a wink. Najah grins, and I have a feeling their relationship might be progressing faster than any of us know.

"Walt is such a tease." She grins. "We're having a good time getting to know each other."

"Well." Josh's dad steps forward. "We won't hold you two up. Molly, you... the ceremony... everything was beautiful. Welcome to the family."

I step forward and give him a warm hug. "Thank

you so much."

He gives me one last smile before escorting Najah away. Joshua's arms go back around me, and we resume our dance, but I'm lost in a cloud of connection, family, love.

"It's something I've never had before."

"What?" Joshua's lips are at my cheek, and he gives me another kiss.

"We're a family. I'm no longer a nobody, daughter of a whore no one ever cared about." My eyes heat, but the tears aren't stronger than the joy swirling around my heart.

Joshua stops dancing and holds my cheeks. "You were never that. You were always mine."

He leans down and kisses my lips. He kisses the line on my chin, and when our eyes meet again, I know my life will never be the same. I'll never be alone, lost, cutting my skin to let the pain out. Not only do I have an adopted father, I have a father-in-law, a baby on the way, and the love of the most beautiful man I've ever met.

"Garter time!" Lara dashes up beside me catching my arm. "It's time to toss the bouquet and the garter. Then you can get out of here and practice making more babies."

"Busted!" Joshua shouts, and Lara shakes her head.

My heart beats a little faster. "I have to take off my garter?"

"It's tradition." Mark catches my elbow. "Just sit on Joshua's lap and he'll slip it off. Then he'll toss it to some lucky bachelor."

Chewing my lip, I meet eyes with Lara. "What?" She's instantly worried. "What's wrong?"

I think of my old habits... habits that don't seem to want to die. "Nothing... it's just this morning, I was thinking how a garter is a great place to hide… something."

Lara's eyes go round, and she hisses in my ear. "If you have a gun in your garter everyone's going to freak out!"

Joshua's hands are around my waist, and he pulls me out onto the floor. I'm on his knee, and the guys form a circle around us. "Only single guys. Do we have any single guys here?"

Dean strides forward, holding up a hand. "Technically!"

Roland strolls forward as well, hands in the pockets of his black tux. He gives me a grin, and I'm glad we're finding a way to be friends after all these years.

Lara is at the edge of the crowd, her hand over her mouth and her eyes worried and wide. My dress slides up my legs and the guys hoot and make catcalls. I laugh and do a little shimmy.

The dress goes higher, and my pale blue garter with the cute little blue bow is on full display. I start to laugh. Lara rolls her eyes and makes a little fist at me.

"Gotcha!" I mouth, and she turns on her heel and walks over to where Mark is holding Jillian. She should have known—I've laid my weapons down.

The garter is off and tossed across the room. Joshua's Uncle Jake catches it, much to Dean's annoyance. "He's already been married once! Garter hog!"

We laugh, and I scoop up my bouquet. The girls rush forward, pushing side to side to make room. "Keep it civilized," I call over my shoulder then toss it high and short.

A scuffle of heels and squeals breaks out, and the girls are in a pile when I turn around. I bend forward laughing harder than I ever have in my life.

Of all people, Candi's hand stretches high over the group, and she yells. "Got it!"

My hand covers my laugh, and Joshua's strong arms surround me. It's the happiest I've ever been in my life. The music changes to a fast dance number, and Joshua leads me off the floor.

"Ready to go?" he whispers in my ear.

Lifting my chin, I kiss him and nod.

I couldn't be more ready to start my new life. I'm leaving the darkness behind, stepping out into the light of a new life for me and for the family we're creating — a law-abiding, peaceful family of love.

THE END.

EPILOGUE

Joshua

Five months of bliss goes by really fast.

The sun is breaking through the clouds, casting long shafts of light across our bedroom, and Molly is curled beside me. She stopped coloring her hair when she found out she was pregnant, and now instead of silver, streaks of rose gold glow around her scalp.

I love it.

She says it makes her look too young and fragile.

I hope our little girl has red hair.

Or boy.

Her pale skin is golden in this light, and I can't resist leaning down to kiss her shoulder. It's how we wake every morning. It's how we've woken since the first night she slept in my bed.

I tried to be a gentleman and take the air mattress.

She said she was crashing my pad, so she should take the air mattress.

In the end, we both took the bed, and I ended up between her sexy thighs.

"You don't think women with giant stomachs are unattractive?" She purrs, turning in her sleep.

"They're my favorite kind of women. Especially the super horny kind."

She giggles with her eyes still closed. "It's pregnancy hormones."

"Oh sure, blame the hormones. It's couldn't be because you have the sexiest husband alive…" I turn her so her back is to my chest. "Who knows exactly where to touch you."

One thing about our growing bundle of joy, he (or she) has made us get very creative with our sex positions. I snake my hand around her the top of her thigh and trace my fingertips lightly up her skin to her core.

Her back arches the closer I get and her hips start to move in time with my fingers. "Mmm…" Her thighs open for me. "Okay… let's go with that."

"I'm going." With a hard thrust, I'm buried, balls-deep in my beautiful wife.

She moans, and I start to rock, still circling her clit with my finger, pinching and smoothing, doing my best to mover her along as fast as I'm going.

"Shit, Molly, you are so fucking sexy." I'm pushing, and she's rocking back against me.

Her hand covers mine, and I let her take the lead, guiding us to the finish line as her insides start to break and shudder, clenching and pulling. I close my eyes and let go, chasing that wave of orgasm as it rises, sweeping us both up in ecstasy.

"Oh, God! Oh, God!" She's crying out, and I'm feeling it… until I'm not. "Oh, oh!"

My eyes pop open, and I realize her cries of pleasure have slowly changed into something different.

"Did you squirt?" I look down at the mattress, where I'm covered in liquid. "I confess, this is kind of a mess, but I'm feeling pretty proud of myself right now…"

"Joshua!" She snaps then rolls forward and lets out a loud wail. "Ooohhhh!"

Panic flashes in my chest. "What is it?"

"My water broke! We've got to get to the… Ooohhhhh! It hurts!"

"Shit!" I jump out of the bed, snatching up my boxer

briefs and jerking them over my hips. "What do you need?"

"Panties... Get my sweatpants... A tee... Ooohhh! Joshua! Oh, OW!"

My throat is so dry, and I go in the bathroom before I realize that's not right. I rush back out and go to her closet, scooping up the little suitcase she packed a week ago to be ready for a situation like this.

"Should I call 911? Can you make it to the hospital?"

"I can make it... Just give me my clothes." She crawls slowly to the side of the bed, stopping every few seconds to let out a loud cry.

I jump to it, digging in the sheets for her panties. Her sweats and tee are on the back of the desk chair from last night. She's made it to the side of the bed and struggles to sit up. I run over and hold her arm, carefully helping her stand, put on her clothes. She pauses to hold her breath, and her face turns red.

"Are you sure you can make it?"

She nods quickly. "Can you drive?"

"I think so..."

Somehow I manage to get us to the hospital and through the emergency room door. We get through the check-in procedure, but we're too late for Molly to have an epidural.

"Were you feeling contractions in the night?" The nurse attaches a million monitors to her arm and stomach and finger.

Molly inhales slowly before groaning. "I felt uncomfortable, but I was sleeping pretty hard."

Her doctor walks in and gives me a wink. "So having sex really does start labor?"

"Apparently it does," I say, feeling like a heel.

"It was going really well until my water broke."

Molly grunts a laugh before it dissolves into another low groan.

"It's going to get crazy for a little bit since we didn't have time for drugs." Her doctor is at the foot of the bed. "The good news is this baby's coming fast. Get ready."

It feels like an eternity of Molly crying and pushing. She holds my hand so hard, I'm sure I'll never use it again. Then she's up on her feet in a squatting position. Her doctor says it uses gravity to help the baby come.

I'm dying as she cries and the two of them work, and I wish there was some way I could reach in there and just pull the kid out. I've been all over Molly's body. Why can't I do this?

Finally, we're on our second eternity, when the most amazing sound in the world breaks through the room. A little cry. Our baby is out, and Molly bursts into tears.

Fuck it, I'm crying, too. My wife's hand is around the back of my neck, and we're both looking down, waiting for the verdict...

"Mom and dad?" The doctor glances up at us for only a moment as the glorious cries of our newborn fill the room. "Meet your new little daughter."

"Oh, Joshua!" Molly cries more, and our daughter is in her arms.

I'm holding both of them, and I've never been more in love in my life. "She's beautiful. She looks just like you."

The most amazing halo of red hair is on her head, and I can't stop touching her. I can't stop kissing my wife. The doctor looks up at us with a satisfied grin on her face, and I swear this is the best day of my life.

The room is quiet. The monitors beep softly, and

our little girl is latched onto her mother's breast, looking at us with big hazel eyes and a serious expression.

"She's very focused on her dinner," I tease, climbing into the wide bed beside my little family.

"She's such a good little eater," Molly says, stroking her cheek.

"Little Squirt takes after you."

That gets me an elbow in the ribs, and I laugh. "You are not calling her that."

"I was going to ask if it was the best orgasm of your life."

"My water broke." Molly turns and gives me a kiss. "You're such a guy."

"Hey, I just want to make you happy."

"And have some weird ego trip."

"It's more about your pleasure."

"Right."

My phone has been going off all day. Dean is in New Orleans with Roland, and all four of the New Orleans crew are frantically booking plane tickets and communicating with us nonstop.

"I'll be home before they get here." Molly looks up at me with a smile. "I'm glad.

"It was such a fast delivery. You're a rock star at having babies. Let's do it again."

She laughs softly. "Give me a year or two."

Our little girl's eyes are drifting closed, and I feel the waves of exhaustion rolling over me.

"Get some sleep." Molly kisses my lips, and I close my eyes in heaven.

* * *

Molly

Heaven is something like this right here.

Joshua's body is curled at my back, and my little girl is sleeping like an angel in the bed beside me. The arms of the bed are raised, and we have pillows all around. It's like we're in a warm, soft cocoon of love.

And I can't sleep.

From the bliss of making love to my husband to the agony of childbirth to the euphoria of welcoming Kaitlyn Anastasia Lara Andrews to the world (we named her after all the moms)...

I'm wide awake.

My phone is in my hand, and I'm answering all the friends sending congratulations. Stas is one of the first messages I return. He's at his villa in Nice and insists we come to visit him as soon as possible so he can meet his adopted granddaughter.

I never missed having a father, but now that he's in my life, I realize what a special relationship it can be.

You need to come here, I text. *Kate won't be able to leave until at least three months. That's too long to wait.*

It doesn't take long before he agrees to fly back and see her. I'm lying my head down, my eyes finally starting to close when one last text pops up.

Hit Girl has a little Doll Baby? Is that right?

My brow quirks and I take a chance.

My little Kate won't have any part of that life.

Congrats, Mama.

It makes me smile. *Thank you.*

When you're ready, I have a job for you.

Shaking my head, I quickly type out my reply. *Hit Girl is retired. Permanently.*

This is a job for the Artsy Nerd Girl who took her place.

"Of all the…" I lean my head back, realizing she knows I'm enrolling in college now, and not just that, she knows my major.

I type quickly. *Still keeping tabs on me?*

Old habits die hard. Maybe you'll feel the same way when you hear my job…

I tell myself I don't want to hear her job. I know I've put that necklace in a safe deposit box in a bank far away… but I'm wide awake now. Might as well satisfy my curiosity.

Go ahead, I reply.

Clyde Banks, code name CyberPop. He's been using Silk Road for years trafficking kiddie porn and underage sex tapes. FBI can't catch him. He deals in BTC only, and he's slippery as an eel. We're the only ones who can bring him in. I'll bet you 2 BTC I turn him over to the feds first. You on?

I remember a time when she said she'd rather match wits with me than cross swords. I think about the challenge of catching bad guys the new and improved way... as opposed to the old-fashioned way. If anybody could do it, it's one of us.

I don't know how much time I have to work on this, but maybe it's something I can do when I'm feeding Kate.

You're on, Shooter.

No Shooter. DPRoberts.

Does that make me Btrcup?

Better than Fezzik.

I'm Rogue.

As you wish.

I grin and put my phone aside. Scooting down in the bed with my husband's arms around me, and my baby in my arms, I think about the long road to here. I wanted justice. I wanted revenge. I guess some people would think by my walking away free, justice still isn't served...

Either way, if I can find a way to make the world a better place and work inside the law, that just might be the best of both worlds. It certainly is better for my family.

I lean down and kiss Kate's little head.

Looks like people can change after all.

* * *

Need More?

The "Bright Lights" duet is Mark & Lara's complete story, including Molly's backstory.

Keep turning for a special sneak peek...

* * *

Want more action and suspense?

The Prince & The Player *is Book #1 of my sexy, action-packed "Dirty Players" series.*

Keep turning for a special sneak peek...

See the inspiration board for *Hit Girl* on Pinterest:
https://goo.gl/vrCtWC

Watch the Book Trailer on YouTube:
https://youtu.be/JDeJUfDhg1Q

* * *

Never miss a new release!

Sign up for my New Release newsletter, and get a
FREE Subscriber-only story bundle!
(http://smarturl.it/TLMnews)

Join **"Tia's Books, Babes & Mermaids"** on Facebook
and chat about the books, post images of your favorite
characters, get EARLY exclusive sneak peeks, and
MORE!
(*www.Facebook.com/groups/TiasBooksandBabes*)

* * *

Get Exclusive Text Alerts and never miss a SALE or
NEW RELEASE by Tia Louise! Text "TiaLouise" to 64600
Now!*
(U.S. only.)

YOUR OPINION COUNTS

If you enjoyed *Hit Girl*, please leave a short, sweet review where you purchased your copy.

Reviews help your favorite authors more than you know.

Thank you so much!

* * *

Books by Louise

Stand-Alone Romances:
When We Touch, 2017
The Last Guy, 2017*
(*co-written with Ilsa Madden-Mills)

The Bright Lights Duet:
Under the Lights, 2018
Under the Stars, 2018

"Sundown" (*A Bright Lights novella*), 2017

Paranormal Romances:
One Immortal, 2015
One Insatiable, 2015

The Dirty Players Series:
The Prince & The Player, 2016
A Player for A Princess, 2016
Dirty Dealers, 2017
Dirty Thief, 2017

The One to Hold Series:
One to Hold (Derek & Melissa), 2013
One to Keep (Patrick & Elaine), 2014
One to Protect (Derek & Melissa), 2014
One to Love (Kenny & Slayde), 2014
One to Leave (Stuart & Mariska), 2014
One to Save (Derek & Melissa), 2015
One to Chase (Amy & Marcus), 2015
One to Take (Stuart & Mariska), 2016

EXCLUSIVE SNEAK PEEK

Under the Lights
© TLM Productions LLC, 2017

Chapter 1
"Show me a hero, and I'll write you a tragedy."

Mark

The first thing I see is the gun on the floor.

Fear tightens my neck, and I'm frozen in the doorway. My backpack slides from my shoulder down my arm as ice trickles into my veins. The room smells like the fourth of July, firecrackers mixed with the musty odor of smoke and damp.

It's hot.

The air barely moves in New Orleans at this time of year.

The dog days.

"Uncle Rick?" My voice is low and even.

My closest living relative, a man I barely know, is hunched in the fetal position on the couch. Eyes closed, both his hands are between his knees, and his lips have disappeared in his teeth.

He could be sleeping, napping while watching a television show. Only the screen is black, and he's not responding.

Fuck. The ice in my veins melts into panic. My eyes dart around the room assessing the scene. Drawers open. Papers spread across the hardwood floor. The corner of the rug is curled under… Signs of a struggle?

I should slowly leave the room, go downstairs, and

call 911 to report a crime.

I don't.

I swallow the fear and pick my way forward, across the small apartment to where my few possessions are stashed. I've been here less than a week, long enough to grow suspicious of his late-night errands, the jerk of surprise when the phone rings after hours, the presence of a .44 Magnum at the dinner table.

Uncle Rick was annoyed when I showed up on his doorstep last week, looking for a place to crash. My plan was to come here, study hard, and get into the police academy.

"You can crash until you've found a place to live," he growled. "By the end of the week."

He was my father's only sibling, and I'd taken a gamble coming here. Then, when he found out my plans, he was even more pissed.

"Why the fuck you wanna be a pig?"

He said I was "part of the problem."

Naturally, I disagreed.

"I want to fight crime, find men like the ones who ruined my dad and bring them to justice," I'd say.

The ones who run the off-track betting rings. The ones who own the prostitutes. The ones who take everything men have and ruin them.

I wanted to be a hero.

He said I was a fool.

Now who's the fool…

My eyes fix on the handgun on the floor. *Don't touch anything.*

Covering my hand with my sleeve, I open the closet door and scoop my few hanging clothes off the rack. A fatigue-green army-surplus bag is in the corner. I shove my extra pair of boots, shirts, underwear… everything I brought with me in it, then I do my best to retrace my steps to the door.

Out on the street, I don't pause before heading up the damp sidewalk. Light mist fills the heavy air, and it's after nine on a Wednesday. Nobody's walking the dark streets. Nobody sees me walking away from a crime scene.

My gut twists, and I feel sick thinking about him dead on the couch. Even if I didn't really know him, he's kin. I have to let the cops know… Leave an anonymous tip or something.

For now, I've got to find a place to go. It helps that I've been searching for my own place since I arrived. Crossing the street, I head toward the river. I remember reading about a few hostels and rooms for rent closer to the shipyards. At worst, I could get a room at the YMCA.

Six more blocks, and I start to encounter the stragglers coming off Bourbon Street. It's the street that never sleeps in the city of excess.

A block away, I stand and watch the bodies slowly passing like a drunk parade in the middle of the night, always moving. Making my way around the perimeter, I read the street signs, looking for the place from memory.

The Marigny is a single door squeezed between a daiquiri shop and a wig and souvenir store. If you're not looking for it, you'll walk right past and never even see it. A skinny guy who looks about ten years older than me sits on the front stoop smoking a cigarette, watching the herd of tourists slowly pass.

"Any rooms available?" I pull my cap lower on my brow. I'm tall, and if I play my cards right, I can look older.

As the guy glances at me, a tendril of smoke curls into his eye and makes him squint. He's dark, Italian or Acadian, and when he pushes off his knees to stand, his head only reaches the top of my shoulder. I dwarf him with my pack on my back.

Black eyes assess my frame. "Where that accent from?"

I've only just gotten used to people swapping *d* for *th* in the Quarter. *Where dat accent from?*

"Evergreen."

"Where that?"

"Avoyelles Parish."

He takes another long drag before he nods. "Are you strong?"

"Who wants to know?" My response is sharp. The shock of the night is wearing off, and unless this guy is the manager, I don't feel like small talk.

"Terrence Price." Cigarette in mouth, he sticks out a hand.

I pause before giving it a shake. "Mark Fitzhugh." His eyebrows rise and my brow lowers. "Family name. You got a problem?"

"No. Fitz. I like it." Cigarette out. "Got a burlesque show at the corner of Royal and Orleans looking for a crew. Go with me tomorrow, and you can have a job."

"What makes you think I need a job?"

"Why you here?"

"I don't know." I don't know if I want to stay in this city. The bad luck of my family feels like it's already found me. At the same time, I have nowhere else to go.

"Come on, you kidding? Pretty ladies showing their tits." He leans closer. "Play your cards right, and you get a private show."

He grins and drives an elbow into my arm. The memory of Rick dead on the couch creeps at the corners of my thoughts, and I shake my head, shake them away.

"Not into girls?" Terrence draws back. "I could see if they need anybody at Oz—"

"No." Clearing my throat, I wave my hand. "I like girls. I'm just... Rough day."

"In that case." He opens the front door. "Get some rest. Take Room 12. I leave in the morning at nine. Meet me here, and you can see what you think."

I leave him on the stoop and enter the narrow building. Two yellow lamps spaced evenly down the length of the passage light the dim hall, and a staircase leading up is at the very back. The hall is lined with doors, and each has a small brass plaque engraved with a number. Number 12 is the first on the left.

Inside, it can't be more than ninety square feet, shallow and wide with no windows. A bed is against the back wall, and a small table and lamp are centered to the left. On the opposite wall is a narrow armoire. I catch the faint whiff of hospital grade ammonia under the stale smell of dust. At least it's clean.

Setting my duffel and backpack in the middle of the floor, I pull the skinny mattress back and check the corners for signs of bed bugs. Going to the head, I pull it back. Not seeing anything, I reach over and kill the lamp before dropping fully clothed onto the blue-striped mattress.

If I decide to stay, I'll have to buy sheets... and food, which means I need money. The muffled roar of street noise filters through the walls, and I consider Terrence's offer. It would tide me over until I make a decision.

Until then...

Reaching into my pocket, I pull out the small burner phone I picked up last week. It's untraceable, which is probably perfect for this. My thumb wavers as I hold it over the numbers. I take a deep breath and slowly dial, 9... 1... 1...

Dread tightens in my chest as I wait for the answer.

"911, what is your emergency?" The voice is robotic,

bored.

"Uh, I need to report a noise." *Shit!* I didn't plan this before I dialed.

"A noise?"

"Sorry." Scrubbing my fingers against my eyelids, I try to think of words that don't sound incriminating. "I thought I heard a car backfire, but—"

"Modern cars don't backfire. You heard a gunshot." Again, bored robot. "Give me your address. Are you in a safe location?"

"Yes… I'm fine. I—it's 216 Evangeline, second floor. Maybe my neighbor?"

"Don't go in or out of your apartment until police arrive. Keep your door locked. Police are on their way. I—"

"Thanks." I press the pad of my thumb against the red *end call* button and drop the small phone onto the bed.

A chill skates over my skin, and I curl my knees into my chest, covering my ears with my palms. The sight of Rick that way unearthed memories of my dad, and that old pain radiates through my spine. I don't cry, but the fist of grief tightens my shoulders. It's oppressive and relentless, demanding action.

Sliding my hands to the back of my neck, I hold on, waiting for sleep to come. Waiting for answers I'll never have.

Terrence is on the stoop holding a paper cup of coffee in his hand when I emerge the next morning. A cigarette is in his mouth, and he smiles when he sees me.

"Good call," he says.

I pause in the entryway and consider my stuff. I don't have much worth stealing, still, it's all I have. "No lock?"

He pulls a key out of his pocket and motions me outside, locking the front door behind me. "Reopens after six."

Key in his pocket, he takes off, headed northeast on Bourbon. I jog after him up the littered sidewalk. It's far less crowded than at midnight, but even at this hour, people still roam, drinks in hand and beads around their necks.

"So you own the place?"

"My aunt does." He takes a drink of coffee. "She lives in Chalmette. I run it for her."

We cut across the street when we reach Orleans in the direction of Royal. Rounding the corner, we're on a narrow lane of wrought iron balconies over narrow doors. Archways blocked off by wooden barriers. It's Pirate Alley.

We're half a block away when Terrence hits my chest with the back of his hand. "Let me do the talking."

A man who looks like the classic dockworker stands in front of a group of similar men giving orders. He's my height, but he outweighs me by at least fifty pounds, with thick hands and cords of muscle.

"Shipment arrives at ten," he growls. "New set design requires a catwalk and series of cranes and pulleys. They'll be mechanically operated, but I need extra men to work late as safety backup during the shows." A trickle of laughter filters through the crowd. "Now get busy. First show rehearses at three o'clock."

He turns, and he's facing Terrence and me. "Who is this, Price?"

"New tenant looking for work. I'll vouch for him." Stepping back, he gestures between us. "Mark, this is Darby Stamp. Darby, Mark Fitzhugh."

"Fitzhugh…" Darby's eyes narrow, and I stand straighter. "You do drugs?"

"No," I answer fast.

"Good. Half these guys do, which means half won't be back, and if they are, they're late." He starts walking and Terrence nods for me to follow. "If I catch you with any of the dancers, you're fired."

"Got it." After all that's happened, romance is not on my mind, and I've never been into drugs. Not that I could afford them.

"Those two rules mean I have to find a new crew about once a week."

He stops at a table holding a coffee dispenser and a large platter of assorted bagels, and dispenses what looks like liquid tar into a paper cup. Then he picks up a bagel and takes a bite, frowns, and tosses it in the trash.

"Pay's seventeen-fifty an hour. Stop by the office to fill out the paperwork before the end of the day."

"Thanks." I hesitate by the table as he heads to the auditorium.

"Help yourself to the food."

I reach over and quickly take a bagel. As soon as I pick it up, I realize it's hard as a rock, but beggars can't be choosers.

Darby keeps talking. "No breaks. You eat while you work. Follow me, and I'll show you the safety backup."

He pulls a metal door open, and we enter the side of a large backstage area. Ropes and boxes are scattered among long strips of red velvet curtain. Metal ladders lead up into the rafters, and squinting overhead, I see a narrow catwalk.

"We'll install two more of them for the performance tonight. The girls wear these belts that are attached to these mechanical pulleys." He motions to an ancient-looking switchboard. "You'll be up there holding the safety rope. It's attached to one dancer, so I need you and a few other guys I can trust to agree to take turns…"

While he speaks, movement catches my eye from the backstage area. Two women dressed in tight black pants and cutoff shirts approach. They're both blonde and stacked. One looks up at me and smiles. Her dark brow arches, and her pink tongue slips out to touch her upper lip. My skin heats at the invitation, and I cut my eyes back to Darby.

He nods in their direction. "Some of the girls live here. Don't go in their rooms unless Gavin or me tells you to. I'd hate to fire you so soon."

"Right."

"Now get back outside and help unload the truck."

I step back as he continues forward and turn on my heel to exit through the metal side door opposite the way the two dancers went. I'm not looking for trouble.

Out of nowhere a small, dark form collides with my chest. She starts to fall, and instinctively, I grab her by the upper arms, pulling her to me.

"Oh!" It's a breathless cry.

"I'm sorry. I—" My voice trails off as bright blue eyes framed by thick lashes capture mine.

I quickly take in full, pink lips and long, glossy waves swishing down her back. She smells fresh like flowers after rain, and as I hold her, I can feel she's slim but strong. She's fucking beautiful.

"I'm okay." Her voice is confident, and… annoyed? Amused?

I let her go. "I'm sorry," I repeat. "I didn't see you in the dark."

She glances down. "I am wearing all black."

I quickly scan the tight halter-top and workout pants she's wearing. It's the same as the other two girls' outfits, but her exposed torso is lined with muscle, not soft like theirs. Her expression is playful as well. I can tell she's younger, more innocent.

"No worries." She starts to go, but I can't help myself.

"Hey… What's your name?"

Her head tilts, and blue eyes meet mine. "Larissa. But everyone calls me Lara. You?"

"Mark." I put a hand in my pocket. "I'm just Mark."

She nods and a smile curls her lips. "Nice to meet you, just Mark."

At that, she takes off toward the food table, and I try to go. Everything in me says don't let my thoughts wander about this girl, follow the rules, turn around and get out of here… but my eyes linger on her slender back, slipping down to her cute little ass. *Larissa.*

"Hey!" The sharp, male growl grabs my attention. "New guy. Get out here and help unload these trucks."

Snapping out of it, I hustle to the door feeling lighter than I have in weeks.

* * *

Get *Under the Lights* on Amazon Today!

EXCLUSIVE SNEAK PEEK

The Prince & The Player
(Dirty Players #1)
© TLM Productions LLC, 2016

Prologue

Zelda Wilder

My legs are wet. Thunder rolls low in a steel-grey sky, and the hiss of warm rain grows louder. I lean further sideways into the culvert, closer against my little sister Ava's body, and grit my teeth against the hunger pain twisting my stomach. There's no way in hell I'm sleeping tonight.

Reaching up, I rub my palm against the back of my neck, under the thick curtain of my blonde hair. A shudder moves at my side, and I realize Ava's crying. We're packed tight in this concrete ditch, but I twist my body around to face her.

Clearing my throat, I force my brows to unclench. I force my voice to be soothing instead of angry. "Hey," I whisper softly. "What's the matter, Ava-bug?"

Silence greets me. She's small enough to be somewhat comfortable in our hideout. Her knees are bent, but unlike me, they're not shoved up into her nose. Still, she leans forward to press her eyes against the backs of her hands. Her glossy brown hair is short around her ears and falls onto her cheeks.

Our parents were classic movie buffs, naming her after Ava Gardner and me after Scott Fitzgerald's crazy wife Zelda. We pretty much lived up to our monikers, since my little sister wound up having emerald green cat eyes and wavy dark hair. She's a showstopper whereas I'm pretty average—flat blue eyes and dishwater blonde. So far no signs of schizophrenia (*har har*), but you can bet your ass I can keep up with the boys in everything, which brings us to this lowly state.

"Come on, now," I urge. "It can't be as bad as all that."

Her dark head moves back and forth. "I'm sorry." Her soft whisper finally answers my question. "This is all my fault."

"What?" Reaching for her skinny shoulder, I pull her up. She's the only person I've ever known who looks pretty even when she's crying. "Why would you say something like that?"

"I tried cutting my hair off. I tried not brushing my teeth—"

"Don't be doing shit like that!" I snap, turning to face front. The rain keeps splashing on my side getting me even wetter. "We can't afford a dentist."

"I don't know what to do, Zee."

Pressing my lips together, I clench my fists on top of my knees. "We ain't going back into no foster home. I'll take care of us."

"But how?" Her voice breaks as it goes high in a whisper.

"Hell, I don't know, but I got all night to figure it out." I press my front teeth together and think. We're not that far from being legal. I'm seventeen, but Ava's only fifteen. Looking at the sand on my shoes, I get an idea. "We got one thing going for us."

"What's that?" My little sister sniffs, and I hear the tiniest flicker of hope in her voice. She'll trust whatever I tell her, and I take that responsibility very seriously.

"We live in the greatest state to be homeless. Sunny

Florida."

"Okay?" Her slim brows wrinkle, and the tears in her eyes make them look like the ocean.

"We don't have to worry about getting cold or anything. We don't have to worry about snow…" I'm thinking hard, assembling a plan in my mind. "During the day, we fly under the radar—keep your head down, don't attract attention. I'll see what I can find us to eat. At night we can sleep on the beach. Or here, or hell, maybe one of these rich assholes forgets to lock his boathouse. Have you seen how nice some of these boathouses are? They're like regular houses!"

Her eyes go round with surprise. "Why are they like that?"

"Hell, I don't know. Rich people are crazy. Some rich men even get their nails polished, and they aren't even gay!"

Air bursts through her lips, and she starts to laugh. I smile and pull her arm so she can lie down with her face on my bony, empty stomach. "Now get some sleep."

The rain is tapering off, and my little sister is laughing instead of crying. I don't have any idea if anything I just said is possible, but I'm going to find out. I'll be damned if I let another foster asshole touch her. It's what Mom would expect me to do. I'm the biggest. I have to take care of us, and I intend to do it.

* * *

Rowan Westringham Tate

The navy fabric of my father's uniform coat stretches taut across his shoulders. It's the tangible warning sign his anger is rising, and the person addressing him would do well to *shut up*.

"Monagasco has been an independent nation for eight hundred years." His voice is a rolling growl pricking the tension in my chest.

The last time my father started on our nation's history, the offending party was thrown out of the meeting room by the neck. He's getting too old for such violent outbursts. I worry about his heart... and my future. My *freedom*, more specifically.

"I think what Hubert was trying to say—" The Grand Duke, my mother's brother Reginald Winchester, tries to intervene.

"I KNOW what Hubert is trying to say!" My father (a.k.a., The King) cuts him off. "He thinks we should cede our southwestern territory to Totrington! Even though their raiders and bandits have pillaged our farms along the border for *generations*!"

Leaning back in my heavy oak chair, I steeple my fingers before my lips and don't say what I want. As crown prince, I've attended these meetings for three years, since I turned nineteen. I've learned when to speak and when to discuss things in private with my father.

I could say I agree with Reggie, we should consider a trade agreement with our neighboring nation-state, but I'm more concerned about the King's health. I've never seen him so worked up before.

"Independence at all costs," he continues, his naturally pink cheeks even pinker. "We will not give those savages an open door to the control of Monagasco."

"No one's suggesting—"

"Shut UP, Hubert!" My father shouts, and I glance down to avoid meeting the earl's offended eyes.

Hubert's sniveling voice is like nails on a chalkboard, and I privately enjoy my father chastising him. I've always suspected him of conspiring with Wade Paxton, Totrington's newly elected Prime Minister, from the time when Wade was only a member of their parliament.

"I've had enough of this." My father walks to the window and looks out. "I'd like to speak to Rowan in private. You can all go."

"Of course." Reginald stands at once, smoothing his long hands down the front of his dark coat.

Tall and slender, with greying black hair and a trim mustache, my uncle embodies the Charmant line of our family. I inherited their height and Norman complexion. My father, by contrast, is a Tate through and through. Short, pink, and round.

As soon as the room is cleared, he stalks back to the table, still brooding like a thunderstorm. "Reggie's in league with them as well," he growls.

"Not necessarily." My voice is low and level, and I hope appeasing. "My uncle does have an idea, and of the two, it's the least offensive. Hubert would combine our countries and walk away —"

"Exactly!" Father snaps, turning to face me, blue eyes blazing. "My own cousin, born and reared in our beautiful land. He's been promised a place in the new government, I'll bet you. They'll throw the lot of us out — behead us if they can."

"I'm pretty sure beheading is no longer tolerated in western civilization."

"Harumph." He's still angry, but at least he's calmer. "It would break your mother's heart. The Charmants founded Monagasco. We can't let those Twatringtons in."

His use of the unofficial nickname for our southwest neighbor makes me grin. Rising from my chair, I brace his shoulder in a firm grasp.

"We won't let that happen." Our blue eyes meet. It's the only feature we share. He's a few inches shorter than me, but he makes up for it in stubbornness. "We're flush with reserves, and the economy can change at any time."

His thick hand covers mine. "I'm doing my best to leave you a strong country to rule. The country I inherited."

"We would do well to reduce our dependence on foreign oil reserves." He starts to argue, but I hold up a hand as I head for the door. He's finally calm, and I'm not interested in riling him up again. "In any event, you'll be around long enough to see the tides turn. Now get some rest." I'm at the enormous wooden door of the war room. "We can't solve all our problems in one day."

"Goodnight, son."

The tone in his voice causes me to look back. He's at the window, and a troubled expression mars his profile. A shimmer of concern passes through my stomach, but I dismiss it, quietly stepping into the dim hallway. It's enormous and shrouded with heavy velvet curtains and tapestries.

I grew up playing in these halls, hiding from my mother and chasing my younger brother. I'm tired and ready for bed when the sound of hushed voices stops me in my tracks.

"Pompous ass. He's going to kill himself with these outbursts. We need to be ready to move when that happens." The glee in Hubert's sniveling voice revives the anger in my chest. I step into the shadows to listen.

"By climbing into bed with Wade Paxton?"

I recognize my uncle's voice, and my jaw clenches. *Is Father right? Is Reginald conspiring with that worm against the crown?*

"Wade Paxton would unite the kingdoms and make us both leaders in the new government."

"Wade Paxton is a thug."

"Not very respectful verbiage for the Prime Minister of Totrington, also known as our future partner."

"He's no better than one of those mob bosses on American television. Savage." Reggie's voice is laced with snobbery. "He'd tax the people and change the very nature of Monagasco."

Hubert's tone is undeterred. "Some things might change, but as leaders, you and I can help maintain the best parts, the heart of the nation. Once Philip is out of the way, of course, which could be sooner than we think."

My fists tighten at my sides. I'm ready to step out of the shadows and shake Hubert's traitorous neck until his teeth rattle. The only thing stopping me is my desire to hear the extent of this treachery.

"You're right about one thing," Reggie says. "Philip's health is tenuous. We need to be prepared to act should a crisis arise."

"What about Rowan? If he's not on our side, we could end up in the same position—and with a much younger king to wait out."

"Possibly." My uncle pauses, and I feel the heat rising around my collar.

"Wade has a plan for managing such a contingency. Should Rowan prove… difficult."

"I'm sure he does," Reggie scoffs. "And Cal? Shall we wipe out the entire Tate line?"

Hubert's voice is low and wicked. "Perhaps being in league with a 'thug' as you put it has its advantages."

How dare these bastards! What they're saying is high treason! My body is poised to move when Reggie's words freeze me in place.

"I'm sure Wade's tactics won't prove necessary. When the time comes to do the right thing, we can count on Rowan."

Count on Rowan? Is it possible he thinks I would even consider a merger with Twatrington? Their voices recede down the corridor as my level of disgust and loyalty to my father rises. The king has had a difficult evening. I'll let him rest tonight, but I will present him with this conspiracy first thing tomorrow. Reggie is right. When the time comes, I will do the right thing.

Looking back, I had no idea the time would come in less than twenty-four hours...

* * *

Get **The Prince & The Player** *from your favorite retailer today! Also available in audiobook format.*

ACKNOWLEDGMENTS

I have so, so many people to thank for helping me with Molly's story.

For starters, HUGE thanks to my beta readers Ilona, Lulu, Tina, Tammi, and Helene for early feedback, notes, and enthusiasm. Love you ladies!

BIG thanks to Lisa Kuhne for helping me get organized and keeping me straight through this new venture. Here's to kicking ass!

I love my readers, my "Mermaids" so much. If you read this book or anxiously awaited it or told me to keep writing, I want you to know this time in particular, I really needed it. THANK YOU for keeping me going.

Thanks to Ena and Amanda with Enticing Journeys and Kylie with Give Me Books for the promo support. Thanks also to Candi Kane for jumping in and spotting me at the last minute—I appreciate your assistance more than I can ever say… High Fives for the dream team!

SO much love to Ilsa Madden-Mills for finding Molly's cover image for me--it's perfect! Thanks to Dana Leah for the gorgeous design, and hugs to Shannon for the sexy teasers. LOVE and thanks to Nita Banks for that superhero book trailer and to Tamara Mataya for the eagle-eyed editing notes. Love you ladies!!!

Finally, to all the bloggers, reviewers, book promoters—YOU are my rock stars. I couldn't do this without you!

Keep in touch, because I'll be back with MORE…Stay sexy,

So much love,

<3 *Tia*

ABOUT THE AUTHOR

Tia Louise is the *USA Today* best-selling, award-winning author of *When We Touch*, the "Bright Lights," "One to Hold," and "Dirty Players" series, and co-author of the #4 Amazon bestseller *The Last Guy*.

After being a teacher, a book editor, a journalist, and finally a magazine editor, she started writing love stories and never stopped.

A lover of the beach, sexy romance, dark chocolate, and sparkling wine, Louise lives in the Midwest with her trophy husband, two teenage geniuses, and one grumpy cat.

Keep up with Tia online:
www.AuthorTiaLouise.com

91265558R00176

Made in the USA
Columbia, SC
19 March 2018